PRAISE FOR
THE MIST-TORN WITCHES

"A well-constructed fantasy with two likable and interesting main characters . . . a fun read." —A Book Obsession

"The murder mystery at the core of this book . . . will hold readers spellbound." —RT Book Reviews

"Hendee knows how to hook her readers with beautiful detailed settings." —Seeing Night Book Reviews

"Incredibly vivid . . . a must read, full of suspense, drama, and magic." —SciFiChick.com

PRAISE FOR
THE NOBLE DEAD SAGA

"A mix of *The Lord of the Rings* and *Buffy the Vampire Slayer*." —*New York Times* bestselling author Kevin J. Anderson

Of Truth and Beasts

"With several twists and surprises, this series is never predictable [and] the impressively shocking, climactic ending left me wanting more. . . . Don't miss this exciting series of magic, mythical creatures, and incredible lore." —SciFiChick.com

"A crowd-pleasing mix of intrigue, epic fantasy, and horror." —*Publishers Weekly*

"*Of Truth and Beasts* . . . once again allows the reader the rare opportunity to travel into the uniquely imaginative realms that only [the Hendees] can create with such power and grace. . . . The Hendees' style of writing is verbally arresting, leaving the reader unable to put the novel down. They are a talented team of storytellers who are able to build a world that is both foreign and familiar. . . . I, for one, am hooked and eagerly await the next incarnation [of] this hypnotizing series." —BookSpot Central

"A fabulous thriller." —*Midwest Book Review*

"The antagonists are strong, convincing forces with private agendas that add satisfying twists to another excellent addition to the series." —Monsters and Critics

continued . . .

"Plenty of action. . . . Fans of the Noble Dead will enjoy the book." —*Booklist*

"The Hendees excel at delivering action and intrigue."
—*Romantic Times* (4 stars)

Through Stone and Sea

"A textured canvas of tangled plots, hidden alliances, secret myths conjured from fantasy's best-known landscapes, and unique characters who will surely take their place in the annals of fantasy." —BookSpot Central

"Suspenseful adventure . . . incredible world building, and intriguing characters are the best part of this questlike fantasy. —SciFiChick.com

In Shade and Shadow

"The Hendees, if given a chance to complete their entire saga, may yet produce a combined fantasy masterwork that will surely stand on the highest pinnacles of literary fantasy lore." —BookSpot Central

"A nicely nuanced tale. . . . The authors use a deft touch to keep the pacing even and set the stage for future adventures in this endlessly intriguing horror-fantasy mix."
—Monsters and Critics

Child of a Dead God

"Readers who love vampire novels will appreciate the full works of Barb and J. C. Hendee, as they consistently provide some of the genre's best. . . . The audience will want to read this novel in one sitting." —*Midwest Book Review*

"Complex and bloody. . . . Interspecies distrust, grand ambitions, and the lure of dangerous secrets protected by the undead drive the action in this neat mix of horror with more traditional fantasy elements." —*Publishers Weekly*

Rebel Fay

"Entertaining . . . a hybrid crossing Tolkienesque fantasy with vampire-infused horror . . . intriguing." —*Publishers Weekly*

"A real page-turner." —*Booklist*

WITCHES IN RED

A NOVEL OF THE MIST-TORN WITCHES

BARB HENDEE

A ROC BOOK

ROC
Published by the Penguin Group
Penguin Group (USA) LLC, 375 Hudson Street,
New York, New York 10014

USA | Canada | UK | Ireland | Australia | New Zealand | India | South Africa | China
penguin.com
A Penguin Random House Company

First published by Roc, an imprint of New American Library,
a division of Penguin Group (USA) LLC

First Printing, May 2014

 REGISTERED TRADEMARK—MARCA REGISTRADA

ISBN 978-0-451-41416-8

Printed in the United States of America
10 9 8 7 6 5 4 3 2 1

*For Gary Jonas, who has kept me on the path of writing
and who's always liked tales about gypsies.*

PROLOGUE

I am called Mariah.

In the mid of one night, I slipped away from the Móndyalítko encampment where I lived and made my way into the trees. I left my perpetually angry sister and my other relatives behind—at least for a little while.

I would not let myself think on any of them tonight. I was going to meet my love.

It still amazed me that he'd been living right under my nose for nearly four months, and we'd never noticed each other. How was that possible? But of course we both had obligations and duties, mine even less pleasant than his. Then . . . only a few weeks ago, we had spoken, and his hand had brushed mine, and I had *known*.

He was kind, not like the other soldiers posted here to oversee the silver mines. He whispered to me softly and touched me as if I were made of glass, and he listened when I spoke. I'd never known how starved I'd been for someone to listen until he filled that empty space.

He was handsome as well, tall and slender, with thick hair and gray eyes.

I couldn't wait to see him.

Once I was far enough from the encampment, I began to move faster, hurrying toward the place where we always met. I longed to touch his face and curl up with him beneath a blanket so we could whisper to each other and keep warm. Even when I'd barely eaten all day, those moments fed me more than the richest venison stew with fresh bread.

Though I knew most men looked at me with hunger—a wild slip of a dark-haired girl—I still could not believe this was happening, that a lieutenant of Prince Lieven's soldiers, connected to the House of Pählen, loved me . . . wanted to marry me.

But he said we must keep our love a secret for now, until he could arrange for a transfer to a new post. I knew he was right, for I was the plaything of his captain, and if the truth came out, neither I nor my lieutenant might ever leave this place, so I guarded our midnight meetings like sacred treasures.

Still moving through the trees, I spotted the small clearing ahead, beside a stream, where we so often met, and I wondered if he was already here.

"Sullian?" I called quietly.

To my surprise, I was answered by a groan—that sounded like someone in pain.

"Sullian?" I repeated, this time in confusion, and I stepped into the clearing.

He was there, in his chain armor and his brown tabard, but he was bent over, holding his stomach. I ran to him. Vomit pooled on the ground before him, and saliva ran from his mouth.

"What is it?" I asked. "You are ill?"

Instead of answering, he stared at his own hand, and when I followed his gaze, my heart nearly stopped.

"No . . . ," I whispered. This could not be happening to him. Not to him.

He gagged, trying to spit the saliva from his mouth.

"Mariah, go!" he choked out. "Run!"

I didn't move.

He managed to stumble a few steps away from me, and I stood, rooted. Fur began sprouting from the exposed skin on his face and hands. He fell to the ground, writhing in pain. His hands continued to change, with his nails growing into claws, and then his chest began to expand. He was crying out in agony, and there was nothing I could do to help him.

I am Móndyalítko, and I have watched the shifters among my people change forms many times. It looked nothing like this. A true shift happened quickly, effortlessly . . . painlessly, from human form into animal form. It was as simple as breathing.

What was happening to Sullian was something else, something ugly and unnatural.

His cries of pain were so loud that he must have alerted the night watch, and I heard shouting.

"Where's it coming from?" someone called.

"Over there!" someone else answered.

If they saw him, they would kill him.

"Get up," I begged without moving any closer. "You must hide!"

He didn't seem to hear me.

His dark brown tabard ripped into several pieces as his body continued to expand. His face elongated, and still I stood staring. A row of fangs grew in his mouth. I knew I should run, that within moments, he would no longer be himself . . . although this, too, was different from the way of my people's shifters, who always remained themselves in either form.

But again, what was happening to Sullian was different.

I choked back a sob. He was all I had, and I was about to lose him.

"Sullian," I whispered.

His body was now larger than those of the great bears that roamed these northern forests, and his cries of pain shifted into low snarls. Unable to move, I took in the sight of him. He resembled a huge wolf in some ways: his head and paws. But his chest was much wider and his eyes were red. Saliva continued to pour from his mouth, and his snarls grew louder.

He dashed forward a few paces on his clawed feet, and then slowly, his head swung back toward me. There was nothing of my love remaining. I saw only rage in his mad red eyes.

Opening his mouth, he exposed his teeth, and I knew that running would be useless. Yet, if I'd wanted to run, I would have done so before now.

His whole body was trembling, and I waited for him to rush me, to end this.

Six men broke from the trees; five were soldiers, and the sixth was old Seth, an aging miner who sometimes looked in on my sister and me. He did not look so old at the moment, however, poised for battle and carrying a pickaxe.

Sullian's head swung in their direction, and he roared.

Two of the soldiers carried loaded crossbows. One of them aimed and fired. The quarrel caught my love in the center of his chest.

"Don't!" I cried. "It's Sullian!"

My words gave the men a brief pause, as so far, none of the officers had succumbed to this horror. Attacking a superior was a hanging offense in the military, but their pause did not last long, as Sullian charged straight at old Seth . . . who didn't stand a chance with his pickaxe. I heard Seth scream, and I wanted to weep, but I still couldn't move my feet.

Another crossbow quarrel sprouted—from the side of Sullian's throat—as three of the soldiers ran toward him with spears taller than they were. I heard the first one strike with a sickening wet sound, and Sullian tried to turn in his madness to attack the nearest man. But a soldier who seemed beyond fear rushed in, gripping his spear with both hands, and somehow drove the point through Sullian's eye, pinning his head to the ground.

My love thrashed a few times, and then he went still.

Finally, I sank to my knees.

I was alone now.

CHAPTER ONE

Céline Fawe worked quietly by herself in her apothecary's shop.

Well, she wasn't completely by herself. Her large orange cat, Oliver, had chased a mouse through a crack in the wall and then stationed himself directly in front of the crack, awaiting his victim. His tail twitched continually, which was most distracting.

"Oliver," Céline told him. "That mouse is long gone. Either take a nap or go and hunt someplace else."

He ignored her, as he usually did, and she tried turning back to her work.

An unfortunate summer cough had set in upon the village, and she'd already run out of cough mixture. So, yesterday, she'd stuffed several large jars full of rose petals and then poured boiling water over them. Today, the liquid would be ready for the next stage—she would combine it with honey and a pinch of salt to make a syrup.

Her sister, Amelie, had gone out to purchase some

bread and apples for lunch, and Céline wondered how soon she might return. It was late summer now, and for the past several months, the only person with whom Céline felt truly at ease was her sister. But the two of them had gone through a painful ordeal in order to achieve ownership of this shop, and Céline was still trying to put some of it behind her.

However, the thought of the shop made her smile. It was her pride. The exterior was painted warm yellow with dark brown trim, and they had named it the Betony and Beech, due to the abundance of betony growing in the herb garden out back and the young beech tree that leaned over their fence from the outside.

Céline did love the shop.

She simply didn't care to remember what she and Amelie had had to do in order to get it. Worse, Prince Anton—who was master of Castle Sèone and its surrounding fiefdoms—had planned one of his banquets tonight and insisted that Céline and Amelie attend. Céline was still uneasy inside the castle, but she couldn't refuse the prince.

Pushing all such thoughts away, she tried once again to focus on preparing the rose petal syrup. When the front door opened, she looked up.

An unfamiliar young woman of perhaps twenty stood nervously in the open doorway.

No matter what her state of mind, Céline believed in being kind and attentive to her customers. Most people who visited an apothecary's shop were facing some kind of difficulty, and she always kept this in mind.

"Come in," she said from behind the table where she

worked. "I'm out of cough syrup at the moment, but I can save you some from this next batch."

The young woman said nothing and finally took a few steps inside. She was thin, with unwashed brown hair coming loose from a single braid. Her dress was threadbare.

"No . . . I don't need syrup," she said.

Céline was a good enough judge of character to see that her visitor was facing more than a family back home suffering from a summer cough, and that whatever was wrong, she was nearing the end of her rope. Most young women who looked and sounded like this tended to be unmarried and pregnant—with a violent father they feared.

"How can I help?" Céline asked, coming around the table. "Would you like some tea? I have hot water in the kettle."

Her visitor answered neither question, and instead looked at Céline's mass of dark blond hair. "You're the seer? The one who can look into the future?"

Céline's stomach lurched, and she tried to keep her expression still. "Not at present," she answered firmly, wondering how fast she could get this woman out of the shop. She had no intention of reading anyone's future. Though it had been several months since her experiences up at the castle, she wasn't ready to practice her other profession again. For now, she chose to be only an apothecary.

"I'm Irmina," the young woman said. "You might have seen my husband, Hugo, out in the village? He's a thatcher, and he's often to be seen working on this roof or that."

"No, I do not think I have—"

"Yesterday morning, he fell off a roof and hit his head," Irmina interrupted, "and he's not woken up."

In spite of her own rising discomfort, Céline couldn't help but feel a stab of sympathy. "Oh, I am sorry. Do you wish me to come and look at him?"

"No. He'll either wake or he won't. The thing is . . . I need to know if he will or he won't."

Céline tried to speak but was again cut off.

"We bought ourselves a little house from Evrard, the wine merchant," Irmina rushed on, "on payments, and we've fallen a bit behind. Then Hugo got himself a job putting a new roof on the smithy, for enough of a wage that once he finished and was paid, we could get caught up, but then . . . he fell."

"You bought a house from Evrard?" Céline repeated. Everyone knew him. He was one of the wealthiest villagers in Sèone, and he'd not become so through any acts of kindness. As a side business, he bought up small dwellings and sold them for a profit—often on payments—and he was merciless to anyone who fell on hard times and could no longer pay.

"Yes." Irmina nodded. "My parents think that I should just give up on the house, have some of the men carry Hugo to their shack, and move back in with them . . . but I can barely face the thought. He and I worked so hard to get our own little place." She pulled something from her pocket. It was a silver ring with a small blue stone of some kind.

"This was passed down from Hugo's grandmother," Irmina went on. "It's the only thing of value we own. If

I know that he's going to wake up, I'll sell this and give the money to Evrard. The ring should fetch enough to buy us a little more time. We can stay in the house, and Hugo can go back to work when he's healed. But if"—for the first time, her voice broke—"if he isn't going to wake up, then I'll be selling his grandmother's ring for nothing more than a few months at best, and I'll lose the house anyway." Reaching out, she touched Céline's wrist. "Do you see? Do you see why I *have* to know?"

Céline did see. She saw only too well.

With her hands shaking slightly, she motioned to a chair. "Come and sit down." She didn't want to do this, but at the same time, she couldn't bring herself to refuse.

Without hesitation, Irmina hurried to the chair, and the flash of hope in her eyes made Céline want to wince. This budding power of hers didn't always work, and even if it did, what if the news was bad?

Reaching out, she grasped Irmina's hand—as this was necessary. She had to be in physical contact with the person she was reading.

Closing her eyes, Céline focused on Irmina, on the spark of her spirit within, and then Céline moved her focus to Hugo . . . to his and Irmina's future together. At first nothing happened, but she kept trying, and a jolt hit her.

She clenched her jaw in preparation. As the second jolt hit, she felt as if her body were being swept forward along a tunnel of mist, and she forgot everything but the sensation of speeding through the mist all around her as it swirled in tones of grays and whites.

This journey was not a long one, and almost immediately, the mist vanished and an image flashed before her. She saw a small bedroom with faded walls. For some reason, her sight often led her into bedrooms . . . deathbeds or childbeds or simply scenes playing out in bedrooms. She didn't know why.

Looking down, she saw Irmina sitting on a stool beside a bed. A young man lay in the bed with his eyes closed. His head was bruised, and he was clearly unconscious, as opposed to sleeping. Irmina was holding a cup of water, and she leaned forward to lift the back of his head and try to pour some of the water into his mouth, probably in the hope that he would swallow it. Most of the liquid ran down the sides of his mouth.

"Please, Hugo," she said. "Try for me."

From where Céline stood, she could see the window, and the sun was setting. The sky was filled with orange clouds. She knew that Irmina could not see her. Céline was not truly there. She was only an observer.

Just as her gaze turned back toward the man on the bed, she heard a cough, followed by the sound of Irmina gasping.

Another cough rang out, this time followed by the sound of sputtering.

"Hugo?" Irmina said.

Céline moved closer to the bed. The man's eyes were open, and he was staring out in confusion while still partially choking on the water. After a moment, his gaze seemed to clear.

"Irmina?"

Sucking in loud breaths, Irmina dropped to her

knees beside the bed. "Can you hear me? See me all right? Do you know your name?"

Céline was surprised at the young woman's presence of mind, to be asking such questions, but . . . they were sensible questions.

Hugo wiped some of the water from his mouth and then licked his fingers as if thirsty. "Course I know my name," he said weakly. "What's happened?"

The small room vanished, and Céline felt herself being whisked backward through the mists.

She opened her eyes to see Irmina sitting rigid.

"Well . . . did you see anything?"

"Yes," Céline answered instantly. "He does wake. I don't know how soon, but the time of day was sunset. I don't think it could be further away than tonight or tomorrow, as his body couldn't survive much longer without him drinking water properly."

"But he wakes up? You saw him wake up?"

"Yes."

Irmina leaned forward as if she was going to be sick. "Oh, thank you . . . thank you."

"It's all right." Céline reached out to help her sit back up.

And suddenly, it *was* all right. She had just used her powers and helped someone, and she felt . . . glad. Before her ability to truly see into the future had surfaced, she'd spent five years pretending to read futures, and in the process, she'd often dispensed advice.

The latter came back to her as naturally as if she'd never stopped. "Listen to me," she said. "Don't sell the ring just yet. Evrard will not throw you out in the next day or two. Wait for Hugo to wake up, and once his mind is clear, ask for his thoughts on this matter. If he feels he'll need weeks to heal, he might counsel you to sell it, but if he thinks he can go back to work sooner, you might be able to arrange something with Evrard— who would prefer to be paid, if possible. This way, Hugo will not accuse you of acting hastily, and you might yet be able to keep his grandmother's ring."

Irmina thought for a moment and then nodded. "Yes . . . yes, of course. I will wait."

"Oh, and one more thing," Céline added. "Since the future has not happened yet, it can still be changed if the people involved take a different course of action. You must continue caring for Hugo exactly as you would have otherwise and try to pretend you never spoke to me. Continue to do just as you would have done for him before."

Irmina nodded again. "I will. Thank you." She suddenly appeared uncomfortable and stood up. "I don't have any money to pay you, but when your roof needs repair, you come to me, and I'll see that Hugo mends it."

In the past, Céline had often bartered for her services. She smiled. "That would be most agreeable, and I'm glad . . . I'm glad I was able to give you good news."

Irmina thanked her again and hurried for the door, probably anxious to get back home now.

Once alone, Céline allowed a few revelations to wash over her. First, she'd used her ability, and nothing horrible had happened as a result. Second, she'd enjoyed reading Irmina, helping Irmina. Perhaps . . . perhaps she could return to being a seer again.

Prince Anton had been quietly waiting for her to return to her previous state, though he never pressed her. As she had been unable to please him in this, being in his company had become a strain, and she'd come to dread being called up to the castle.

But now she felt a little lighter.

Walking through the shop, she made her way to the bedroom she shared with Amelie and opened up their wooden wardrobe. A few fine gowns hung there, and her gaze stopped on one of rich amber silk that Anton especially liked.

Suddenly, she wasn't dreading the banquet tonight anymore.

Amelie Fawe wandered aimlessly through the market stalls in the village, in no hurry to make her purchases and head back to the Betony and Beech . . . not that she wasn't proud of the apothecary's shop. She was. Nor that she wasn't grateful that she and her sister, Céline, had been given a home here in Sèone. Of course she was grateful.

Even the market here was a cheerful place, filled with stalls of colorful fruits and vegetables and steaming bread and bolts of cloth and candles. The people glowed with health and had nothing to fear while they remained inside the thick wall surrounding both the castle and the village.

No, it was more that in this safe place, Amelie didn't feel useful.

Only this past spring, she and Céline had been living in a dark, lawless village called Shetâna. The sisters had been orphaned just over five years ago when Céline was fifteen and Amelie was twelve. Shetâna was under the control of Prince Damek, and Damek's soldiers had viewed the people of the village as little more than prey to be abused.

Two orphaned girls had seemed easy targets at first, but Amelie had quickly proven that assumption wrong. She'd taken to wearing a dagger on one hip and a short sword on the other. She'd learned to rely on speed and the element of surprise, and she could cut a man open in a matter of seconds with her dagger.

Céline had learned to play the part of "seer" and had increased her knowledge of herb lore and healing. Amelie saw to their protection and day-to-day needs, while Céline earned most of their living. They depended upon each other.

However . . . here in Sèone, Prince Anton's soldiers had come as quite a surprise. They actually viewed it as their *duty* to protect the people who lived here. Of course, this was a good thing. It simply left Amelie with little to do herself.

In addition to adjusting to this new state of affairs, she was also coming to terms with something else. Shortly after arriving here, Céline revealed that she was truly developing the ability to see the future—like their mother—and then Amelie discovered that she could read pasts. The latter was a revelation, as Amelie had never viewed herself as special, certainly not like Céline.

Céline had always been uncommonly pretty and could make most people do anything she wanted. Amelie was, well . . . different.

To begin, the sisters looked nothing alike. Céline was small and slender, with a mass of dark blond hair that hung down her back. She often wore a red velvet dress that fit her snuggly—in order to look the part of the seer—and her eyes were lavender.

Amelie had inherited their mother's lavender eyes, but that was all.

Having recently observed her eighteenth birthday, Amelie was even shorter than Céline. But where Céline was slight, Amelie's build showed a hint of strength and muscle. She despised dresses and always wore breeches, a man's shirt, a canvas jacket, and boots. She'd inherited their father's straight black hair, which she'd cropped into a bob. For years, she'd kept it at jaw-length, but of late, she'd let it grow, and now it hung to her shoulders.

Most people found her a bit peculiar, but she didn't care.

Then . . . she'd made this discovery that she too had been born with a power—like her mother—only she could read pasts and not futures. She longed to put this ability to use, perhaps even to earn her and Céline some extra money. People often came to Céline to hear their futures, but there might be many reasons why someone would wish for a past to be read . . .

To find a lost object that had been put away and then the hiding place forgotten.

To solve a disagreement in which two people remembered a situation differently.

The possibilities were endless. But Céline was still so fragile after their experiences up at the castle—in which they'd been engaged to catch a murderer—that so far, she'd not been up to presenting the sisters as a pair of seers.

Amelie didn't wish to press her and had decided not to use her own new power until Céline was ready as well.

But this all left Amelie with nothing to protect and nothing to do.

In addition to feeling useless, she was beginning to feel restless—and that only made her angry with herself for not appreciating their good fortune enough.

"Morning, Lieutenant," a voice called out from behind her.

"Morning, Simon," a familiar voice called back.

Amelie froze in front of the market stall where she stood.

Slowly, she turned her head to see Lieutenant Jaromir walking into the market, wearing his chain armor and tan tabard. He hadn't spotted her yet. Other villagers began calling greetings to him now. Jaromir was well liked by the people he protected.

What was he doing out here, just walking in the streets? The summer had been awfully quiet. Perhaps he was bored, as she was.

Ducking down slightly, Amelie couldn't help looking at him for a few moments.

Perhaps thirty years old, he wasn't exactly handsome, but he wore a small goatee around his mouth and kept his light brown hair tied back at the nape of his neck. From his weathered face to the scars on his hands, most elements of his appearance marked him as a professional soldier. He was tall and strong and seemed comfortable inside his own skin. However, he was also arrogant and too fond of being in control, and he would do anything—*anything*—he deemed necessary to protect Prince Anton.

Both Amelie's opinion of Jaromir and her relationship to him were . . . complicated. In truth, there was no relationship, but he'd made hints that he'd prefer to alter that state of affairs.

So, at the prospect of him walking into the market, she did the only thing she possibly could do and dashed around the back of a stall to hide before he spotted her. Yes, it was cowardly, and she knew it, but facing him in the street would have been much worse.

She'd had to politely greet him the few times that Anton had insisted the sisters come up to the castle for a banquet, but once formalities were over, she'd been able to avoid talking with Jaromir due to the various activities that took place in a crowd, such as everyone eating too much food or the inevitable card games that followed.

Out here, in the market by herself, she'd have no excuse not to speak with him if he approached her.

So—though partially ashamed of herself—she crouched behind the stall of a wool seller and peered around the edge toward the street.

"What are you doing, girl?" asked the aging wool seller.

"Quiet," Amelie told him. "I don't want someone to see me."

He glanced down the street. "The lieutenant? Did you break the law?"

All the people here referred to Jaromir as "the lieutenant," as if it were some kind of title. He had authority over everyone except Prince Anton. He liked it that
way.

"No," Amelie answered. "I just don't want to have
to talk to him."

The old man raised an eyebrow.

But he had no chance to respond, as a loud commotion broke out from the direction of the outer village
gates. Amelie moved up from her crouched position to
see what was happening.

A rider came pounding up the narrow cobbled
street, straight toward the market, pushing his horse at
a pace much too fast to be considered safe inside the
wall surrounding the village and the castle. The popu-
lation here was large and condensed. People were not
allowed to gallop their horses through the streets.

But the rider didn't slow down. Villagers screamed
and dodged out of the way. A few fruit carts were over-
turned, and he just kept coming.

Amelie stood, wondering what was about to happen, when she saw Jaromir position himself directly in
the rider's path.

"Stop!" he ordered.

What a show-off, Amelie thought.

The rider fought wildly to pull up his horse and
nearly smashed into Jaromir before he managed to get
the creature stopped. Jaromir didn't even flinch.

It was then that Amelie finally noticed the rider
wore chain armor and a dark brown tabard: the color
worn by the guards of Prince Lieven, who was father

to both Anton and Damek, as well as the current head of the House of Pählen.

Though the rider was panting hard, upon getting a better look at Jaromir, he leaned down and said something while wearing an urgent expression. Amelie couldn't hear what was said, but Jaromir's eyes widened, and he seemed to forget all about the public disturbance. Turning around, he ushered the rider to follow, and they both headed toward the castle.

Finally, something had happened.

Amelie was dying to know what.

Once inside the castle, Lieutenant Jaromir sent a guard upstairs to find Anton, and then he led the messenger into the vast main hall—whereupon he immediately began second-guessing himself. Due to the banquet planned for that night, the hall was in a state of uproar, with far too many servants bustling about moving tables and dragging benches into place.

The messenger in the brown tabard looked around at all the activity. He was still puffing, and Jaromir couldn't help noting his grizzled face, gray hair, and wide chest. The man was too old to be riding at top speed all the way from Castle Pählen.

A serving girl in an apron stood just inside the hall, and Jaromir motioned to her. "Could you fetch this man a mug of ale?" he asked. It sounded like a request, but of course she dropped what she was doing and ran for the kitchens.

"Can you not tell me something of your message?" he asked the burly man beside him.

"No," the man answered bluntly. "This comes straight from Prince Lieven to his son."

Even though the man was possessed of a strong voice, Jaromir could barely hear him over the din in the hall. Still, Jaromir balked at the idea of bringing a stranger up to Anton's private rooms. Such a prospect went against all his instincts.

No, it was better to wait here.

Suddenly, the hall fell silent as Prince Anton walked through the large open archway. Of medium height, he was slender, with dark hair tucked behind his ears. He wore black breeches and a midnight blue tunic. At twenty-three, he looked young to be in charge of so many people, but his bearing was noble, and Jaromir was proud of the man he served. Anton was more than his lord. The two had become good friends.

All the servants bowed their heads, but Anton didn't seem to notice them.

"Leonides?" he asked, looking at the messenger.

The grizzled man offered a tired smile. "Yes, lad, it's me."

Jaromir couldn't help bristling at this lack of respect. Everyone here addressed Anton as "my prince" or "my lord." But when Anton did not insist on a proper correction, Jaromir suddenly felt at odds, uncertain of the situation.

"Look at the state of you," Anton said, walking closer.

"I've been riding all night and half the day. I've a message from your father."

The girl came trotting back in with the ale, and the

aging messenger took it from her, downing it in a few gulps and handing back the mug.

There was a small side chamber in the hall with a door that closed, and Jaromir motioned toward it with his head. "Perhaps in there?"

Anton nodded and led the way. As soon as all three men were inside, Jaromir closed the door. The room was small indeed, with a single table, two chairs, and no window. Several candles glowed from the table.

"Jaromir," Anton said, "this is Leonides, my sword master when I was a boy. He has served my father for years."

The affection in his voice was undisguised and unusual, as Anton almost always guarded his emotions. Again, Jaromir felt uncertain. So, he simply offered a polite nod.

"Sit and rest," Anton said.

With a grateful expression, Leonides dropped into a chair.

"Is my father well?" Anton asked.

"He's well," Leonides grunted. "But he's got a problem, a tricky one, and he needs you to see to it right away."

"Me?"

Leonides leaned back, and his brow furrowed as if he was gathering his thoughts. "Do you remember about five years ago when your father bought the Ryazan silver mines up in the Northwest Territories?"

Anton didn't answer, but Leonides didn't seem to notice.

"Those mines proved a good purchase," the sword

master continued. "Your father sent a contingent of his own guards to set up an encampment and hire workers to mine the silver. Over the years, he's rotated the men posted there . . . as it's foolish to leave anyone in that wild country for too long. But the miners are still digging and silver is still coming out."

Anton shook his head in confusion. "And now there is a problem?"

Leonides didn't look at him. "A few months ago, your father got a report he almost couldn't believe, didn't believe at first. The present contingent has been out there for only about four months, but even in a short time, those forests can do things to a man's mind. A Captain Keegan is in charge, along with a Lieutenant Sullian. Keegan wrote to your father that several of the young soldiers under him had . . ." He paused. "Well, they had turned into beasts and gone mad and had to be killed."

"What?" Anton asked.

Leonides nodded. "Your father sent a small number of reinforcements, but when more reports arrived at Castle Pählen, he started to think these stories were more than a bit of forest madness. By that point, eight of our guards out there were dead, and then . . . two weeks ago, Lieutenant Sullian changed into one of these beasts and had to be killed."

"This is nonsense," Jaromir said, unable to keep silent. "Prince Lieven's initial instincts were right."

"It's not nonsense," Leonides stated flatly, his voice carrying across the room. He looked back to Anton. "And these men who become beasts are too often killing the mine workers before they can be killed themselves. Some of the workers, with signed contracts, have been caught trying to slip away in the night. Production has come to a near halt, and your father wants this solved. He wants the silver flowing again."

If anything, Anton appeared more puzzled than before. "Why would he engage me for this?"

As if in agreement with the confusion, Leonides shrugged and answered, "Honestly, lad, I don't know. He said you were clever—which I don't dispute—and he sent me here as fast as I could ride." Reaching beneath his armor, he pulled out a piece of paper. "Oh, and he sent a letter."

Quickly, Anton scanned the contents of the letter and then held it out for Jaromir.

Jaromir took it and read an account of everything Leonides had just related, but his eyes stopped on two carefully worded sentences:

> I've learned that you were recently troubled by a similar, seemingly unsolvable problem, and yet you managed it. I engage you to solve this one for me, as quickly as possible, but if it proves too much for you, I can turn the matter over to your brother.

His gaze flew up to Anton's face. First, how did Prince Lieven know about their "problem" this past spring? They hadn't told him. Second, this was a test, plain and simple. Anton's father wanted this solved and had given the task to Anton . . . along with a veiled threat to engage Damek instead if necessary.

Jaromir couldn't help feeling angry. Anton and Damek were always being pitted against each other, and if Jaromir had any say in the matter, Anton would not only survive but also come out on top.

Droevinka had no hereditary king. Instead, it was a land of many princes, each one heading his own noble house and overseeing multiple fiefdoms. But . . . they all served a single grand prince, and a new grand prince was elected every nine years by the gathered heads of the noble houses. This system had served the country well for more than a hundred years. At present, Prince Rodêk of the House of Äntes was in rule.

But within two years, a new grand prince would be voted in.

Anton and Damek were sons of the House of Pählen. Their father, Prince Lieven, controlled a large portion of the western region. He'd given Damek, who was the elder brother, an aging castle and seven large fiefs to oversee. He'd given Anton a better castle but six smaller fiefs. These "assignments" were a chance for each young man to prove himself. However, Prince Lieven had been aging in recent days, and it was rumored he would soon be naming a successor as leader of the House of Pählen. It was his right to choose between his sons, and should a victor be chosen within the next two years, then that son would have the right to place his name on the voting list for the position of grand prince.

More than anything, Jaromir wanted Anton on that list.

But this task Prince Lieven had just demanded

hardly seemed fair . . . to stop a contingent of soldiers in an isolated, heavily forested area from turning into beasts?

Anton looked at Leonides. "You must be weary, and I won't have you riding back out today. I'll have you brought to a guest room to eat and rest while I write a response. You can take it to my father tomorrow."

The aging sword master sighed. "Thank you, lad. I'll admit I'm not as young as I once was."

Jaromir opened the door and called to the same girl from earlier. "Can you have this man taken to a guest room?" he asked, and again it sounded like a request. "He'll need a hot meal as well."

"Of course, sir. Right away."

Leonides followed the girl. Jaromir closed the door again and turned back to Anton.

"What do you think?"

"I don't know. But my father is not given to fancies. If he believes these stories, then there is some truth."

Though Jaromir didn't want to agree, he realized Anton was right. Prince Lieven was not given to fancies.

"All right," Jaromir said. "The main thing your father wants is production at the mines restored. Ryazan is a four-day day ride from here, and after that, there's no telling how long this will take to solve. We both cannot be away from Sèone for so long a time. I suggest you let me handpick a contingent of our own men and ride out to see to this myself."

Anton was silent for a few moments, and then he said, "My father has men . . . far more men than I do—

along with captains and lieutenants he trusts. Damek certainly has more men than me. Father wouldn't be giving me this task if he thought it could be solved by sending a stronger contingent with a better leader." He paused. "Besides, I've met Captain Keegan, and if he's in charge of the mines, he'll bristle at you riding in with a show of force, and then you'll be at odds. No, he has to believe that he's being sent 'help,' and not a challenge to competence. This must be approached differently."

"Differently?"

Again, Anton hesitated. "Somehow, my father knows about the murders that took place here in the spring. I don't know how he knows, but those murders were solved and stopped by three people." He locked eyes with Jaromir. "Only three."

Jaromir stared back at him and didn't like where this was going.

CHAPTER TWO

Céline and Amelie arrived at the castle that evening and made their way toward the great hall for the banquet. As they walked from the entryway down the main passage, braziers along the walls provided light. For the first time this summer, Céline wasn't forcing herself to attend such an event. She wasn't dreading Anton's thinly veiled concern as he attempted to politely inquire whether or not she was using her abilities again.

Tonight . . . when he asked, she could give him some relief, for she knew his concern was partially motivated by unexpressed guilt—that what he'd asked her to do in the spring might have permanently damaged her. Tonight, she could erase his guilt, or at least ease it.

In addition, she'd worn the amber silk gown he especially liked. The square neckline was cut just above the tops of her breasts, with a point at each shoulder. The sleeves were narrow, the slender waistline fit her perfectly, and the skirt was full, draping about her in yards of fabric. The color reflected just a hint of gold, and it suited her dark blond hair, which she had worn loose.

Amelie, as always, was dressed in her breeches,

faded blue shirt, and short canvas jacket. Céline knew better than to even suggest anything else.

"Something's wrong," Amelie said as they approached the large archway of the great hall. "We haven't passed any other guests, and I don't hear any voices."

Paying more attention to their surroundings, Céline realized her sister was right. Normally, from this range, they would hear the sounds of laughter and chatting echoing from the hall.

Céline and Amelie passed through the archway, expecting to see a hundred well-dressed guests—perhaps all hushed to silence for some reason—only to find the vast chamber nearly empty.

A light supper had been laid out on one of the long tables, and a few of the castle guards were eating cold ham with bread and drinking mugs of ale. One of the guards glanced over at them.

Before either of the sisters could inquire further, a deep voice sounded behind them.

"Céline."

She turned to see Lieutenant Jaromir walking toward them.

"Did we get the night wrong?" she asked.

He shook his head. "No, the banquet was canceled."

At the strained expression on his face, she felt a sudden coldness in the pit of her stomach.

"Canceled? Why weren't we sent word? Is Prince Anton ill?"

"No, he's not ill, and you weren't sent word because something has come up that . . ." He faltered and glanced at Amelie. "You both need to come upstairs with me, to his apartments."

As Amelie followed her sister and Jaromir into Anton's apartments, she struggled with a mix of excitement and apprehension. Part of her couldn't help feeling glad that something, *anything*, seemed to be happening, but she and Céline would never be called for a private meeting like this unless it was serious . . . and unless Anton wanted something from them.

Amelie closed the door behind herself and glanced around.

Most princes lived in some luxury, but Anton appeared to prefer austerity. There were tapestries on the walls and a large hearth. But the furnishings consisted of a messy writing desk, a few heavy wooden chairs, and rows of bookshelves along the walls. It looked more like the chambers of a scholar than those of a prince. A closed door stood on the same wall as the hearth, but Amelie knew it led to his sleeping chambers—as Céline had tended him once when he was ill.

Anton himself stood beside one of the heavy wooden chairs, wearing a simple blue tunic and black breeches. The expression on his face was no less strained than Jaromir's, causing Amelie's apprehension to increase. But then Anton's gaze stopped on Céline, and he started slightly. She'd put some effort into her appearance tonight, and it showed.

"Céline . . . ," he said, his eyes lingering on her silk gown.

"What's happened?" Céline asked him, sounding openly worried.

Anton motioned them all further inside. He opened his mouth as if to speak and then closed it again.

"I hardly know where to begin," he said finally. "Jaromir . . . perhaps you could . . . ?"

Jaromir ran a hand over the top of his head, and Amelie's apprehension turned to alarm.

"What is going on?" she asked. "Does this have anything to do with that messenger who arrived from Castle Pählen today?"

"How did you know that?" Jaromir shook his head quickly. "No, it doesn't matter. The prince needs your help to help solve a . . . difficulty for his father."

"What kind of difficulty?" Céline asked, and suddenly Amelie regretted coming anywhere near the castle tonight. Earlier today, Céline had seemed more herself than she had in months, and now she was getting that haunted look in her eyes again.

"Have you ever heard of the Ryazan silver mines?" Anton asked, entering the conversation again.

Both sisters shook their heads. They'd both lived their entire lives in Shetâna before coming here.

"My father has owned these mines for the past five years, and they have proven quite . . . lucrative." He hesitated for a few breaths, as if steeling himself, and then began speaking again, spilling out a bizarre story of the soldiers assigned to these mines turning into beasts, killing the contracted laborers, and then having to be killed themselves.

Amelie stood tense, waiting to see where this was going.

"At last count, my father had lost nine men to this affliction, at least one of whom was an officer," Anton finished quietly, "and production at the mines has come to a standstill. He's asked me to solve this for him, and he's threatened to turn to Damek if I cannot." He locked eyes with Céline. "It's a test of leadership."

Céline didn't respond, but her left hand was trembling slightly.

"Even if any of this wild tale is true," Amelie said, stepping in front of her sister. "What does it have to do with us?"

Jaromir sighed, looking beyond miserable, but Amelie was not about to make this easy on him. She wanted to know exactly why she and Céline had been dragged in here to listen to this.

"Prince Anton believes that sending a new contingent won't help," Jaromir finally answered. "He wants the three of us—you, me, and Céline—to solve this . . . as we did before."

"No!" Amelie spat at him. She'd been feeling useless and restless lately, but Céline wasn't going anywhere near some pack of Pählen soldiers reportedly turning into "beasts."

"I can keep you both safe," Jaromir insisted. "I'll be there with you. While you and Céline use your abilities to figure out what's happening, I will have no other task than protecting you. Once you know the truth, you turn it over to me, and I will take action . . . just like our plan last time."

"You want us to read these soldiers," Céline asked quietly, "their pasts and futures and figure out what is happening to them?"

"I'd never ask this of you, Céline," Anton answered raggedly. "I don't want to send you to . . ." He trailed off. "But this is the first time my father has asked me for a personal favor. I cannot refuse. I cannot fail, and this cannot be solved through force." He stepped closer to Céline. "Jaromir and I have been planning all afternoon, and we've come up with several provisions. I will send you and Amelie as ladies of my court, as my personal healers and seers, to ensure you are given due respect from the soldiers stationed at Ryazan. For the journey itself, Jaromir will take a small contingent of our own guards, and as added protection we will dress you both in red cloaks."

Amelie wanted to shake her head at his "provisions." Droevinka was often in a state of civil war, even small wars between the houses. In years past, traveling healers who attempted to help wounded soldiers had often been killed along the road as spies or enemy combatants. Somehow—and no one quite knew where this started—they began wearing red cloaks to try to distinguish themselves. Still, too many of them were being lost, and the country was facing a shortage of skilled healers. As a result, all the princes had gathered and agreed that no factions would harm those in red cloaks.

"And you think those cloaks will protect us from madmen turning into beasts?" Amelie asked angrily.

"No," Jaromir stated. "*I* will do that."

To Amelie's further discomfort, so far, Céline had not refused, but the tremble in her left hand was growing worse.

"You'll need to dress as traveling ladies of my court," Anton added, glancing at Amelie's breeches.

Oh, this just got better and better.

"We haven't agreed to go anywhere," she told him.

His expression darkened, and she fought to hold her tongue. Anton was normally well-mannered, but like all princes of this nation, he was a warlord vying to hold on to power, and he expected to be obeyed.

"I am asking you to do this for me," he said tightly.

Without thinking, Amelie exploded in the only way she could, by making her own demands. "What's in it for us?"

Céline gasped, and Jaromir's face tightened in shock. He stared at her as if she were a stranger.

Instantly, Amelie regretted her words and wished she could take them back. They might have done a service for Anton last spring, but he had not only given her and Céline a safe refuge and his protection; he'd given them an apothecary shop with an herb garden and a built-in livelihood. They owed him more than they could ever repay.

Only Anton did not appear affected by her demand. Instead, he looked her up and down as if she were a simpleton. "As reward, you might receive me as grand prince of your nation. Unless you would prefer Damek?"

Amelie glanced away, embarrassed.

"We cannot refuse," Céline whispered.

Everyone fell silent, and as Anton again took in the sight of Céline's silk gown and loose hair, it was his turn to appear embarrassed. But the expression passed quickly, and he drew himself to full height.

"Go home and rest tonight," he said. "Come back up to the castle and see Helga tomorrow. Don't bother about packing anything other than medicinal supplies you might wish to bring. Helga will get you both packed and prepared for the journey. You'll ride out at midday." He paused. "I swear Jaromir will keep you from harm."

Céline didn't meet his eyes, but she nodded.

After a nearly sleepless night in her own bed, the following morning Céline found herself back up at the castle, inside a guest room, trapped between two very strong-willed women.

"I am *not* wearing those," Amelie insisted.

"Oh, yes, you are, girlie," Helga countered, shoving both a green wool gown—which laced up the front—and a white cotton shift at Amelie. "His lord majesty lieutenant says you're going in disguise for your own safety, so go in disguise you will! Now, get those breeches off or I'll pin you to that bed and pull 'em off myself."

Amelie's eyes narrowed. "You can try."

Helga squared off with the gown and shift over one arm, and her hands clenched into fists. She appeared to be at least in her seventies, with thick white hair up in a bun that was partially covered by an orange kerchief. Her wrinkled face had a dusky tone, and she wore a faded homespun dress that might have once been purple.

"And what of your sister?" she accused. "His lord majesty lieutenant says you'll be safe if you arrive as *ladies* of the court who've also taken up the red cloak. Mistress Céline's safety depends on this as well. If you show up dressed like a hooligan boy, Jaromir's story won't hold water for a minute, and if those soldiers don't believe it of you, they won't believe it of her either. Then what happens?"

Amelie stood shaking with rage, but with gritted teeth, she finally held her out hand. "Oh, give them to me."

Céline breathed softly in relief, but it was the first and only hint of relief she'd felt since last night. No matter how important this task might be, a part of her couldn't believe what Anton was asking. She had begun to think he cared for her, that he'd been giving her all the time she needed to heal. But . . . it seemed he'd simply not required her abilities until now, and the moment he did, he'd not hesitated to ask. Worse, in spite of Jaromir's skill with a sword, Céline and Amelie were being sent into danger—and Anton knew it.

Céline couldn't help feeling numb. Nothing was as she'd thought.

As Amelie angrily pulled off her faded blue shirt, Helga stepped back and examined the lavender wool gown Céline had arrived wearing. "Good. That will do nicely. Ladies wear wool when traveling. Now, come and look at what I've packed for you."

With little choice, Céline moved to obey, but she couldn't help viewing Helga with affection. Though the old woman was officially a servant here in the castle, Céline suspected she was more. For one, everyone else treated Jaromir with deference and respect—even fear on occasion—but Helga often referred to him sarcastically as "his lord majesty lieutenant" and had a tendency to boss him around . . . and for some reason, he let her.

Even more, Helga had been responsible for helping Céline and Amelie understand at least the roots of who they were and where their mother had come from: the Móndyalítko, or "the world's little children," traveling gypsies.

Before arriving in Sèone, Céline and Amelie had known little of their origins.

Their father had been a village hunter for Shetâna, and one year, he'd been on a long-distance hunt, lasting several weeks, and he'd come back with their mother and married her. Then the couple had built an apothecary shop in Shetâna and started a small family. Once Céline and Amelie were old enough, their mother taught them to read. She taught Céline herb lore and the ways of healing—while saying nothing of her own past.

Neither of the sisters had ever heard the term "Mist-Torn" before Helga explained it to them, that not only were they born of a Móndyalítko mother, but they were of a special line called the Mist-Torn, each of whom possessed a natural power. As sisters, Céline and Amelie were two sides of the same coin, one able to read the future and one able to read the past.

This knowledge had changed their lives.

"I've packed a second wool dress for each of you," Helga was saying, "and a formal gown for both of you as well, should Captain Keegan be one of those officers who likes to entertain."

Amelie looked over with her face turning red. "I thought we going to be in the middle of a forest."

Helga nodded sagely, causing her kerchief to fall further askew. "Yes, and some of those captains posted to the middle of nowhere insist on bringing their own wine and goblets and putting on airs to try to pretend they ain't in the middle of nowhere. His lord majesty lieutenant has no idea what you're walking into, and he told me to make sure you were prepared."

"Thank you, Helga," Céline said. "We know you're trying to help."

Helga grunted and turned back to the large travel bags. "I've got stockings and clean shifts and brushes for your hair. Do you have any potions you need to need to pack?"

Céline bit the inside of her mouth at the word "potions" and went to the door to retrieve a large box of supplies she'd brought up from the shop. Like Jaromir, she had no idea what they were walking into and wanted to be prepared for any contingency.

"Will there be room in the provisions wagon?" she asked.

"The lieutenant will make room," Helga answered, hefting the box.

"I can barely move in this thing," Amelie complained.

Glancing over at her sister, Céline saw that she was

trying to swing her arms while wearing the green gown.

"You'll get used to it," Céline said, almost crossly. Really . . . they had bigger worries than Amelie being forced to abandon her breeches and put on a dress.

"The color suits you," Helga said.

Indeed, the shade of forest green did suit Amelie's pale skin. The gown was simple, long sleeved, with a straight neckline. The skirt was not too full, though it did seem rather long. Hopefully, she wouldn't trip over it.

Crouching, Amelie tucked her dagger into a sheath inside her boot.

Helga picked up a set of bright red cloaks lying on the bed. "You'd best put these on." She held one out. "Prince Anton had them purchased down in the village this morning. I heard he paid a fortune."

Céline didn't doubt it. Both cloaks were of fine quality, dyed a rich shade of scarlet. Only a prince could afford to buy two such ready-made garments at a moment's notice.

Amelie reached out and touched one. "Won't these make us look more like ladies of court just playing at being healers?"

Céline took a cloak and put it on, leaving the hood down so that it rested on her shoulders. "It doesn't matter. The only thing that matters is that this Captain Keegan believes we're seers and healers from Anton's court sent to help him."

Ironically, they both *were* seers from Anton's court, and Céline was a skilled healer, but no one at Ryazan could know they were peasants who, until a few months ago, had been scraping out an existence in a tiny, muddy village under the harsh thumb of Damek's rule. They would need to command respect if they intended to conduct a proper investigation.

By way of answer, Amelie donned her cloak as well.

Turning, Céline looked into a tall mirror on the stand in the corner. Amelie stood beside her, and they appeared as two respectable young healers preparing for a journey.

"What about my hair?" Amelie asked.

"If anyone asks, we'll tell them you had a fever and I had to cut it off, and it's just now growing back out."

"Right, then. Are we ready?"

Céline didn't answer. This was all happening much too fast, and she didn't feel remotely ready.

Near midday, Céline found herself in the courtyard of the castle, standing just outside a bustling collection of soldiers and horses as Jaromir called out orders in preparation for departure. He was dressed in chain armor and a tan tabard of Castle Sèone, with a sheathed long sword on his left hip.

Amelie was overseeing their travel bags being packed into a wagon, but Céline didn't seem able to speak or move. A part her still couldn't believe that only last evening, she'd walked up to the castle looking forward to attending a banquet.

Now she felt lost and out of control, as if she was being swept along on a current instead of guiding her own path.

"All right," Jaromir called. "Get the provisions tied down and covered."

Céline glanced over the men he'd chosen. Though not surprised, she was slightly unsettled to see Corporal Pavel at Jaromir's side. Pavel was tall with a lanky build and dark close-cropped hair. He was considered quite good in a fight, and so Jaromir often brought him on journeys. But Céline was cautious around Pavel. He had a well-hidden temper, and although he'd never actually hurt Céline, he had come close once, and she avoided him when possible.

She was surprised, however, to see Guardsman Rurik in the mix. He was a smaller man with a wiry build and curly light brown hair he wore to the top of his shoulders. He was known as the swiftest rider of anyone under Jaromir's command, and so he'd been offered the position of messenger between Anton and his father.

It seemed unlikely that Anton would wish to part with him for any length of time.

Still, Jaromir appeared to have great trust in Rurik, and when Céline and Amelie had first arrived in the courtyard that morning, Jaromir had explained his preparations a bit more carefully. He'd chosen fifteen men—whom he knew well—from the Sèone ranks as escort, and he'd had a wagon loaded with provisions. Once they neared Ryazan, he would keep Corporal Pavel with him and send the rest back to Sèone, as Anton did not want him riding into the encampment with a contingent. Jaromir would later send Pavel to arrange for an escort to come and see them safely home again, once the . . . difficulty had been solved. Anton and Jaromir had considered having the contingent camp somewhere in the woods and wait. But there was no telling how long it would take Amelie and Céline to solve the situation—possibly weeks—and so in the end, they'd decided it was a better option to have the men simply return to Sèone and go back when necessary.

However, the gist of all this suggested the trip would not be brief. That much was clear. So Céline had asked Erin, the blacksmith's daughter, to come check on Oliver at the shop each day, to bring him milk and make certain he had fresh water. Céline had left a back shutter open, so he could get in and out easily, and he was perfectly capable of hunting for himself, but she wanted him to know that he'd not been abandoned, that the shop was still his home.

And now she was simply waiting to ride out on a journey she could not refuse.

"I chose your horse myself," said a soft voice behind her.

Turning, she found Anton standing there, taking in the sight of her red cloak.

"Would you like to meet her?" he asked.

His face was unreadable, but his voice was strained and his eyes shone with misery. Suddenly, all her numbness faded away. He didn't want to send her on this task. He looked as lost as she by all the activity taking place in this courtyard.

Trying to smile, she answered, "Yes, please introduce us."

She followed him over to a dappled gray mare with a cloth bridle and a blanket over her sidesaddle.

"Her name is Sable," Anton said. "She's gentle but swift."

Céline didn't know how to ride, so she simply nodded, petting Sable's soft nose. "Thank you."

The misery in his eyes increased, and he leaned closer. "Céline, I didn't want to ask this of you . . . any of this. But I cannot fail my father, and I cannot see any other way. You and Amelie have a chance of finding out what is happening at those mines, and then Jaromir can stop it. There is no one else." He paused. "You understand? This isn't about me. It's about the future of Droevinka."

His normally haughty voice sounded so pained, she wasn't certain how to respond. She did understand, and she could not fathom even the prospect of Damek as grand prince, with the power of life and death over the nation.

"Mount up!" Jaromir called.

Céline glanced over at Amelie, who was scrambling up into the sidesaddle of a small black gelding. Amelie didn't know how to ride either, and sitting with her legs on the same side of the horse would hardly make it easier. The very concept of a sidesaddle struck Céline as ridiculous, but she and Amelie were supposed to be ladies of court.

Anton took hold of Sable's bridle and helped guide Céline's foot into the stirrup. Thankfully, Céline managed to lift herself and settle into her own saddle with a modicum of grace.

Then she looked down. Before leaving, she needed

to tell Anton something. She felt different from only moments ago. His coming out here to see her off, to express his regret and reluctance, had made her understand the importance of what he was asking.

"We won't fail," she said. "I swear that your father will not be disappointed, that he will see you as a leader who can step up to any task, any problem, and find a way to solve it."

He stared up. "Céline—"

"I swear," she repeated.

Then she managed to steer the mare around and follow Amelie and Jaromir toward the castle gates, with a contingent of fifteen soldiers and a wagon coming behind her.

CHAPTER THREE

Two days later, Amelie's backside had never been so sore. Perhaps riding on a horse saved wear on one's feet, but she didn't find the trade-off worthwhile. Every step sent a new jarring pain up her spine. As the contingent traveled up a heavily forested dirt road, she seriously considered asking Jaromir if she and Céline might tie their mounts to the back of the wagon and ride on top of the provisions for a while.

Only two things stopped her.

First, "ladies of court" should probably not be seen sitting on top of the provisions like so much extra baggage.

Second . . . Jaromir hadn't looked at her once since the journey began. In fact, he hadn't looked at her since the night up in Anton's apartments. She'd both expected him to tease her about the green dress and make jokes about someone finally getting her into a skirt—and dreaded that he would do so.

But he hadn't.

He hadn't said a word.

With a sinking feeling, she thought she knew why.

His face had been so shocked when she'd demanded of Anton, "What's in it for us?" and he hadn't looked at her since. In truth, she should be thrilled, dancing with joy that she'd finally done something to make him stop teasing her, flirting with her, attempting to make her like him. She knew his reputation for going through women, and she had no intention of being just another girl on his long list.

But still . . . was he angry with her? Had he been so appalled by her words to Anton that his opinion of her was forever changed? Quite unexpectedly, she found the prospect upsetting.

"Are you all right?" Céline asked tiredly, wincing at another jarring step of her own horse.

"Fine."

Realizing her face must have given something away, Amelie pushed down all thoughts of Jaromir. Instead, she tried to ignore her aching backside and focus on the journey. A part of her had always wanted to travel, but she'd seldom had the chance. Once when she was younger, she'd visited the great city of Enêmûsk, but the actual journey had been somewhat of a blur.

Now she tried to keep track of the path they followed.

Castle Sèone was located in southwest Droevinka, not far from the Belaskian border. Even though Jaromir was well traveled, he carried a map, and he occasionally stopped and consulted it. He'd led them on a well-maintained road straight east at first, and then he'd turned north. She'd heard several of the soldiers mention that the Ryazan silver mines were at the top of

Droevinka, right on the Stravinan border. But she couldn't help noticing that the farther north they traveled, the thicker the trees seemed to grow and the more narrow and potholed the road became. It must turn to mud in the autumn.

The weather in Droevinka leaned toward cold and gray—sometimes even in summer. Amelie was accustomed to this.

But toward the end of this second day of the journey, she was beginning to find their surroundings downright oppressive. Daylight was fading, and old trees along the side of the narrow road were dotted with moss that dangled in scant beards from a few branches. Beneath the aroma of loam and wild foliage was an ever-present thin scent of decay. By the way several of the soldiers glanced around at the trees, she could see she wasn't alone in noting the eerie quality of the forest.

"Small clearing ahead," Jaromir called. "We'll make camp for the night."

"Oh, thank the gods," Céline said quietly. "I can't wait to get off this horse."

Within moments, they were off the road and dismounted, and a now somewhat familiar routine began. Several soldiers saw to the horses while others found branches for a fire and still others unpacked provisions. Whenever possible, Amelie and Céline tried to help, but Jaromir's men were well trained, and Amelie felt more in the way than anything else.

"Voulter and Rimoux," Jaromir said to a pair of men as he pointed west. "There's a stream just below that drop-off. Go and fetch some water."

Had he already known about the stream before stopping? Jaromir seemed to have planned for everything, and he knew how to give orders. Thankfully, he'd packed a small tent, and each night, one of the soldiers had set it up for Amelie and Céline so they wouldn't have to sleep in the open.

By the fall of full darkness, camp had been set, water was boiling for tea, and several men were passing out rations of jerked beef, apples, and biscuits. Amelie moved to sit by the fire with her supper balanced in one arm. She had to keep her other hand free to lift the more than annoying hem of her skirt. She still hated wearing this dress and didn't think she'd get used to it. The red cloak didn't bother her so much. At least it was warm.

A few of the soldiers sat down beside her. The routine for setting camp and eating had been exactly the same last night, but tonight . . . something felt different. The men kept glancing into the thick, dark forest, and the long, dangling beards of moss from the nearest trees looked like black ropes, waiting to tangle whoever was foolish enough to go near.

Even Guardsman Rurik, who was known for his cheerful nature, sat down silently and kept his eyes lowered as he bit into an apple.

"Shall we have some entertainment?" Céline asked, smiling as she walked through the seated soldiers and stood near the fire. "You all look a glum lot to me."

She wasn't carrying any food, and her cloak was thrown back over her shoulders so that her arms were free. Amelie couldn't help but feel a stab of admiration for her sister. Céline had a few faults, being overly sensitive for one, but at times that sensitivity could be useful. She'd probably felt the men's trepidation over the past few hours even more keenly than had Amelie.

The difference was that Céline could do something about it.

"Guardsman Voulter," Céline said, turning toward a young man with carrot red hair. "I saw you in the market last week, trying to win over Esmeralda, the butcher's pretty daughter, and I could see she left you in some doubt."

A few of the soldiers stopped eating and grinned as Guardsman Voulter's face turned as red as his hair.

"Would you like to know how she will receive your attentions next time?" Céline asked.

"I'd like to know," Rurik called out through a mouthful of apple.

Several of the others laughed.

Standing there with the darkness behind her, light from the flames glinting off her hair, and her red cloak thrown back, Céline looked every inch the beautiful gypsy fortune-teller.

"Would you like to know?" she asked Voulter more gently, and he nodded once.

Walking over, Céline took his hand.

"Oh, this is promising," she said, gazing into his palm. She wasn't really attempting to use her abilities and see his future, but the men didn't know that. For five years, before her true power surfaced, Céline had made a good living pretending to read futures. She knew exactly what to say and do.

"Esmeralda's father makes her family eat far too much meat," she announced, still looking into Voulter's palm. "I see here that the next time you see her, you bring her a small loaf of cinnamon bread and some strawberries—which are her favorites—and she is most welcoming and pleased to see you. Your attentions are gladly met."

Most of the men were smiling in amusement now, and Céline turned to a soldier with a hint of gray at his temples. "You have a question. I can see it in your face."

She was skilled at reading faces. She always had been.

The soldier hesitated and then said, "I'd like to get one more foal out of my mare, Aspen, but she's growing older, and I don't want to lose her. Will she be safe if I try?"

This was a trickier question. Céline had many friends in the village and had probably known that Esmeralda harbored a taste for cinnamon bread and strawberries. However, though this new dilemma was not as much fun as Voulter's had been, all the men at the fire were listening intently, interested in the answer.

Céline didn't hesitate. Walking over, she took the man's hand and looked into his palm, running her finger down the centerline. "No, you are wise to be concerned. I see her in trouble if she breeds again. If you wish to keep her safe, you should not try."

Amelie had a feeling this would be the answer. When in doubt, Céline normally erred on the side of safety, but she'd also managed to compliment the soldier on his wisdom and at the same time probably told him what he'd wanted to hear.

Céline looked around the circle and smiled again. "Who's next?"

Amelie stopped listening and turned her head slightly, attempting to glance behind herself.

Jaromir was standing outside the circle of seated men, watching Céline with gratitude on his face. He was no fool, and he must have felt the nervous energy of the men as they made camp. Now Céline had lightened the mood.

Yet an unwanted wave of unhappiness flooded through Amelie.

For some reason—and she had no idea why—she didn't want Jaromir to think badly of her. It was outside her nature to either explain or apologize. In her entire life, she'd only managed it a few times with Céline. But Céline had always forgiven her with great warmth.

Jaromir was not a man known for his warmth.

Still, without allowing herself to think, Amelie climbed to her feet. She could not go another day leaving things the way they were.

Making her way outside the circle, she almost balked when Jaromir saw her coming and his expression closed up. How would she feel if she tried to explain herself and her attempt changed nothing? The humiliation would be too much.

But she couldn't stop.

"Jaromir . . . ," she tried to begin.

He looked back toward the fire, and her heart sank.

"I wanted to . . . ," she stammered. "I wanted to tell you that I didn't mean what I said in Prince Anton's chambers."

His head turned quickly, and his eyes dropped to her face.

"Céline and I grew up so poor," she rushed on. "We had to ask for payment or trade for anything we did for others. What I said . . . it just came out. I felt backed into a corner, and when that happens, I always say the wrong thing. But I didn't mean it. I am grateful for all Anton has done for us, and I'm . . . I'm sorry."

All the hardness in his face vanished, and his brown eyes grew soft. "Don't be sorry. You know I lived as a hired sword once, poor and hungry, and those scars never heal. I should have realized. You're here now, and you're ready to help. Let's say no more about it."

Amelie blinked in near disbelief. She'd reached out to someone besides Céline, and he had reached back. He'd been kind. She didn't know what to say.

"Besides," he added. "So far, the journey has been worth it just to see you in that dress."

"Well, don't get used to it!" she snapped before she could stop herself.

He flashed her a grin.

She didn't return the smile, but she felt much, much better.

Céline continued entertaining the men until they'd finished their suppers. By trade, she didn't read palms, and this certainly wasn't how it was normally done, but she knew how to lean upon her deeply ingrained skills at gauging facial inflections, and her only goal tonight had been to create a distraction and help the men relax a bit in this oppressive forest. She'd succeeded. Glancing over, she saw Amelie talking to Jaromir, and the sight made her glad. Jaromir had been a bit standoffish on this journey, and no matter how much Amelie pretended otherwise, it was clear she'd been bothered.

"All right," Céline said, "I need to eat my supper, too." She took a step from the campfire.

"Oh, just one more," Guardsman Rurik begged, his brown curls looking frizzy in the damp night air. "Sergeant Bazin's wife threw him out again, clothes in the street and all. It was quite something. Can you see if she'll take him back?"

A stocky, middle-aged guard choked on his tea and looked over. "Rurik!"

"Well, don't you want to know?" Rurik asked him.

But Céline would not be tempted. Waving Rurik off, she began walking again. Nearing the edge of the circle, though, she stopped.

Corporal Pavel stood beside a dark tree, staring at her. She realized he must have been standing there in the shadows, watching her the whole time without joining in. His expression was sad, almost hungry, and she fought against feeling sorry for him. His moods could change swiftly. She'd underestimated him once, and it had almost cost her.

Changing directions, she walked more in the direction of Jaromir and Amelie.

"I'm going down to the creek to wash," she said as she passed them.

"Do you want me to come?" Jaromir asked.

There was probably some water left in one of the

buckets, but Céline was really after a few moments to herself. "No, I won't be long, and I can see well at night. I just need to wash off the dust."

Overhead, the clouds parted and moonlight shone down through the trees. She made her way down a slope, hearing the water rushing a short distance below. Up above, she could still hear the voices of the men as they talked around the fire, and she sank to a crouch, dipping her hands in the cold water and bringing them up to her face.

Her first moment of solitude in several days.

A part of her didn't want to dwell on what lay ahead . . . on her promise to Anton that she wouldn't fail, but success was going to involve more than making a few men laugh around a campfire. She would have to read the soldiers at Ryazan for real, to invoke her ability, and in all likelihood, to see blood and death in someone's future.

Could she bear to go through that again?

"Céline," said a quiet voice from behind her.

Still in her crouched position, she whirled in alarm to see Pavel standing a few paces away. Had he followed her down here? His expression was still sad and hungry.

In the spring, when she'd been engaged in solving the series of murders for Anton, she and Pavel had become friends. She'd known he was attracted to her, and she had used this to her own advantage once. When she and Jaromir disagreed over the best way to protect a potential victim, she'd tried to circumvent Jaromir's authority and ended up offering Pavel a cup of tea laced with opium—as he had been guarding the victim. He took the tea from her hands, thinking she was favoring him with her attention. Shortly after drinking it, he'd fallen asleep, allowing her to sneak the victim outside the castle for better protection.

Yes, this had been a questionable action on her part, but at the time, it seemed her only possible course.

Pavel had been reprimanded, and afterward, in his anger, he'd cornered Céline inside a shack and terrified her. Later he regretted this, but it didn't matter. She no longer trusted him. Though he kept this dark side of himself hidden away much of the time, she had seen it.

"Why won't you talk to me?" he asked. "Are you so angry that you won't even talk?"

Glancing up the slope, she became very aware that they were alone. She wasn't remotely angry. She was afraid of him. "I need to get back to Amelie."

She tried to walk past, but his right hand snaked out, grabbing her wrist. Before she realized what was happening, he had her back pressed up against a tree. She gasped, instinctively pushing against his chest. He didn't seem to notice she was struggling.

"Are you punishing me?" he whispered in her ear. "You know I'm sorry about . . . about before, but you played with me, tricked me, made me look a fool to the lieutenant." He raised his left hand and touched her cheek. "That's all done now."

Her mind raced for a way to stay calm and get herself free, but when he moved his hand down her face, toward her throat, she couldn't help trying to cry out.

"Amel—"

Instantly, his hand was over her mouth, and his eyes flashed in anger. "You're going to stay here and talk to me! Tell me what I have to do to make you forgive me, to stop punishing me."

She couldn't move in his grip, and she was struggling to breathe though her nose. Somehow, she got one hand up around his wrist, trying to pull it off her mouth.

"Pavel, please," she tried saying into his palm, but the sound was muffled.

"Corporal!" a deep voice barked.

Pavel's body jerked. His grip eased slightly, and Céline managed to look to the left. Jaromir stood there with moonlight washing over his face.

"Step away," he ordered.

For only a second or two, Céline thought Pavel was going to refuse, which would mean he was more unhinged than even she'd realized. Jaromir's men didn't disobey his orders.

But with a sharp jerk, Pavel stepped backward, glaring at her as if she'd caused this.

"Céline, get up to camp," Jaromir said.

This was embarrassing for all of them, but she didn't need to be asked twice. Dashing past Jaromir, she ran up the slope, hearing his low voice behind her, followed by Pavel's short, clipped replies.

Though she was glad Jaromir had come down to check on her, a part of her couldn't help regretting what he'd seen. While she certainly didn't blame herself for Pavel's behavior, she also couldn't help feeling that because of her, there was now a rift between two soldiers who needed to depend on each other.

Walking back into camp, she tried to appear calm—and apparently failed.

"What's wrong?" Amelie asked.

"Nothing."

She would say no more.

Though Amelie expected the following day to be less rife with tension . . . it wasn't. Jaromir once again treated her in the same easygoing manner as before their misunderstanding—which made her both glad and mildly annoyed—but something else felt wrong, and now he and Pavel seemed to be avoiding each other.

No matter how much Céline denied it, *something* had happened the night before, and Amelie was hurt that Céline wouldn't tell her. The sisters had never kept secrets from each other.

However, as the day progressed, Amelie's sore backside took precedence over all other concerns, and she began to focus on just making it to dusk.

The forest around them continued to grow darker and denser. The path they traveled, which barely passed for a road, became so narrow that the entire party began riding single file, and Sergeant Bazin, who drove the wagon, was having difficulty as brush kept getting caught in the spokes of the wheels.

Somehow, they all pressed onward until Jaromir called a halt at dusk. Amelie slid off her horse, putting both hands to her back. Once again, the soldiers worked quickly to set up camp, but they seemed just as angst ridden as they'd been the night before, glancing into the dark trees.

When the campfire fire burned brightly and supper had been passed out, Céline stepped in again to try to distract the men. Tonight, she switched to storytelling.

"Have you heard the tale of the ungrateful prince?" she asked, holding up both palms.

Her first story was an adventure about a haughty young prince transformed into a wolfhound by a wizard to whom he'd been rude. The young noble then roamed the land, attempting to lift the curse using only his brains and his paws while learning more about the people of his province in the process.

Céline walked around the glowing campfire, using her arms and hands to help tell the story, and altering her voice to make the characters seem more real.

By the time she was halfway through, all the soldiers had stopped eating and were leaning forward, just listening.

Of course the young prince negated his curse in the end by undertaking one unselfish task, helping a village plagued by trolls.

Céline acted out the final battle with great flair.

The next tale was a comedy about three brothers vying for the love of an unworthy woman by playing foul tricks on one another. When Céline reached the point at which one brother tainted another's bathwater with blue dye, the soldiers were laughing out loud.

Although Amelie had been enjoying the stories, too, she glanced back and noticed Jaromir watching Céline with the same gratitude as he had the night before.

At the sight of this, Amelie couldn't help feeling useless again. She possessed skills and gifts, but entertaining other people was not among them. Though she longed to be useful, Céline's gifts were simply much more . . . apparent.

Soon, everyone bedded down for the night, somewhat cheered both by the stories Céline had woven into the night air and with the hope of reaching their destination the following day.

But on that next day, Céline's gifts only proved ever more visible and indispensable.

The morning started off well enough. Once they were packed and ready to leave, Jaromir mounted his horse and consulted his map. Amelie settled gingerly into the saddle of her black gelding and then rode up beside him.

"How far?" she asked, already gritting her teeth at the pain shooting up her spine.

"It depends," he answered, holding the map down for her to see. "We're going to have to cross the Vudrask River, so we have two possible routes from here."

"Cross the river? Isn't that the borderline between Droevinka and Stravina?"

"Generally, yes," he answered. "But over the past hundred years or so, a few territories directly on either side have been traded. Ryazan is one of them."

Drawing her attention back to the map, he pointed his finger at their current location and then began sliding it. "If we want an easier time of things, we turn off onto this wide northeast road, follow it all the way up to and around Enêmûsk, and then keep going until we reach this bridge." He pointed to a symbol representing a bridge. "Once across, we can head west again, but that route will take us longer." His finger moved back to their current location and then upward. "Or we can continue straight north on this current narrow path and ford the river here where the water is more shallow. Following that route, we should reached Ryazan by late afternoon."

"Oh, the shorter one, please," Amelie blurted out.

"Are you in a hurry to arrive there?"

"No, I am in a hurry to be off this horse. My backside will never be the same."

Instantly, she regretted her words, expecting him to make some joke about her backside, but he simply nodded. "All right. Straight north it is."

She rode behind him as he led the way, with Céline directly behind her. The single-file column did not leave much opportunity for conversation, but in a way this was better. She wanted to just focus on getting through one more day. If all went well, tomorrow she would not have to climb back onto this horse.

However, in the early afternoon, she heard the sound of rushing, gurgling water, and within a few more steps, the sound grew louder.

"What is that?"

"The river," Jaromir answered.

The road broke through the trees, and he walked his horse down the bank to make room for those behind him. Following him, Amelie felt her first hint of doubt over her impulse to take the fastest route. When Jaromir had said "shallow," she'd been envisioning slow water over a rocky streambed.

The sight before her looked nothing like the image

in her mind. The river was wide and the current appeared swift. Through the water, she could see to the bottom and gauged that the depth would nearly cover the wagon's wheels.

"You said it would be shallow."

Jaromir glanced down at her. "This is shallow. This is the one place where barges can run into trouble."

Céline pulled up beside them and went slightly pale. "We're going to cross that?"

"Soldiers from the northern houses do it all the time," he assured them. "We'll be fine."

After that, more horses came from the forest out onto the bank, and Jaromir started giving orders. "I'm going to take Amelie and Céline over first," he called. "Pavel and Rurik, you help Bazin with the wagon, one of you on each side of the team."

"Yes, sir," they both called at the same time.

Amelie remembered that the stocky, middle-aged guard driving the wagon was the one whose wife had apparently thrown him out of the house.

But she didn't have time to think long on this, as without delay, Jaromir nudged his horse forward. "Follow me," he said.

With little choice, Amelie urged her gelding after Jaromir's oversized chestnut stallion—named Badger due to his penchant for biting anyone he didn't like. Amelie's smaller horse didn't hesitate, walking right into the water. She glanced back once to see Céline's gray mare coming after them. The water rose to the level of Amelie's mount's stomach and the current rushed swiftly. The bottom of her gown and cloak were soaked, but her horse managed to keep walking at a steady pace, following Jaromir's lead, and soon, all three horses broke into a trot as they reached the bank on the other side.

Céline was still pale, but she managed a smile. "Not so bad after all."

Amelie turned to look back and see how the others were faring. The soldiers on horseback were having no trouble, but Bazin was trying to force the harnessed team into the water, and both horses refused. To help, Rurik leaned over and took hold of one bridle while Pavel did the same with the other. Jaromir watched tensely and then seemed to relax a bit as the team finally moved forward, pulling the wagon into the current.

"Well done," he called.

As Amelie had guessed, the water quickly reached more than halfway up the wheels, and the team snorted as they struggled forward, with white ringing their eyes. Halfway across, it seemed they would make it without incident, but then the harnessed horse on the left side tripped over a rock and started to go down. It screamed out as it fought to right itself. Unfortunately, Pavel had been holding its bridle, and his horse panicked and tried to bolt. It slipped as well . . . going down with him in the saddle.

"Pavel!" Jaromir shouted, kicking his own horse back into the water.

Amelie watched helplessly as Pavel's horse landed on him and then thrashed to jump back up. Pavel came off the horse, but his foot was still in the stirrup. Amelie heard a cracking sound over the rush of the water, and then he was free of the saddle but caught in the current.

Céline drew in a loud breath as Jaromir reached him and swung off his horse. Catching Pavel under both arms, Jaromir somehow managed to pull him the rest of the way across the river and up onto the bank. Pavel's horse had managed to reach the bank as well. Céline was already running toward them, and then, finally, spurred from her shock, Amelie dashed after her.

Pavel was crying out in pain, and Céline was already giving orders.

"Jaromir, don't move him anymore. Just lay him flat. It's his right leg."

The next few moments were a blur of confusion as more of the men came running over. Jaromir used a dagger to cut Pavel's pant leg open, and Amelie put one hand to her mouth. She wasn't squeamish, but the white bone of his shin was poking through his torn flesh.

"By the gods," one of the soldiers said, "that cannot be fixed. He's going to lose that leg."

Pavel's eyes went wide. "No!" He tried pulling himself up the bank.

Amelie wanted to punch the soldier who'd spoken.

But Céline was at Pavel's head, talking to him. "Don't listen to him. You won't lose your leg." She looked around as the wagon came up out of the river onto the bank. "Amelie, run and get my box." She turned back. "Jaromir, I need flat boards. Can you break one of the apple crates and bring me several of the boards?"

Amelie and Jaromir both ran for the wagon. Amelie's errand was quicker, as she simply needed to get Céline's box and run back. She left Jaromir breaking the side off a crate.

"Here!" Amelie called, skidding to a stop.

Pavel was in so much pain, he was panting, and his features were twisted.

The box was large, and Céline opened it carefully. The inside was filled with bottles, jars, powders, and bandages. She took out a bottle filled with a white milky substance. "Amelie, hold his head."

Amelie knew what to do and moved to cradle Pavel's head.

"Swallow this," Céline told him. "It will stop the pain."

Her words must have gotten through, because he let her put the bottle to his mouth, and he took a drink.

"One more," she ordered. "A large swallow."

He obeyed her.

Everyone else just stood watching, but in a few moments, Pavel began to relax in Amelie's arms. Carefully, she laid him on the bank, and his eyes closed halfway. Jaromir came jogging up with the boards.

"What did you give him?"

"Poppy syrup," Céline answered. "He'll be asleep soon. I have to set the leg, and you will not want him awake for that." Scooting down, she frowned at the broken bone. Pavel's boots were made of stiff leather and came halfway up his shins. "This boot must have protected his ankle and foot when the horse jumped back up, but then his leg took all the force." She glanced at Jaromir. "We need to get the boot off without causing any more damage. I'm going to hold the leg, and I need you to slowly, very slowly, inch off the boot."

For all his strength, Amelie suspected Jaromir was capable of being gentle, and he proved her right in the next few moments as Céline held Pavel's leg below the broken section and Jaromir took his time inching the boot off bit by small bit.

Céline took a deep breath once it came away from Pavel's foot in Jaromir's hand.

"All right," she said. "Now I need to cut off the rest of this pant leg and then set the bone."

"Have you done this before?" Jaromir asked, his voice tight.

"Yes, many times. My mother taught me how to set everything from broken bones to dislocated shoulders."

That seemed good enough for him, because he fell silent and let her work. She glanced up at Pavel to make certain he was out cold; then, with a scraping sound, she set the broken shinbone until the parts lined up perfectly and the leg was straight. After that, she quickly but carefully dabbed the jagged wounds around the bone with a cleansing and healing ointment made from adder's-tongue. Then she splinted his shin with the narrow boards and began the slow process of wrapping them tightly with strips of bandages.

This took some time.

Wiping her head with the back of her hand, she finally said, "All right. That's all I can do. The bone is secure, and it should knit. But he cannot travel until he wakes, and even then, we'll need to make a space for him in the back of the wagon, so he can sit up with the leg straight. He can't put any weight on it for weeks. Once he's back home, he should be able to use crutches as long as he keeps his weight off." Looking up at Jaromir, she hesitated. "I'm sorry, but you'll have to choose another man to remain with us in Ryazan."

To Amelie's puzzlement, a flash of relief crossed Jaromir's face, as if a burden had suddenly been taken from him.

"Yes, of course." He stood up. "We'll make camp here and see if he's fit to travel in the morning."

Amelie raised an eyebrow. Why would Jaromir be relieved that Pavel couldn't remain with them in Ryazan?

The following day, at midmorning, Céline pronounced Pavel fit to travel, and she supervised as Rurik, Jaromir, and Bazin lifted her patient into a cleared space in the wagon's bed.

"Don't try to help us," Rurik told Pavel. "Just let us do the work."

Once they had him settled, they leaned him against a large rolled-up piece of canvas, and he glanced down at his splinted leg. Céline had no idea how he was feeling. His expression was dark, and she guessed he was probably torn between gratitude that his leg had been saved and angry disappointment that he'd lost his place on the mission.

"Remember what I said about not putting weight on it," she told him, playing the part of the healer to avoid speaking of anything else. "The bone must be allowed to knit."

He didn't answer and didn't look at her.

She turned to Jaromir. "I think it's safe for him if we press onward."

Jaromir exhaled through his nose, as if considering something, and then he stood up in the back of the wagon. "Everyone," he called out, "over here."

Faster than Céline would have expected, all the men had gathered round. Amelie was among them, looking up at Jaromir curiously.

"Ryazan is not far up this road," he began, pointing north. "Guardsman Rurik will stay with me, but I'm sending the rest of you back now." Turning his body slightly, he motioned down a wide, well-maintained road to the east. "I don't want you crossing the river again, so head east and use the bridge up above Enêmûsk." He handed the map to Bazin. "Then head straight home and make sure Pavel stays off his leg."

Almost everyone nodded in agreement . . . all except for Guardsman Rurik, who was aghast.

"Me?" he asked. "Sir? Shouldn't you choose someone else?"

Jaromir wasn't accustomed to having his orders questioned. "Guardsman?"

"What if Prince Anton needs a message sent to his father?" Rurik rushed on.

Jaromir's jaw twitched. "He can send someone else." His voice held an edge of threat, and Rurik fell silent, but he looked shaken.

Céline wondered why. She'd found him to be a good

choice on Jaromir's part. Rurik might not be as strong a fighter as Pavel, but he was steady and of a cheerful disposition, and on this task, those two qualities might be of more use. Why was he reluctant to stay? Had he heard any hints about what she and Amelie had come here to do? Even so, he was a soldier and didn't strike her as someone easily frightened.

"Guardsman Voulter," Jaromir said. "Tie the women's travel bags onto one of the extra horses." He continued giving orders in preparation for them to separate from the group, but Céline stopped listening.

She turned and gazed up the road to the north, forgetting about Rurik's strange reluctance and Pavel's broken leg.

Ryazan waited.

CHAPTER FOUR

By midday, the already narrow road had turned into little more than a path, but when Jaromir saw a clearing up ahead, he knew they'd arrived at their destination. As his horse broke through the tree line, he had no idea what to expect.

But . . . he had anticipated at least seeing a number of small buildings. From what he understood, Prince Lieven had had men stationed here for five years.

"Tents?" Amelie asked in equal puzzlement, pulling her horse up beside his.

Six enormous tents and numerous smaller ones were the only dwellings in sight. Behind the tents stood a large, makeshift wooden barn, but it appeared to be the only permanent construction.

Several soldiers in dark brown tabards—and carrying spears—turned their way, but they all froze as Céline rode up beside her sister and then Rurik brought up the rear.

Jaromir raised a hand in greeting. No one responded, and the soldiers milling among the tents stood staring at Amelie and Céline. These men appeared unwashed and on edge, with tight, anxious expressions. Following his instincts, Jaromir decided not to advance until someone approached him.

Finally, an overweight guard came walking over, gripping his spear but holding the point straight up.

"You lost?" he asked.

Two other guards came up behind him, looking even more unkempt up close. One was young, maybe seventeen, with long tangled hair and mismatched eyes: one blue, one brown. He appeared more skittish than edgy. His companion was a little older and taller, with two missing front teeth. The younger one hid halfway behind him, as if seeking protection.

But all three men continued to stare at Amelie and Céline.

Jaromir tensed at the complete lack of military discipline, and he pitched his tone to cold, angry authority. "I am Lieutenant Jaromir of Castle Sèone. We've been sent at the request of Prince Lieven. I would speak with Captain Keegan."

There was still a soldier inside the rotund guard directly in front of him, because the man winced, as if remembering something forgotten. Then he straightened and touched his chest. "Guardsman Saunders, sir." He pointed first to the youth behind him and then to the other man. "Guardsmen Graham and Ramsey."

"Where is your captain?" Jaromir asked.

Saunders turned around. "This way, sir."

Remaining mounted, Jaromir nodded to Amelie and then followed Guardsman Saunders through the tents. Many of the temporary shelters they passed looked years old, with patches and untended holes. It wasn't raining, but the sky was overcast and gray, adding to the dismal quality of their surroundings. Saunders led them toward the back of the encampment to the second-largest of the tents—the size of a small house—only this one appeared newer than the others.

Jaromir dismounted and turned to help Amelie off her horse. She looked at his outstretched hands and seemed about to push them away, but he shook his head once, hoping she'd have the sense to play her part. Thankfully, she seemed to realize this as well and let him lift her down. Rurik was on the ground, doing the same for Céline.

"Announce us and then see to our horses," Jaromir ordered.

Saunders stuck his head inside the open front flap of the tent. "Captain, visitors here to see you . . . from Castle Sèone."

Without waiting for an invitation, Jaromir walked past him, inside, motioning to his companions to follow. After the shabby visage of the camp outside, he was somewhat taken aback by the luxury now surrounding him. The floor was covered in thick furs. Tapestries hanging from the ceiling had been tastefully arranged to create partitions. There was a long polished table with six wooden chairs in the center of the main area, decorated with silver candlesticks. Looking through the partitions toward the rear, he could see a round, stone-bordered fire pit with a ventilation hole up above, so this tent could be kept warm when necessary.

At present, the tent held only two occupants, both men in chain armor and dark brown tabards. Jaromir pegged Captain Keegan right away, but only by virtue of his age. Keegan was of medium height, with a stocky, muscular build that was just now going to fat. His hair had gone gray, and he wore a close-trimmed beard that completely covered the lower half of his face.

The other man was in his late twenties, tall, well built, and clean-shaven, with sandy-colored hair and light blue eyes.

Keegan immediately bristled at the visitors walking into his tent. "What is this?" he barked.

Again, Jaromir hesitated. Had all semblance of military professionalism broken down here?

"Lieutenant Jaromir," he answered stiffly, "of Castle Sèone." He held one hand toward the women. "May I present the ladies Céline and Amelie Fawe of Prince Anton's court?"

As with Saunders, his manner had an immediate effect, and both men came to attention but seemed at a loss for words.

Céline smiled. "Forgive our appearance, Captain. We have been traveling for days."

This had an even more rapid effect than Jaromir's words, and both Keegan and his companion hurried to the table, pulling out chairs. "Ladies, please," Keegan said, "come and sit."

Saunders was gone now, and Rurik stood in the doorway. "You're dismissed," Jaromir told him quietly. "Make sure the horses are cared for."

"Yes, sir."

Keegan was pouring wine for Amelie and Céline, who were seated at the table, and he motioned to the tall, sandy-haired man. "This is Corporal Quinn. He is my current second-in-command." Glancing back at Jaromir, he asked, "You were sent by Prince Anton?"

"Via his father, to offer our assistance," Jaromir answered, stepping forward and pulling two letters from inside the quilted shirt beneath his armor. "The first is a letter from Prince Lieven to my lord, and the second is a letter from my lord to you."

He and Anton had decided to hold nothing back and allow Keegan full access to all pertinent information.

With a confused frown, Keegan took the letters from him and took his time reading them both. The first one was the same letter Leonides had carried from Prince Lieven, explaining the situation and clearly asking Anton to handle the matter. The second letter was from Anton, written directly to Keegan, explaining that Céline and Amelie were seers and healers from the court of Sèone, who were to be given full cooperation. Anton blatantly stated that if Keegan wished to have the heart of this problem rooted out and solved, he must grant Céline and Amelie's every request.

Finally, Keegan looked up and handed both letters to Corporal Quinn. But the captain seemed on the edge of strained disbelief.

"Let me understand this . . . ," he began. "So, instead of sending a replacement for me or even reinforcements from Pählen, my prince appealed to his youngest son . . . who in turn has sent two women who claim to be 'seers.'" His voice was rising toward the end of this short speech.

"Your prince already sent reinforcements once," Jaromir answered. "They were no help."

"Please, Captain," Céline said. "I know how this must seem, but Prince Anton had a similar, seemingly unsolvable . . . problem in the spring, and my sister and I were able to stop a series of unnatural deaths. We would not have been sent here unless your prince and mine believed we could help you."

Corporal Quinn was listening to her with interest. He had the same haunted, exhausted look of everyone else Jaromir had encountered here so far, but the man's light blue eyes were more alert. "Did you ride all this way with no escort?" he asked.

"No, of course not," Jaromir answered. "We had a small contingent, but I sent them back."

"Sent them back?" Keegan repeated. "Why?"

Again, Jaromir decided on honesty. "Because my lord thought you might feel challenged or that your authority was being threatened if I rode in with a contingent of men from Sèone under my command."

When Keegan glanced away, it suggested that Anton's instincts had been correct.

"My lord wishes you to understand that we are here to help," Jaromir went on. "That is all we wish to do. And he wanted to show his confidence that he trusts you to keep these ladies safe." The last part was a mere compliment. He would protect Amelie and Céline himself.

Keegan let out a long exhale. "If he wanted to keep them safe, he shouldn't have sent them here at all."

*   *   *

Céline listened as the men talked, but on the inside, she was trying not to panic over everything she'd seen and felt since riding in.

This was a place deserted by hope. She could see it in the faces of the men, in their shabby living conditions, in the fact that they'd long since ceased to wash or have a care for the proper manner of soldiers on duty.

Worse, the inside of this tent only increased her concerns, as it suggested their leader had cut himself off and lived apart with his thick furs and his red wine and tapestries. And still . . . the entire encampment felt so temporary, as if for years, none of the rotating groups of men stationed here had ever harbored any intention of staying long enough to put up wooden barracks.

So far, Amelie had remained silent, but Céline knew she must be just as troubled by what they'd walked into.

It was difficult to help men who appeared to view themselves as beyond help—and that's what she was sensing.

"Forgive me," Corporal Quinn said cautiously, looking at Céline. "But I don't quite understand the word 'seer.' What is it exactly that you claim to be able to do?"

She studied him. While Captain Keegan appeared to be a man letting himself go to seed, Quinn was in his prime. He, too, had been under great strain, but unlike those of the men outside, his tabard and face were clean. He had a coiled energy about him, as if he was capable of quick action when necessary. Céline thought he might be useful if she could win his trust.

"We each have a different ability," she answered. "I

can read a person's future, and Amelie can read their past."

Gulping half a goblet of wine, Captain Keegan made a loud, derisive snort, and Céline realized it was too soon to ask him to allow her to start reading his men. He would first need to understand they were not charlatans. Besides, she needed a better idea of the situation, and it seemed she was going to have to fall back on the authority that Anton had provided by sending his letter.

"Your prince mentioned that some of the workers here have been killed, but . . . where do the workers live?" she asked. "Riding in, we saw only your own encampment."

Quinn glanced at his captain, and Keegan pulled out a chair, sitting down himself. He pointed north. "There's a path through the trees, toward the mines. The workers live in a cleared area over there. I've been posting guards for them at night."

She nodded and then steeled herself. It was time for more difficult questions.

"Captain, can you tell us . . . what exactly did you mean by reporting that your men are 'turning into beasts'? What sort of beasts?"

A short silence followed, and this time Quinn answered.

"Like wolves, only larger, with wide chests and red eyes. It seems to happen quickly, with no warning."

"But this is only happening to your own men," Jaromir broke in, "not to any of the miners or their families."

"So far, yes," Quinn responded. "But you can't imagine . . . these things, these wolves are savage, mad, and they start killing anything in sight within moments of the change. Not long after this started, our workers began trying to escape, and we've had to actually ride some of them down and bring them back."

"Ride them down?" Amelie spoke up for the first time. "They're not allowed to leave?"

The question appeared to baffle both Keegan and Quinn.

"Well . . . of course they've signed contracts," Keegan answered. "My only duty here is to ensure the silver continues to flow. I cannot do that without enough workers."

Céline digested this quickly. What he was describing sounded a good deal like slavery, via these "contracts."

"How many soldiers have you lost?" she asked.

"Ten have been infected," Quinn answered, "including one officer, Lieutenant Sullian, and we lost the tenth man only three days ago. But we've also lost several more of our own men who were killed by the wolves, so the captain hasn't been able to spare anyone to carry a report to our prince about this last case."

"Infected?" she repeated.

"Well, what else could it be?" Keegan snapped, taking another swallow of wine. "And it's intentional. At first, I thought that one of the men had somehow . . . contracted this and it was spreading at random. But only my men have been affected. There is someone behind this."

Céline had been coming to this conclusion as well,

but the captain seemed so certain. Did he know something he wasn't sharing?

"Have you noticed any warning signs before the men begin to change? Or made any connections between them?"

Quinn shook his head. "I've only seen it happen twice, and it was sudden both times. One moment the man was fine, and then he began to retch, and then . . . we have to kill them as soon as possible."

"Do the bodies revert back to human form once they are dead?" she asked.

Both men were taken aback by the question, and she was aware that she probably didn't sound anything like a lady of court, but these things had to be asked.

"No," Quinn said. "And we burn them soon after."

"You burn the bodies of the wolves?" This was not good news. Céline wanted to examine one. "What about the miners and other soldiers who've been killed? Are they burned too?"

"I've seen no reason to enforce that," Keegan answered. "Some of our workers are Móndyalítko, and they have their own way of doing things, and I'm certain the infection is not being spread through the bodies of dead miners."

"Móndyalítko?"

That hardly seemed likely. From what she understood, her mother's people were nomadic.

But neither Quinn nor Keegan responded, and she glanced at Jaromir, who so far was allowing her to run most of the questions.

"Captain," she began, wondering how to word her next request, "it is a pity that you do not have the body of someone who has undergone this . . . change for me to examine. When it happens again, it would be best if you could incapacitate the victim for me to study."

She'd already begun to think of the men being turned as victims.

Keegan's mouth fell open for a moment, and then he closed it again. "Begging your pardon, my lady, but you have no idea with what we are dealing. Trust me, you will not want one of these *things* merely incapacitated."

"Oh, but I will," she countered. "I cannot even guess what is happening to your men until I examine someone who has been afflicted. My prince wants this situation solved, and therefore I will do whatever I deem necessary." Standing up, she said, "Until I have one of these . . . soldiers turned wolves to study, perhaps I might see the body of someone who has been killed by one of these creatures? The wounds might tell me something."

If Keegan found her first request disturbing, he found this one distasteful and curled one side of his upper lip. "It's been three days since the last attack. There were several injuries. One miner was killed, but he's been buried."

Céline pondered this and knew any useful evidence would probably be too compromised at this point for her to insist on a body being dug up.

"You mentioned injuries. Does anyone have wounds in need of attention?"

Keegan frowned thoughtfully, as if this had never occurred to him. "Possibly . . . yes, I think so."

As if on cue, Amelie stood.

"We brought a large box of medicinal supplies," Céline said. "If you would be so good as to assign us private quarters, my sister and I will change our clothes and then go see what help we might offer the miners."

At first, she thought Keegan might refuse, but he nodded. "Of course."

Céline and Amelie were provided with a medium-sized tent to themselves—about the size of their work-room back home, with an entrance tall enough that neither one had to duck to enter.

"Not bad," Amelie said, looking around. "Considering."

Céline agreed. Most of the floor was covered with furs and there were no holes in the roof. There was a bed with a wooden frame and a down-filled mattress, along with a small table and three chairs. A plain wash-basin and pitcher had been provided. She wondered who had previously been assigned here.

"Here," Jaromir said, handing their travel bags through the entrance. "Change your clothes, and I'll walk you north."

Céline took the bags, and he closed the flap over the entrance from the outside, giving them some privacy.

"What do you make of that captain?" Amelie whispered. "I don't think he's going to be much help."

"Me either," Céline whispered back, taking off her

cloak and opening one of the bags. "But I was surprised Jaromir was so quiet. I thought he might press a few points."

"He can't. Keegan outranks him."

"What?"

"Keegan is a captain. Jaromir's a lieutenant. He has to follow the chain of command."

"Yes . . . but Anton put Jaromir in charge of the investigation."

"Doesn't matter," Amelie said as she began to get undressed.

Troubled, Céline began unlacing the front of her own wool gown. Jaromir was in charge of the security of a great castle and everyone who lived around it, and Keegan was in charge of a pack of motley soldiers in the middle of nowhere, and yet Keegan had more power due to what she considered a slight difference in official rank. That somehow seemed wrong to her. Jaromir was the most capable man she'd ever met.

After struggling out of the lavender dress, she shivered slightly in only her long white shift and stockings. The poor dress looked far worse for wear after the journey. Its hem was filthy, and the sleeves and bodice were dotted with some of Pavel's blood.

"I'd give anything to put on my blue shirt and breeches," Amelie sighed, looking down at the shift she wore.

"Well, let's see what else Helga packed."

They found two evening gowns and a set of silver hairbrushes in the first bag, so they moved on to the second. Inside, they found clean stockings, extra shifts, and a pair of serviceable wool dresses, one of tan, about the color of Céline's hair, and another of pale blue. Amelie took the pale blue, as it was slightly shorter, and Céline wore the tan. Then they tied on their red cloaks and Céline picked up her large box of supplies.

"We're ready," she called.

Jaromir drew the flap back and entered, seeing the box in her arms. "Let me carry that."

He took it, and they followed him out.

"Where's Rurik?" Amelie asked.

"Seeing the horses are properly fed," Jaromir answered. "I don't trust this lot with Badger, and Anton is fond of that gray mare."

Out among the small sea of tents, Céline kept close to Jaromir as he led the way north, and a number of dirty soldiers in dark brown tabards turned to watch them walk past. There must have been women among the families of the miners, but Céline wondered how long it had been since these men had seen a pretty girl like Amelie in a pale blue gown and scarlet cloak.

However, with Jaromir as their escort, none of the soldiers tried to speak to them, and soon they left the collection of tents behind.

"There," he said, pointing.

Following the direction of his finger, Céline spotted a path leading through the thick trees. Some of the gray clouds above were parting, and though the air was cool, patches of open sky peeked though.

The three of them took the path into the trees and had walked only about a hundred paces when it emptied into an open area with small hills in the background . . . and Céline found herself looking upon the Ryazan miners' encampment.

To her right stood a collection of about thirty-five shacks or huts so haphazardly placed that they could have sprouted up only over time with no sense of planning. Some were made from old boards, but most were circular wattle-and-daub dwellings with thatched roofs.

To her left stood six more of the wattle-and-daub dwellings, surrounded by four decaying wagons with what looked to be small homes built on top of the beds. From what she could see, some of the wagon-homes had once been painted in bright colors, but now much of the paint had faded or been chipped away. Empty harness poles stretched out from the fronts of these wagons, with no sign that they had been used in some time.

There were no horses in sight. In fact, there were no animals at all, no goats or milk cows, not even a few chickens scratching at the dirt.

But there were people milling about.

"Which side?" Jaromir asked.

"Left," Céline said. She didn't know why, but she was drawn to the scattered collection of wagon-homes.

The largest of these was also in the best condition, with a solid-looking roof and shutters over the windows. Two women were busy out front. One was hanging clothes, and the other was tending a fire. Both straightened as Céline approached.

The one tending the fire was perhaps sixteen years old, but Céline stopped upon getting a better look at her. She was beautiful, slender and small boned, with a mane of black hair. Her skin was pale, and her eyes were as black as her hair. Her slight body tensed, and she reminded Céline of a young doe about to spring. There was something wild in her eyes.

Céline smiled. "Hello."

The woman hanging laundry approached, protectively stepping up beside the girl. This one was about twenty-five, though thin lines were already etched about the corners of her eyes. Her thick hair was a shade of brown-black and pulled back into a braid. While she lacked the girl's beauty, she was pretty, and Céline thought them alike enough to be sisters.

"What do you want?" the older one asked, glancing at Jaromir, her tone a mix of anger and anxiety.

Céline had to admit that he did look rather intimidating, especially in comparison with some of the soldiers stationed here.

"We've been sent here to help," Céline said quickly, turning to open the box in Jaromir's arms. "I'm a healer from Castle Sèone, and Prince Lieven asked his son, my lord, to send you some assistance. He's heard of your troubles and these terrible attacks." She motioned the woman closer and pointed to various pots, jars, and bottles inside the box. "There is cough syrup, healing ointment, salve for aching joints, bandages, insect and burn salves, and, oh, this is a cleansing tonic."

The woman's eyes flew over the contents of the box. Her body gave off waves of slow-burning anger, but something akin to hope passed across her face at the same time. The slip of a girl took a step or two closer, just enough to peek inside the box, still moving like a forest animal come in from the trees.

Céline smiled again. "I am Céline, and this is my sister, Amelie. This man is Lieutenant Jaromir. He is our bodyguard, but I do assure you, we've been sent to help."

The woman's eyes moved up to Céline's face as if searching for something, and then, satisfied, she nodded. "I am Mercedes. This is my sister, Mariah."

The girl studied Amelie curiously, but she would not move closer to where Jaromir stood.

"Do you have any injured or ill here who need attention?" Céline asked.

Mercedes shook her head in seeming disbelief. "Do we have any . . . ? Yes. We have a number of people in need."

Céline motioned to the wagon. "Perhaps I could set up here, and you could tell the others?"

Mercedes glanced back at the box.

"Mariah," she said finally, "bring these ladies inside and give them what help they need. I'm going to find Marcus and have him round up any wounded men. I'll speak to the women myself."

The girl tilted her head to one side and waved Céline forward. Then she sprang up the back steps of the wagon and opened a door.

Céline followed.

Watching Céline head up the steps, Amelie turned to Jaromir. "You'd better wait out here. We'll be fine, and

I don't think there's much room in there." She looked over toward the shacks and huts. "You might even try walking around and talking to some of the men. See what you can learn that Captain Keegan didn't tell us."

"I doubt any of them will talk to me."

"They will," she insisted. "After only a minute or two, they'll see that you're here to help. You have that effect on people. All the villagers at Castle Sèone trust you."

He blinked several times and then nodded. "All right, but I won't go far."

Turning, she hurried up the stairs to help her sister.

Inside, the covered wagon felt even more like a house. Toward the front were two bunk beds nailed into the wall. A bench was built into one sidewall with a stationary table. Pots and pans hung from the other wall. Threadbare curtains covered the shuttered windows.

"Mariah, would you open the shutters for some light and air?" Céline said as she took off her cloak and began setting out a collection of jars and bottles on the table.

"That soldier won't come in, will he?" the girl asked.

It was the first time she'd spoken. Her voice was soft and wild, like her eyes, but she spoke with real fear—and something deeper, possibly hatred. Amelie wondered what she might have suffered at the hands of the soldiers here.

"No," Amelie answered firmly. "He won't. But even if he did, he wouldn't hurt you."

Sounds of footsteps came from the stairs, and Mercedes returned with Céline's first patients, a bone-thin woman and two children, all coughing.

"Come in," Céline said.

Mercedes sent the family in, but she remained outside.

The rest of the afternoon became a blur. Mariah slipped out so there would be more room inside. Amelie stayed to help her sister, but the condition of the people here soon began to wear upon her. She had seen poverty, true poverty, in Shetâna, but this was different; a string of half-starved women and children flowed through, suffering from deep coughs, ringworm, infected insect bites, and shingles. Some of the women were pregnant. Céline did what she could for them.

Things only got worse when the men began arriving. Mining must be a dangerous business, as the equally underfed men coming through the door bore old injuries of poorly set broken bones. Most of the men over thirty were beginning to succumb to their joints stiffening to the point of constant pain.

There was nothing Céline could do for poorly set bones, long healed, but she'd brought along two jugs of a dense liquid she made from monkshood that worked well on aging joints, and she spent several hours just rubbing it into elbows and shoulders and knees to help relieve pain. She told some of the men that she'd come back tomorrow, and if they brought her a small empty jar or bottle, she'd send some of the monkshood home with them.

Several times, Mercedes came up to stand in the open doorway, just watching Céline.

In the late afternoon, a father arrived with a boy of about fifteen who was holding his left arm with his right hand. The arm had been loosely tied up with a stained rag that was not wide enough to serve as a proper sling.

"Broke his arm three days back," the father said. "We were among the few still willing to go back into the mines, and then one of those beasts attacked. The boy was standing in a cart and scrambled to get out. He fell."

Amelie was attempting to straighten up the bottles on the table. "Inside the mines? One of the . . . wolves attacked you there? Were you working at night?"

"No, it was midday. But no one has gone back in since."

Amelie took a moment to get her head around that. One of the Pählen soldiers had transformed and attacked the miners at work in the middle of the day?

"Bring the boy inside," Céline said.

The boy was brought in, and she sat him on the bench and removed the makeshift sling to examine his forearm. Amelie winced. The bone had been broken and had not been set at all. Although the skin wasn't torn, from what she could see, the bone was still in two pieces. If something was not done, he'd lose use of the arm.

Céline looked up at the father. "If it's only been a few days, I should able to set this." She picked up the bottle of poppy syrup. "But it will be painful enough that I'd need to put him to sleep first, and splinting the injury will take some time. Once the bone is secured, it will need to remain splinted and in a sling for at least a moon, probably longer. He'll not be able to work for a while, but once the bone knits, he will have use of his arm again."

The man was clearly unaccustomed to anyone trying to help him or his family, and he wrung his hands in indecision. Although he himself had not thought to do anything for the boy's injury, Céline's talk of pain and setting bones had clearly upset him. He seemed uncertain about entrusting his son to a stranger.

The man looked to Mercedes, who was standing in the doorway.

She wore the same quietly angry expression, but her head moved up and down once. "She's one of my people, from the line of Fawe. If she says she can set the bone, she can set it."

Amelie was startled. How would Mercedes know they were Móndyalítko, from the line of Fawe? But she bit back any questions. She didn't want the miner to begin to doubt.

"How can I help?" the man asked.

"Get some boards," Céline answered, "strong, but narrow and short, so I can splint his forearm."

And so for the second time in two days, Amelie helped her sister drug someone senseless, set a bone, brace it with boards, and wrap it tightly. By the time they were done, Céline was pale and wiping her forehead with her sleeve. Since entering this wagon, she'd not stopped to rest for hours.

"Now we need something to make a proper sling," she said, looking around.

Mercedes was still in the open doorway. "Use one of the curtains. They're clean, and I cannot think of anything else."

"Are you sure?"

"I'm sure."

The curtains were one of the few homey touches inside the wagon, but Céline took one down and fashioned a sling, tying the boy's arm against his chest.

"He should wake soon," she said.

Mercedes turned to call outside somewhere, "Shaldon, you can come carry him home." Then her voice lowered, and she spoke to someone else outside. "Mariah, go and tell Marcus not to bring any more men. The healer's done in. But tell him that I want him to come himself."

A few moments later, the still-sleeping boy was carried out, and Céline finally sank onto the bench.

Céline's hands and arms were nearly numb as she allowed herself to sit still for a few breaths.

Mercedes stepped inside the wagon. "You did well. I'd forgotten . . . I've forgotten a lot of things."

"How did you know she's from the line of Fawe?" Amelie asked.

Céline looked up, as she had been wondering that herself.

"Her hair," Mercedes answered. "Only the line of Fawe has hair that color. You see any Móndyalítko here with tan hair? And you've both got lavender eyes."

"But how did you know we're Móndyalítko?" Céline asked.

Mercedes snorted. "You think I'd let you in here, let you treat these people, if you weren't? I know my own kind when I see one."

Perhaps unconsciously, Amelie reached up and touched her hair. Ironically, she'd inherited her dark hair from their father, who was not Móndyalítko.

Then Céline felt rather than heard something in the doorway and turned her head. She froze. The man standing there was a taller, more muscular version of Mariah, though he was closer to Mercedes in age. His coal black hair hung down past his collar, and his eyes were locked on Céline. She would never have described him as handsome. He was . . . beautiful. Like Mariah, he had something almost feral about him, as if he didn't belong inside any four walls. More important, even though she'd never seen him before, there was something familiar about him, as if she'd known him for years.

"This is my cousin Marcus," Mercedes said. "I want you to look at his shoulder. He'll be the last one today. I promise."

"My shoulder's fine," Marcus answered.

"It's not fine," Mariah snapped at him, "and we have a proper healer. Let her see it." She moved to the back of the wagon, to the bunk beds, to give him room to enter.

Slowly, still staring at Céline, he came inside.

"Please sit," she managed to say, and he sank onto the bench.

Amelie went to sit with Mercedes on one of the beds.

"Take a look at the back of his right shoulder," Mercedes instructed.

His shirt was dark brown, but when Céline moved to examine his back, she could see spots of blood soaking through.

"Please take off your shirt," she told him.

This he did without hesitating.

"Oh, Marcus," she breathed, as if she'd spoken his name a thousand times before. "What happened?"

Four deep gouges ran from the top of his shoulder halfway down his back. They were angry and swollen and looked as if they'd not even begun to close.

"One of those soldier-wolves slashed me. I was trying to draw it off that boy you just helped." When he spoke the word "soldier," the hatred in his voice was unmistakable.

"Inside the mine?" she asked.

"Yes. We managed to kill it, but it cost us."

Céline didn't ask what it had cost. Right now, she didn't want to know. "These wounds are on the verge of infection. I need to do a deep cleaning . . . and it's going to hurt." She picked up the bottle of poppy syrup. "I want you to drink just a spoonful of this, not enough to put you to sleep, but enough to dull the pain."

He glanced at the bottle skeptically.

"Do it," Mercedes ordered him.

Céline poured a wooden spoonful, and he let her feed it to him.

"We need to wait a few moments," she said, "and let that take effect."

Mariah appeared in the doorway, looking in. The resemblance between her and her male cousin was astonishing. Then it occurred to Céline that although these three were slender, they weren't starving. Marcus's bare shoulders and arms showed lean but developed muscles.

"You helped the children," Mariah said to Céline. "That was good."

Her words and speech were so simple that Céline wasn't certain how to respond for a few seconds. "There wasn't much I could do. What they need is food."

"They won't find much of that here," Marcus said, "except in the soldiers' provisions tent."

"Why don't you have any animals?" Amelie asked. "Chickens or a milk cow?"

"Can't afford to buy a cow," Mercedes answered. "And we ate the last of the chickens years ago, before we even arrived."

"How many years have you been here?"

"Three."

Listening to the exchange, even with what little she knew of her mother's people, Céline couldn't imagine a group of Móndyalítko remaining in this awful place for three years.

"Where are your horses?" she asked Marcus quietly.

"Gone." He glanced away. "I hunt for us, and we eat whatever Captain Keegan doesn't take." Again, when he said Keegan's name, the hatred in his voice was thick. "We share what we can with the others here, and Mariah does what she can for the children."

He looked at Mariah, in the doorway, and she looked back. Something passed between them, but Céline had no idea what.

Picking up the jar of adder's-tongue ointment and a clean rag, she said, "All right, this won't be pleasant."

Turning her attention to his wounds, she remembered that one of the reasons she'd come here was to examine anyone injured by the afflicted soldiers. Judging by the distance between the claw marks on Marcus's back, whatever had done this to him must have had enormous paws.

She started at the top of his shoulder and began to work her way down. He didn't gasp or flinch once, and she knew the poppy syrup could not be dulling all the pain. When she finished cleaning all the wounds, she put away the adder's-tongue and switched to a mixture of ground garlic and ginger in vinegar.

"This is going to sting, but it will ward off infection," she said, dabbing the mixture onto a clean rag and touching it to his back.

Again, he didn't flinch.

When she'd finished with that, she wrapped his shoulder as best she could and helped him get his shirt back on. He let her.

Mercedes stood up suddenly, seeming uncomfortable. "We can't pay you anything."

So weary by now that she was having trouble staying on her feet, Céline leaned on the table. "We didn't come for payment." Then something occurred to her. "Oh . . . there is one thing, perhaps a favor you might help us with."

Mercedes's entire body went rigid. "A favor?"

"Yes, we had to pack light for the journey, and Amelie and I were only allowed one extra wool dress for day wear. We nearly ruined the ones we wore on the journey here. I have blood on mine from tending to an injured soldier. How can we get them laundered here? Could you allow us to use your washtub and clothesline?"

Mercedes's expression turned incredulous, and then she barked out a single laugh. "That's your favor? Help with washing a few gowns?" She shook her head. "You bring them to me, and I'll launder them myself. I can get blood out of wool."

"Thank you."

Still sitting on the bench, Marcus was watching Céline with his black eyes, as if trying to figure her out. She put on her cloak and gathered up the box of supplies as Amelie moved to join her.

"We'll be back tomorrow," Céline said, hoping she sounded businesslike. "Marcus, don't take off those bandages, even if the wounds itch."

Mariah made room in the doorway, and Céline headed out, nearly tripping on the stairs from exhaustion. The sun dipped low. Was it only that morning that she had waved good-bye to Corporal Bazin and the other soldiers from Sèone and then followed Jaromir into this encampment? It felt as if whole days had passed.

Jaromir was waiting for them near the path up ahead, but as Amelie walked beside her, Céline whispered, "What do you think of those three back there in the wagon?"

"I think someone in their family has a penchant for names starting with the letter *M*."

This attempt at humor was so unexpected that Céline couldn't help the corners of her mouth turning up. Amelie could almost always make her smile.

"In truth," Amelie added, "I think Mercedes is angry, but she lets it out. Marcus and Mariah are holding in a lot of hatred."

That was Céline's assessment as well.

"Marcus and some of the Móndyalítko men must have signed contracts with Keegan," she said. "Horses to pull the wagons or not, I can't think of any other reason why they'd stay here . . . and Marcus hates the soldiers."

"Yes, but how much does he hate them?"

How much indeed?

Jaromir came walking to meet them. "You look done in."

"You've no idea," Céline answered. "Can we go to our tent and rest for a while?"

"Of course." He took the box from her and led the way down the path back toward the soldiers' camp.

"Did you learn anything from the men?" she asked.

"Not a lot, only that there have been three attacks by these . . . wolves during the day, inside the mines themselves. The miners are refusing to work at all now, and Keegan's soldiers won't let them leave but also won't enforce any work because that would mean the soldiers would have to enter to mines themselves to oversee, and they're just as afraid of being trapped or caught down there."

Céline absorbed this. "I think you learned quite a bit. If someone is doing this on purpose—infecting the soldiers, I mean—it almost sounds like they are *trying* to shut down work in the mines."

The path emptied into the Pählen encampment.

As the collection of tents came into view, Céline heard raised voices. Turning, she saw that Captain Keegan was out among his men. In fact . . . he was shouting at five of them. She recognized three of the soldiers from earlier in the day, the rotund Guardsman Saunders, the skittish young Graham, and the tall, semi-toothless Ramsey. She'd not met the other two.

"We have guests here from the court of Sèone!" Keegan shouted. "Sent at the request of our prince! And you're all wandering around out here with no one placed at his designated post. You're all filthy, and you look a disgrace. I won't have it! You'll clean yourselves up and act like soldiers or I'll have you on night watch in that gypsy camp. Do you hear me?"

Had Jaromir ever given his men such a speech, they would have been groveling. He rarely made threats—as he rarely needed to—but a threat from Jaromir was taken seriously.

Céline expected the soldiers to bow and scrape and express a chorus of "Yes, sirs."

They did not.

Ramsey glared at the captain in thinly veiled hostility and spoke so softly that Céline had to read his lips, but it seemed that he said, "I'll not take orders from a man who can't pay his own debts."

Captain Keegan went stiff. "What did you say?"

No one answered for a moment, and then Ramsey mumbled, "Nothing."

"Get to your posts," Keegan ordered.

The men shuffled away, but Céline was somewhat shaken. She'd never seen anything like that. Even back in Shetâna, the chain of command was unquestioned and soldiers followed the orders of a superior officer.

Discipline was breaking down here . . . and these men would need discipline if they hoped to organize themselves and survive.

However, as she, Amelie, and Jaromir walked up, they pretended not to have witnessed the scene.

"Good evening, Captain," she said.

He turned and saw her approaching. "My lady, I was coming in search of you."

"Yes, we were detained in the miners' encampment."

He frowned. "All afternoon?" But then he offered Amelie a polite bow of his head. "I've had a small dinner prepared, to be served in my tent. Could you be ready in an hour?"

Céline wanted to groan. She wanted her bed. The last thing she wanted to do was put on an evening gown and sit at a table making polite conversation. But they were here for a reason, and she glanced at Jaromir. He nodded once.

"Of course," she said. "We'd be honored." As she started to walk away, something occurred to her, and she was uncertain of the protocol. Amelie had stressed that as the ranking commander, he was in charge of everyone here. Did she need his permission to conduct any readings? "Captain . . . per our inquiry, I would like to do a reading of a young woman named Mariah and a man called Marcus. Do I have your permission?"

His frown deepened. "Mariah? Why?"

By way of answer, she looked him up and down, as would any haughty lady of Anton's court.

He glanced away, embarrassed. "Yes, do as you see fit."

CHAPTER FIVE

Though Céline was still feeling weary as she entered Captain Keegan's tent that night, she was aware enough to be somewhat unsettled by the state of her gown. At Jaromir's request, Helga had packed for the two sisters, including two fine dresses from the castle—which had probably once belonged to Anton's aunt. Both gowns were silk. Amelie wore a seafoam green, and Céline's was a dark shade of pink. But . . . even though both garments had been carefully folded, they'd still been jostled about for days inside a bag. Céline wished a travel chest had been used instead, but she supposed that Jaromir felt bags would be easier to tie onto the back of a horse if necessary.

As a result, no matter how she'd tried to smooth both gowns, there were creases in the skirts, and as there was no way the delicate slippers Helga had packed would have survived the walk to Keegan's tent, both sisters ended up wearing their boots. Somehow, this combination made Céline feel less like a lady of court.

Worse, she'd almost had to wrestle Amelie into the

seafoam green dress, as both gowns were cut rather low across the bosom, and at first Amelie had refused to wear either of them, but when forced to choose she'd decided that she disliked the pink more than the green. Once she'd finally been laced in and her hair had been brushed, she looked both startlingly pretty and painfully uncomfortable at the same time.

Again . . . the latter was hardly reflective of a lady of court.

However, neither Captain Keegan nor Corporal Quinn appeared to notice the creases as they watched their guests enter. Jaromir brought up the rear of the trio. Apparently, as a mere guardsman, Rurik had not been invited, and Céline hoped he was faring all right among a group of unfamiliar soldiers.

"A sight for sore eyes," Keegan said, appraising Céline, who had put up her own hair with soft fringes hanging down. "I've not seen a lady in a proper gown since this past spring."

While she found this rather forward, she managed a smile. The table was adorned with more silver candlesticks and pewter goblets.

As Quinn pulled out a chair for her, Jaromir stepped in to hold one for Amelie. He'd not teased her once about the silk gown, but he also seemed unable to take his eyes off her. This had not helped Amelie's comfort level.

Once they were all seated, Keegan snapped his fingers. A Pählen soldier entered from the back of the tent and began pouring wine like a servant. When he finished, he vanished again.

Keegan looked down the table at everyone seated there and cleared his throat.

"Lady Céline," he began with what could only be called a lecturing intonation. "I've been informed you spent the entire afternoon tending to that filth living in the miners' camp."

Céline's hand stopped with her goblet halfway to her mouth. "I beg your pardon?"

He took a long swallow of his own wine. "I thought you were going in order to attend to a few injuries for the workers. But most of those miners and gypsies will do nothing to help themselves. Of course you have my full cooperation in your efforts here, but you must not tire yourself out or waste medicine by giving it to those little better than animals. It does them no good, and they won't thank you."

Céline stared at him, and Amelie's face had gone red.

"Lieutenant," Quinn blurted out, as if trying to change the subject, "how was your summer crop back in Sèone?"

"Abundant," Jaromir answered, perhaps equally glad to be speaking of anything else. "The weather has been kind."

Two more soldiers entered, one carrying a plate of steaming flatbread and another carrying a large tray with two roasted birds on top. The tray was placed directly in front of Keegan, who picked up a knife and two-pronged fork to carve. Both soldiers vanished.

"We have a well-stocked provisions tent, with a stove, and I brought a cook with me from Pählen." He gestured to the tray before him. "But we also have plenty of game here. These are wild pheasants baked with pears. I think you'll enjoy the dish."

At the sight of the pheasants, Céline heard Marcus's voice in her ears.

I hunt, and we eat whatever Captain Keegan doesn't take.

Marcus had probably caught those birds himself. Thinking of the tragic conditions she'd seen in the miners' encampment, she wondered if she could manage to swallow a bite. Looking across the table, she guessed Amelie was thinking the same thing.

Thankfully, Keegan seemed oblivious to their discomfort, nor did he expect conversation from the women at the table, and he proceeded to carve while continuing the discussion of the summer harvest with Quinn and Jaromir. Somehow, Céline managed to get through the meal and eat enough for the sake of manners, hoping she might be excused soon. Between the wine and the overly long day, the table was beginning to swim before her eyes.

Through the pointless dinner talk, she heard Jaromir ask, "How many men do you have stationed here now?"

Keegan and Quinn both went silent, and then Quinn answered, "Subtracting current losses, I believe we are down to forty-one."

"Forty-one?" Amelie repeated. "With the women and children added in, I'd guess there are maybe two hundred people or a little more over in the miners' encampment. Do you need forty-one armed guards to keep them here?"

Keegan shifted in his chair. "Well . . . some of those

men are reinforcements my lord sent to assist with recent difficulties."

Yes, Céline thought, *and those reinforcements have not helped.*

A commotion sounded outside the front of the tent, and to her shock, four soldiers dragged Mariah and Marcus inside. Mariah was openly frightened, but Marcus shoved both the soldiers holding him away, and he glared at one as if daring the man to touch him again. Then he looked as if he was about to strike the nearest man holding Mariah.

Céline jumped to her feet, knocking her chair backward. "What is this?" She spoke to the soldiers. "Take your hands off that girl, *now!*"

They let go of Mariah and looked to their captain.

Keegan stood and frowned at Céline. "You told me you wanted to read them. You claim to be Anton's seer? As does your sister?" From his tone, it was clear he believed she and Amelie possessed no real power at all and were merely bored ladies playing up to Anton.

And this was not at all what she'd intended when she'd spoken to Keegan earlier.

"Now that they're here, you should read them," Jaromir said, his voice tight.

She turned back to him and knew what he was thinking. They were here to play a part, to do a job. If she was to convince Keegan that she was a true seer who should be allowed to read his men, she'd better start proving it.

"Mariah," she said softly, "it's all right. If you can come here and sit with me, I just want to touch your hand. That's all I want to do. Afterward, you can go home to Mercedes. I promise."

Some of the panic in Mariah's eyes faded, and Céline reached out with one hand. "Come and sit with me."

She straightened her chair and pulled another over for Mariah. Hating herself for doing this in front of Keegan and Quinn and all these men, she kept her hand out, and Mariah came to her, gripping her fingers. The girl's hands were so small. She couldn't be more than two years younger than Amelie, but somehow she seemed much younger.

Céline sat, and Mariah sat, too, almost as if she would find protection by close proximity. "It's all right," Céline said again. "I'm just going to close my eyes and see your future. No one will hurt you."

It might have been more useful to have Amelie read the girl's past, but Amelie was not skilled at soothing or comforting someone frightened. Céline needed to show Mariah there was nothing to fear.

Holding the girl's hand, Céline closed her eyes and tried to shut out everyone and everything else in the tent. She cleared her mind and focused on Mariah's spark of spirit . . . on her future. The first jolt hit almost instantly, and Céline steeled herself for the second. Then she was rushing forward on the white mists.

The journey was short.

A scene materialized around her, and for a moment, she was confused. She found herself standing in this same tent, only at the back, near a bed. The tent was much darker and only a single candle lantern burned on a small table. There was a basket of food on the floor near a hanging tapestry that divided this section of the tent from the front. Moving closer, Céline saw that it contained jerked beef and biscuits: the staples of traveling soldiers.

Suddenly, Keegan stepped past the tapestry and into the back section of the tent. He wore only his breeches and shirt, with the tails of his shirt hanging loose, and he carried a goblet of wine.

"Is that you?" he said, squinting out the back exit. "Hurry up."

A shadow moved in the doorway.

Céline tensed as Mariah slowly came inside. Her feet were bare, and she again looked like a doe about to spring.

"You know what to do by now," Keegan said. "Just get on with it. Unless you and your sister want to move on now that your father's dead and you have no man to work the mines." He waved his hand toward the basket of food. "And you want those vermin children to go hungry."

In the light of the candle lantern, Mariah's young face was even more beautiful, but her black eyes glowed with hate and fear.

She didn't run or move closer to him.

With a disgusted sound, he reached out and grabbed her arm.

Céline wanted to shout and push him away, but she was only an observer, and she had a sick feeling in her stomach that she knew exactly what was coming.

Keegan dragged Mariah toward his bed. As he reached it, he turned and roughly pushed the top of the dress down over her shoulders. Her breasts were pale and small, like the rest of her.

Céline started choking. She wanted this to end. She wanted to be away from here.

Then Keegan had Mariah pinned down on top of the bed. He shoved her skirt up, and she began to whimper. Inside the vision, Céline forced herself to turn, to look away.

The image vanished.

"Céline!"

Opening her eyes, she could hear herself choking and see Jaromir crouched beside her chair. Amelie was right behind him.

Céline feared she was going to be sick.

"Come out of it," Jaromir said. "I'm right here."

Captain Keegan walked up behind Amelie. "What is happening?" he demanded.

Céline couldn't bring herself to look at him. Mariah sat tightly in her chair, with her head swiveling back and forth, and Céline realized she'd need to get a quick hold of herself. She had no intention of humiliating the girl further in this company.

"What did you see?" Amelie asked.

"Nothing," she answered. "It didn't work."

Both Jaromir and Amelie would know she was lying, but neither would give her away. Putting her hand on the arm of her chair, she tried standing. Marcus was staring at her.

Keegan appeared uncertain, but he motioned toward Marcus with his head. "You want to read him now?"

"No," Marcus said, his voice resounding through the tent. "Not like this."

Two of the soldiers moved to grab him, and Céline couldn't stop herself from crying out, "Don't touch him!" For some reason, she couldn't stand the thought of those filthy soldiers putting their hands on Marcus again.

Both soldiers froze in place, and again, she fought for control of herself. "Forgive me," she managed to say to Keegan. "The day has been too long, and I am weary. Could we please forgo this for the night?"

The walls of the tent were swimming around her now, and she barely heard his reply, which seemed to include some kind of apology.

"Please allow Marcus and Mariah to go home," she said.

The next thing she knew, Jaromir was on one side of her and Amelie was on the other, and she was being ushered out the tent's front flap. She didn't remember the walk back to their own tent, but she was aware of Jaromir coming inside when they reached it.

As Amelie helped Céline inside their tent, her concern was growing into open worry. She'd seen her sister this distraught only once before, and it had taken Céline a long time to recover. A candle lantern glowed from atop the table. Someone must have entered and lit it for them.

"What happened back there?" Jaromir asked. "I know you saw something."

Amelie helped Céline into a chair and almost couldn't believe it when her sister let out a single sob. They didn't cry. Either of them.

"Keegan is abusing the girl . . . ," Céline managed to get out. She wiped her eyes and took a breath. "I saw him, and I could tell that it wasn't the first time."

Amelie straightened. "What do you mean, 'abusing'?"

"You know what I mean," Céline answered quietly. "It's not exactly force, but he's coercing her with food for the children and threats of making her and her sister leave."

Amelie whirled toward Jaromir. "You have to stop it. Tell him he has to stop or you'll report him to Prince Lieven."

In all the time she'd known Jaromir, she'd never seen him grow so uncomfortable. He shifted his weight from one foot to the other and couldn't seem to meet her eyes.

"Amelie . . . ," he said. "Prince Lieven won't care, and I can't threaten a superior officer. I know this kind of thing is unfortunate, but it happens all the time when men are stationed in outlying places like this."

"Unfortunate?" she repeated.

"Men trading food for the favors of a woman has been going on as long as warfare," he said.

"It wasn't like that," Céline whispered. "You didn't see it. It was awful."

"Jaromir, you have to do something!" Amelie insisted. "You protect people. It's what you do." She couldn't believe he was standing there arguing with her. Why wasn't he already striding to Keegan's tent?

His expression hardened. "I can't. There's nothing I can do." He backed toward the entrance. "We're here to solve a problem for Prince Anton, and I think you'd both do well to remember that." He paused but still wouldn't look at either of them. "You're both tired. Get some sleep, and we'll press on with the investigation in the morning. I'm in the tent next door. Call out if you need me."

Though it seemed impossible that he would turn and walk out and leave things like this, he did.

Amelie stared at the empty doorway for a moment and then turned back to her sister. "Oh, Céline."

Poor Amelie appeared so stricken by Jaromir's behavior that Céline forced herself to stand.

"We'll do something for the girl ourselves," she said. "I don't know what yet, but we will." She reached out for Amelie's hand. "Jaromir is right about one thing. We must get some sleep. Help me out of this dress."

Both the assurance that they would help Mariah themselves and the sensible words about getting some sleep moved Amelie into action. They helped each other undress down to their shifts and stockings, and then they went to examine the bed. The mattress and bedding were dry, but the blankets were thin, so Céline spread their red cloaks over the top for added warmth. Then she blew out the candle lantern.

Soon they were huddled beneath the covers, and

Céline hoped that her sister would not wish to talk anymore tonight. After all that had happened today, she was not up to speaking to anyone, even Amelie.

Thankfully, Amelie's breathing soon grew steady and even, and Céline assumed that sleep would come to her quickly as well. She could not remember having been so tired.

Unfortunately, it didn't.

Could she be too tired to sleep?

Or was it something else? She couldn't explain it, but as she sat up, her gaze moved through the darkness toward where she knew the closed flap of the tent door to be. There was someone out there. Someone waited for her.

Leaving Amelie to sleep, Céline got up from the bed and donned her red cloak. She made her way to the tent flap and went outside. There were no soldiers milling about, but a few lamps on poles allowed her to see as far as two or three tents away.

Movement near a tent up ahead caught her eye, and someone stepped from the darkness into the light of a hanging lantern.

It was Marcus.

Then it struck her that she might be asleep, that this might be a dream.

Without thinking, she walked toward him, and he drew her back out of sight, between two tents. She followed. His face was so beautiful, almost unreal, with his black eyes and sharp cheekbones. No, this wasn't a dream. She was awake.

"I saw what Keegan is doing to Mariah," Céline said.

"I know you did."

"I never meant for him to drag you into his tent like that."

"I know. I saw your face."

This man struck her as dangerous, but for some reason, she wasn't afraid of him.

"I can't stop Keegan," he said. "The only thing I can do to help is to take Mercedes and Mariah away from this place, and I can't until the end of autumn, when my contract is finished, and that's only if Mariah will leave."

"Why wouldn't she leave?"

"Because we've been unlucky, and believe it or not, some things were worse before we arrived here and our men started signing contracts with the House of Pählen." He sounded accusatory, as if blaming the men in his family.

Céline couldn't imagine that a life traveling as Móndyalítko nomads could be worse than the Ryazan mines. "But you signed a contract."

"No, I did not. Not at first. I was our hunter. I stayed because my people needed me, and I watched our men get caught in a web as they were promised work and pay. But the miners only get paid if they complete a contract. During the year, they're allowed to take out vouchers to be traded for food from the provisions tent, but those vouchers later come out of their pay. That's why so many of the children go hungry. Their fathers try to avoid falling back on the vouchers."

He looked at the ground. "Both Mercedes and Mariah's parents are gone, and so is my mother. But my father still lives. My older brother signed a contract every year, and he was one of the first killed in the attacks by these soldier-wolves. Keegan told me that unless I completed his contract, my father had agreed to work in my brother's place. My father isn't well, and I couldn't let . . . I took over the contract. It's finished at the end of autumn. But with my brother gone, I have some power in our decisions. Once I'm free, I am taking Mercedes, Mariah, and my father out of here if we have to walk and I have to carry Mariah on my shoulder. I wish I could save the entire family, but I can't, and those three matter the most to me."

"Where will you go?"

"To the Autumn Fair outside of Kéonsk. Some of our people gather there, and I'll ask another family group to take us in. They won't refuse. I have certain . . . attributes that make me valuable."

She wondered what those might be but thought better of asking. He was just now beginning to trust her. "Why are you telling me all this?"

"Because I couldn't stand for you to see what you saw tonight and think that I was doing nothing to stop it. I'm going to get Mariah and Mercedes free of these soldiers."

The hate in voice was so thick, she almost backed up. Again, she knew his anger wasn't aimed at her. But if anyone had a motive to sabotage the mines, he did. If the mines were closed permanently, would the miners be paid and set free?

Without warning, his manner changed and he moved closer, backing her up against the tent.

"Do you still want to read my future?" he whispered. "You won't even have to try. Just touch my hand." He raised one slender hand. She hesitated.

"Afraid?" he asked.

Reaching over, she touched two of his fingers. Without her even having to focus, the world around vanished.

She wasn't drawn into the mists, and she didn't feel herself rushing forward in time. The scene took on the quality of a dream again. To her amazement, she was not a mere spectator. Instead, she found herself seeing through someone else's eyes. She was closer to the ground and running on all fours through a forest. The feeling of freedom flowing through was exhilarating . . . as was the speed. She could smell life all around her, and she longed to hunt . . .

Whipping her hand from Marcus's, she stepped away.

His eyes glinted in the moonlight. "Stay inside your tent tonight," he said, "no matter what you hear."

Was he worried for her safety? "Why would you want to help me?"

"Because I know my own kind when I see one."

He turned and vanished into the darkness.

Turning slowly, Céline walked to her tent and got back into bed. She wanted to separate and examine what he'd told her and what she had seen and experienced when she'd touched him. But this time, sleep overwhelmed her as soon as her head hit the pillow.

Maybe it had been a dream.

CHAPTER SIX

Later that night, Amelie was lost in such a deep sleep that when the world exploded in a series of sounds, she was slow to react.

The first sounds to register were growls and snarls, followed by screams . . . coming from somewhere outside.

She sat up.

What was happening? At first she wasn't even certain where she was. It was dark, but she could see Céline sleeping beside her, and she remembered they were inside a tent.

"Everyone who can hear me, light torches and move to the perimeter!" Jaromir shouted from somewhere beyond the tent wall. "Don't let it out of the encampment!"

Jumping out of bed, Amelie pulled on her boots. There was no time to lace up a dress, so she tied her cloak over the top of her shift. Drawing her dagger, she gripped the hilt tightly, cursing the fact that she had no sword.

Céline stirred and sat up.

"Amelie? What's happening?"

"Stay here," Amelie ordered. "I need to help Jaromir, but don't you leave this tent!"

She ran out, following the direction of Jaromir's voice.

At the sound of savage snarls and someone screaming, Jaromir had grabbed several weapons and run from his tent with Rurik at his side. He'd arranged for Rurik to bunk with him in a small tent beside the sisters' assigned quarters. Both men had been sleeping fully clothed.

"Sir, where's it coming from?" Rurik asked, his head moving back and forth.

The snarls and screams seemed to be echoing off the tents. The sounds were close, but Jaromir couldn't tell where they came from. Rurik was poised with his sword drawn, but Jaromir's blade was still sheathed. He strapped it on and gripped a stout cudgel that he'd brought from home. Having fought wolves in the past, he'd found a short, heavy weapon to be more effective at close quarters.

Also . . . Céline had mentioned she needed one of these beasts alive.

Glancing at Rurik's sword, he said, "Defend yourself, but don't kill it unless you have to."

Closing his eyes, he listened for a moment, and then all sounds vanished. A second later, he heard other soldiers shouting.

"Over there," he said, pointing north.

Both men ran between the tents, and Jaromir skidded to a stop at the sight of Corporal Quinn, wearing breeches and an untucked shirt, carrying a loaded crossbow in one hand and a long spear in the other. His gaze was fixed on the ground.

Looking down, Jaromir let out a long breath, and Rurik said, "Oh . . . by the gods."

There was a soldier Jaromir had not seen before, dead, with his face and throat slashed. Light from hanging lanterns illuminated the sight of dark blood running from the wound in his throat and soaking into the dirt. Other men with spears were running up now, but the world seemed a mass of shouting and confusion.

"Where's Captain Keegan?" Jaromir asked Quinn.

"I haven't seen him, but we need to organize. We can't let the wolf escape. If it reaches the forest, it'll double around and go straight for the miners' encampment."

With Keegan absent, Jaromir took charge. "Everyone who can hear me, light torches and move to the perimeter!" he shouted. "Don't let it out of the encampment!"

The men around him moved quickly, lighting torches from the flames of hanging lanterns and running for the edges of the camp. They seemed almost relieved to have someone giving orders.

"I'll take the north side," Jaromir told Quinn. "You take the south. I'll listen to the west, and you to the east. If it tries to get out, one of us should be able to reach the men trying to keep it in. If it doesn't appear, I'll call an order for everyone to start moving inward."

Quinn nodded and turned to head south.

"Jaromir!"

To his utter disbelief, Amelie came running up, wearing nothing but her shift and her cloak . . . wielding a dagger. What could she be thinking?

"I need a better weapon," she said. "Quick."

Men were shouting to one another at the perimeter, and Quinn looked back. "Get that woman out of here!"

Fighting the anger rising inside him, Jaromir leaned down toward Amelie's flushed face. "Go back to your tent right now."

"No, I can help. Just get me a weapon."

"I don't have time for this!" he shouted, knowing he should have reached the northern perimeter by now. "For once, just do as I say and get back to your tent!"

She didn't move, but her features twisted to match the rage he was feeling.

One of Quinn's men was still within earshot. "You!" Jaromir called. "Get this lady back to her tent."

Then he bolted, with Rurik on his heels, leaving Amelie behind.

"Amelie!"

Céline watched her sister run out of the tent, and for a moment, she sat in fear and uncertainty. She'd been so tired and had fallen so deeply asleep. Now she could hear shouting from all around outside . . . and Amelie had just gone out there.

Struggling to gather her wits, Céline got out of bed and pulled on her boots and cloak.

She slipped out the flap of the tent, looking both ways. Her sister was nowhere in sight, and although she could see none of the soldiers, the camp seemed to have erupted in the sounds of men shouting to one another.

What was happening?

A low growl sounded from behind, and slowly, she turned around.

She froze.

Beneath the light from a hanging lantern crouched something akin to a wolf. It was huge, with a wide chest, and paws larger than Jaromir's hands. Its eyes were red, and saliva dripped from the fangs of its long, open mouth.

Céline didn't move, breathing softly, but it growled low again.

She saw nothing but madness in the creature's eyes.

Tensing its body, it charged.

Céline dashed forward, running as fast as she could, not even looking where she was going.

"Amelie!" she screamed.

Amelie shook with humiliation and anger as she was "escorted" back to her tent by a Pählen soldier. She'd find a way to make Jaromir pay for this. Though the soldier carried a short, thick spear, he appeared beyond nervous and looked into every shadow as he ushered her along.

Then . . . over the shouts of soldiers calling out to one another, a scream rang out.

"Amelie!"

At the sound of Céline's cry, Amelie whirled, catching the Pählen soldier in the back of his ankle with the toe of her boot, sending him sprawling. As he fell, she grabbed the spear from his hand.

After crouching to shove her dagger back into the sheath in her boot, she gripped the spear in both hands and ran toward the sound of Céline's voice.

Jaromir had just reached the north perimeter when he heard Céline scream.

"Amelie!"

He jerked to a stop, with Rurik skidding beside him.

"That was Céline!" Rurik cried, stating the obvious.

"Quiet," Jaromir ordered, listening.

He heard no loud snarls, and Céline did not scream again, so he was torn. What if her plight had nothing to do with the beast stalking these tents? He had a responsibility to help Quinn keep the wolf from breaking into the trees.

But . . . he had a greater responsibility to Anton, and that meant protecting Céline and Amelie.

"Rurik, you take my place here, working with Quinn. Listen for him. If he calls for help, you run to him, understand?"

"Yes, sir."

Leaving Rurik behind, Jaromir jogged to the west, around the edge of the camp, and was unsettled to see how sparsely guarded it was on this side. He'd need to do something about that quickly.

But he never had time.

A second later, Céline burst from between two of the outer tents about forty paces ahead of him, and she ran for the trees. A large, furred creature on four legs burst out after her, closing the distance, and they both vanished into the surrounding forest.

"Quinn!" Jaromir shouted. "Rurik! Over here!"

He bolted forward.

With little choice, Céline fled blindly into the forest, thinking of nothing but escape.

She could feel and hear the great wolf right on her heels, and she tried dodging around a tree, hoping it might run past and give her a few seconds.

But both its speed and its control of its body were astonishing. As she dodged, it dropped down on its haunches and turned to charge. All she could see were teeth and fur and mad red eyes.

I'm going to die, she thought.

But before the wolf could launch, something smaller and darker—and just as heavily furred—came dashing through the trees and leaped, catching the slathering wolf in the side and knocking it off its feet. Snarls and growls filled the night air.

Céline gasped, unable to see well in the darkness, but then she heard the sound of booted feet crashing through the forest, and Jaromir broke into sight carrying some kind of heavy club.

Whirling her head back toward the wolf, she found that the smaller creature—which she'd never seen clearly—was gone.

The red-eyed beast was on its feet, charging at her again.

Jaromir closed in from the side, swinging his club

downward, catching the wolf across the side of its head. The sound resonated so loudly, she thought he must have cracked its skull.

"Céline, stay back!" he shouted.

The massive wolf didn't stay down. It rolled several times, snarling in rage, and gained its feet again, rushing Jaromir. He gripped his club, but Céline didn't see how he could withstand a full onslaught from something so large, and she looked around wildly for a branch, for anything with which to help him.

As the wolf raced past her, someone blurred into view from the other side of the tree, swinging a narrow object downward. A loud crack sounded out, and Céline whirled to see Amelie, in her red cloak, with a short spear in her grip, and . . . she had just landed a blow on the beast's head with the spear's butt.

Whipping the spear back up, Amelie brought it down again, hard, on the back of the wolf's neck, and the already stunned creature collapsed. She swung again, this time with another strike for its head, and it lay still, with its eyes closed, but it was breathing.

Then all Céline could hear was Jaromir and Amelie both panting as they stared at each other.

"There's your captive, Céline," Amelie breathed.

Corporal Quinn, Guardsman Rurik, and three other men broke through the trees, and Quinn raised his spear at the sight of the wolf on the ground.

"No," Jaromir said, still panting but holding up one hand. "We need it."

Quinn looked uncertain and didn't lower the spear.

Feeling dizzy and sick to her stomach, Céline some-how stepped between them. "Please, Corporal . . . just tie it up somewhere and don't give it any water."

The world around her began to spin, and the ground came rushing up.

CHAPTER SEVEN

"Céline?"

Opening her eyes, Céline found herself in a bed, inside the tent she shared with Amelie, and her sister—fully dressed—was leaning over her, holding a plate of bread and a mug of steaming tea. The tent flap was partially open, revealing bright daylight outside.

"Amelie? What time is it?"

"Almost midday. We haven't wanted to wake you, but Jaromir thought it was time."

"Midday?" Céline couldn't remember ever having slept so late, but something had happened last night . . . something . . .

Bits and pieces came rushing back.

"It's all right," Amelie rushed to say. "You just fainted."

Céline blinked, suddenly feeling less disturbed and somewhat annoyed by Amelie's suggestion. The Fawe sisters did not cry, they did not sleep until midday, and they most certainly did not faint.

Seeing the expression on her face, Amelie held up one hand in surrender. "You need to eat and get dressed. Quinn has the wolf tied up in the barn, but he's getting anxious for us to do whatever we're going to do."

"Oh . . ."

Céline climbed out of the bed and reached for her tan wool dress as a number of questions rose in her mind.

"What of Captain Keegan?" she asked. "I never saw him last night."

"He's fine," Amelie answered without attempting to hide her disgust. "But he looks even worse for wear. I think he kept on drinking long after we left last night, and he probably slept through the whole ordeal of having his camp attacked. One of the Pählen soldiers was killed. I saw the body."

Céline shook her head. "Poor man."

Keegan had no business being placed in charge of anyone. He abused the women and neglected the men. Trying to focus on something else, she began lacing up the front her dress.

"Céline . . . ," Amelie started and then stopped.

"What is it?"

"You and I have met the man who was . . . changed last night. Quinn did a head count, and Guardsman Ramsey was the only one unaccounted for."

Céline's hands stopped lacing the dress. Ramsey was the tall man who'd been arguing with Keegan at sunset last night. Neither she nor Amelie knew him, but it was still sad to put a face to this tragedy. Ramsey was a victim just as much as the soldier he'd killed in his madness.

As she finished dressing, she realized she was hungry and started in on the bread and tea.

"I think I should read Ramsey," Amelie said. "Seeing his future won't tell us anything . . . as I'm not certain he has much of a future in his current state. But maybe I can see something that happened just before the change, something that triggered it."

Taking a long swallow of the warm tea, Céline considered her sister's words and nodded. "Yes, you're right. Let me do an examination, and then we'll have you do a reading." She walked over to the table and picked up the empty water basin and the pitcher. "Here, you carry these. Have they kept him thirsty as I asked?"

"Yes. Why?"

Céline hurried to her box of supplies and took out the bottle of poppy syrup. "Because tied up or not, he'll still be dangerous. I don't want him senseless or you won't get a reading, but we do need him calm."

With that, she headed for the tent flap and stepped outside. Guardsman Rurik was waiting, and he offered a good-natured but mock bow. "My lady Céline."

"Oh, stop." She was glad to see another familiar face. His shoulder-length hair looked even curlier than usual, and in the sunlight, she noticed he had a light smattering of freckles. "Have things been all right for you here? We've hardly seen you, and I was worried you'd been cut off and rather on your own."

"I've been fine. Most of the Pählen soldiers have taken to sleeping in the large tents. Safety in numbers and all that. But I'm bunking in the small tent next to yours with the lieutenant. I'd take my chances with him any day." He flashed a grin.

In spite of everything, she smiled back. "So would I."

Amelie came up behind them, carrying the basin and pitcher. "We should get to the barn."

Rurik looked at her. "You'd best be careful around the lieutenant. He's fit to be tied about you disobeying his orders last night."

"I saved his life!"

"Doesn't matter."

By way of answer, Amelie grunted, and the three of them started off, walking through the tents toward the only wooden structure in the soldiers' encampment. The day was fair, with clear patches showing through the clouds above. Both sisters had forgone their cloaks, and Amelie seemed to be somewhat more comfortable as she strode along in her pale blue dress.

"How soon do you think we'll be done with all this?" Rurik asked. His previous good nature seemed strained, as if the answer mattered to him very much.

Céline remembered how reluctant he'd been to take Pavel's place, and again she wondered why.

"I don't know," she answered honestly. "We haven't learned anything of use yet. We don't even know if these transformations are due to some kind of infection or if someone is doing this to the soldiers on purpose."

The barn loomed ahead, with a small collection of hens pecking at the ground out front, and then she saw that Jaromir was waiting outside with two men. As she drew closer, she recognized Guardsmen Saunders and Graham. Saunders's expression was bleak, but Graham's eyes were red, as if he'd been weeping, and again the whole face of these tragedies hit Céline. Graham was young, and Ramsey had been his friend—possibly even a protector.

"I'm so sorry," she said, walking up. "Amelie just told me that it was Ramsey."

Graham looked at the ground.

"Keegan and Quinn are inside," Jaromir said quietly. "I thought you might like to question these two before we go in."

That was good thinking on his part. Though yesterday and last night had been trying, the sleep and the tea had left her feeling much more like herself today. She turned to Saunders.

"Please understand that we are only trying to find out what is happening here so we can stop it," she began, "but were you with Guardsman Ramsey last evening?"

Both men nodded.

"Did he eat anything you did not?" she asked. "Or drink something you did not? Can you think of anyone unusual that he spoke to?"

Graham lifted his head. "No, we all ate our normal rations and then played cards for a while, but an hour past dark, we split up to go to our night posts, and that . . . that was the last time I saw him."

"Was he still angry at Captain Keegan?" Amelie asked suddenly.

Both men's eyes widened and neither spoke.

"It's just that we overheard the captain dressing you down," she went on, "and Ramsey spoke back to him."

Saunders shook his head. "That's just Ramsey's nature. He blows up easy and gets over it easy. He wasn't angry for long."

"Miss . . . my lady," Graham said. "Can you do anything for him? He . . . he always looked out for me. Can you give him one of your potions and bring him back?"

Poor young man. Céline couldn't lie to him. "I don't think so. I don't even know what's happened to him, so I wouldn't begin to know how to fix it."

His chin dropped toward the ground again, but she would not offer him false hope. "If either one of you remembers anything, anything out of the ordinary that happened yesterday, please come and tell one of us."

Jaromir turned to open the barn door, and she realized that he appeared to be pointedly ignoring Amelie, who was pointedly ignoring him back. Céline wanted to sigh. She sensed a loud argument in their near future.

Before entering, Amelie walked over to the horse trough and filled the pitcher.

Céline turned and stepped through the door. Inside, she took in the sight of the barn, which also served as a stable for a number of horses—and two cows that she could see. It was a large construction, with high windows along both sides. Light flowed in to show dust hanging in the air, and the horses were restless, moving anxiously in their stalls as if they wished to get out.

Amelie and Rurik joined her inside.

Jaromir stepped past and took the lead, heading through the line of stalls, straight for the back. The quartet emerged into a large open room with a dirt floor, where Captain Keegan and Corporal Quinn waited. Quinn was his usual well-groomed self—and holding a spear—but the captain looked awful, his hair a mess and his skin tinged green. He put one hand to his mouth and belched quietly.

However, she did not stop to appraise him for long, as the growling creature tied to a stake consumed her attention. She'd not gained a clear look at it last night, and now she moved closer. Its growl rose to a snarl, but she could see it had been secured with some kind of makeshift leather harness and tied to a stake pounded into the ground.

The beast appeared to be an enormous wolf, larger than a bear—though she had seen that much last night. Now she had full view of its teeth and the details of its massive claws. Its fur was brown peppered with white. Its eyes were still red, and its body gave off a strange, musky odor.

"I'm sorry it's not muzzled," Quinn said. "We got it tied up last night, and I was just about to arrange for a muzzle when it woke up, and I pulled my men back. If you need me to, I can knock it unconscious again."

"No, that's quite all right, Corporal. Amelie and I need it at least partially awake."

"This is absurd," Keegan said angrily, turning on Jaromir. "And I would think you should have had the good sense to stop it last night. You cannot possibly allow these *ladies* of court to go near that thing and pretend to read its future or its past."

Well, there it was. At least he was openly admitting he believed them to be wealthy, silly frauds playing games at court for Anton's amusement.

The skin over Jaromir's cheekbones drew back. "I am here at the request of Prince Anton, and I serve him. Since you were not present last night, as the ranking officer, I handled the situation as I saw fit."

Keegan's green skin blanched, and Jaromir turned to Céline.

"Now what?" he asked.

"We need to drug Ramsey," she said, walking to Amelie. "Set the basin on the ground and pour the water. He'll be thirsty by now."

At her use of Ramsey's name, all the men winced slightly, as if she'd said something in poor taste. She ignored them.

Amelie half filled the basin, and Céline measured and poured in several spoonfuls of the poppy syrup, though she was uncertain quite how much to use. She wanted the wolf calm but still awake.

"I think that's enough," she said finally, reaching down to pick up her concoction.

"What are you doing?" Jaromir asked in alarm, striding over. "Give me that!"

Rocking back on her heels, Céline watched helplessly as he grabbed the basin.

"Bully," Amelie said under her breath.

Jaromir pretended he hadn't been close enough to hear and headed for the wolf, which snarled and jerked against the harness as he drew closer. He stopped a few paces out, put the basin on the floor, and slowly slid it over until it was just close enough for the wolf to begin lapping thirstily.

Captain Keegan watched all this with his arms crossed. "Madness," he muttered.

"Thank you," Céline told Jaromir. "Now we wait."

No one spoke for a while, and then the wolf ceased growling. It stumbled. After another few moments, it sank to the ground. Céline took a few steps toward it, and Jaromir was at her side, hand on the hilt of his sword.

"Come and help me with this next part," Céline told him as she moved even closer. The wolf lay awake but in a stupor.

"Help you with what?" Jaromir asked.

"I think you must have some experience looking for small wounds? We need to go over its body and see if we can learn how Ramsey was infected. Was he bitten? Slashed? Poked with something? It may be none of these, but we need to look."

Nodding with interest now, Jaromir knelt beside her. He was always happiest when he had something solid and clear to *do*.

Amelie hung back and let Céline and Jaromir go over the body of the wolf carefully. Céline started with the paws, while Jaromir started at the head, examining the ears first.

For the first time, Keegan appeared less disgusted and watched silently, as if even he could see the sense in what they were doing. Céline ran her hands over every inch of the wolf's body, her fingers prodding through its coarse fur to feel a thick hide over its muscle structure. In the end, to her frustration, they found nothing other than several lumps on the wolf's head from when it was bashed unconscious.

She shook her head. "Nothing." Then she looked back at Amelie. "I guess it's your turn. I can't think of anything else to search for here."

Although Amelie was the one who'd suggested that reading Ramsey's past would be far more useful than reading his future, now that the prospect was upon her, she found herself reluctant to touch this creature and try to form a strong enough connection with its spirit to read its past.

Her ability worked slightly different from Céline's in several ways. While Céline could see someone else's future only as an observer, if Amelie wished, she could bond with her target and see the past through his or her eyes. Also, in some cases, the people Amelie read could be just as conscious as she was of the scenes being replayed, and afterward they were aware of exactly what she'd seen. The people Céline read never had any idea what she was seeing. The two sisters had discussed these differences, and Céline guessed they might be due to the fact that the past was set in stone, and the future could still be changed—that she was seeing just one possible line unless something was done to alter it.

As Amelie slowly approached the wolf, she was determined to go back only as an observer, and though she believed herself to have courage, even that much filled her with dread.

The moment of doubt must have shown on her face,

because Jaromir stood up from where he'd been crouched beside the creature.

"What's wrong? Can you do this?"

That was all it took to stiffen Amelie's backbone. He'd been insufferable since last night, first refusing to do anything to help Mariah, then treating Amelie like a child and ordering her back to her tent when she belonged in the middle of the fight, and now he was behaving as if *she* was the one in the wrong for having come to his aid in the forest.

She would not allow him to see her in fear of anything.

"Of course I can do it."

Striding over, she crouched down, and so did he.

"Céline," he asked, "how long will this beast remain drugged?"

"I don't know. I don't know anything about its internal workings. I had to guess at how much syrup to put in the water."

Jaromir looked across the wolf at Amelie. "Go ahead and do your reading, but if this thing starts to wake up, I'm going shove you hard. Céline, you get back near Quinn and Rurik."

As Céline hurried away, Amelie gritted her teeth. When it came to the three of them, why did Jaromir always have to insist on making sure everyone knew he was in charge?

Trying to forget he was there, she reached out and closed her eyes. Her hand rested on the wolf's shoulder. She'd expected the fur to be soft, but it was surpris-

ingly coarse. Letting go of all her fears, she focused on
the wolf . . . on Ramsey, and she tried to feel for the
spark of his spirit.

After first, she felt nothing, sensed nothing.

Refocusing, she forgot the wolf and focused only on
Ramsey, picturing him in her mind.

Without warning, without a single jolt, she was jerked
back through the gray and white mists, rushing backward down the corridor of time. Now she could defi-
nitely feel a spirit, and it was strong. It was grabbing for
her own, clinging to her, and she tried to fight back, to
keep herself separated, to be only an observer, but the
spirit meshed with hers, and she knew she had lost the
battle. Struggling to keep her head, to make certain this
reading was not a waste, she focused on Ramsey's recent
life in this camp, on trying to make him show her what
had happened to him, what had caused him to change.

But the mists jerked her to a stop and would not allow her to cross a certain point. Then the mists cleared,
and she found herself standing in the darkness on the
edge of the soldiers' encampment, looking inward at
the tents.

Nausea hit her.

Pain like she'd never experienced flowed through
her body in waves, and she couldn't help crying out
and choking as she retched up the contents of her stomach. Raising her hands before her eyes, she saw a man's
hands, with fur beginning to sprout and claws beginning to grow.

Terror exceeded pain.

She was inside Ramsey as he was last night, and he

knew what was happening to him. He was so afraid and in so much pain. She heard his clothing tear, and she felt his body expand.

And then . . . all she felt was rage, the need to kill . . . and she rushed forward on four legs . . .

"Amelie!"

The scene vanished, and she was choking. Opening her eyes, she found herself partially on the barn floor and partially in Jaromir's arms. Céline was running toward her, falling to her knees.

"Are you all right?" Céline asked. "Jaromir had to pull you away. You were gagging so badly."

Trying to draw in a few breaths, Amelie couldn't help the waves of despair washing through her. Ramsey was gone. There was nothing left of him inside the wolf.

"I couldn't . . . ," she tried to say. "I couldn't get past last night when he started to change. I felt it. I felt everything."

Jaromir held her, rocking her back and forth.

For a moment, she let him. Then she pulled away and tried to sit up on her own. "Is there any water left in that pitcher?"

Rurik grabbed the pitcher and hurried over.

Once Amelie had washed out her mouth, she shook her head in strained sorrow. "I tried, Céline. I can't see anything of Ramsey's life. I can only see when the wolf began."

Looking at Amelie, Céline hated that her sister had been forced to endure this. She couldn't imagine what Amelie had seen and felt in the past few moments.

Climbing to her feet, Céline turned to face Keegan and Quinn.

Keegan looked more unsettled now and less disgusted.

Good, Céline thought. *He should be unsettled.*

"I had hoped this would work," she told him, "but it seems that there is not enough left of Ramsey's spirit for my sister to see into his past." She paused and steeled herself. "It's time to change tactics. Captain, you must give us permission to begin reading your men. If I can pinpoint the next victim, we might be able to find out what is happening."

His mouth fell open, and this time, his green-tinged skin began turning pink.

"Absolutely not!" he spat at her. "I'll not have my men subjected to two ladies playing at being Anton's seers, only to have you single one man out as the next 'victim,' as you so gracefully put it. Do you know what would happen to him? The others would kill him on the spot."

Jaromir stood up. "Captain, your prince requested help from his son, and his son sent us, and you were asked to afford us every cooperation."

"Not to the point where it endangers my men," Keegan shot back.

His derision of their abilities didn't surprise Céline, but he'd seemed uncertain after watching Amelie—as if he was beginning to wonder if they could do as they claimed. Until this moment, he'd not shown much concern for his men. But what other reason could he have for not wanting her or Amelie to read them?

Keegan turned back to the wolf, and the horror in his bloodshot eyes was clear enough. "Lady Céline," he said, clipping off his words, "is there anything more you can learn from this beast?"

Perhaps he wished to dismiss her. She struggled for something else to try—anything. If he wouldn't allow her to read the soldiers, she was at a dead end. But nothing came to her, at least not yet.

He seemed to take her silence as an answer, and she expected him to break up the group so they could all leave this barn. Instead, he motioned to Quinn and then to the wolf. Quinn hefted his spear and took a few steps forward.

Céline went cold. "Stop! What are you doing?"

Amelie climbed to her feet but didn't say anything.

Jaromir drew his sword and said, "Céline, go outside."

She could feel her eyes widening. "Jaromir, no! He's tied to a stake and unable to hurt anything. You cannot just kill him. He is a victim here." She couldn't believe they were even considering this. "Amelie, don't let them!"

But her sister glanced away, and Jaromir nodded to someone behind Céline. An arm reached around her stomach and lifted her feet off the ground. She kicked and tried to break free.

"It's just me," Rurik said in her ear. "Don't struggle."

"Rurik, put me down! Jaromir, you cannot allow this!"

Rurik turned and began walking swiftly though the barn, carrying her past the stalls and finally through the door outside. Only then did he place her back on her feet, and she jerked away, pressing her back up against the outside of the barn.

"Rurik, how could you? How could you let them?"

"The lieutenant's right!" His voice was ragged. "You heard Amelie. Guardsman Ramsey is gone. He died last night, and all that's left is that *thing* in there. What if it got loose? Do you want it running around camp? You want it to kill one of the miners' children or Amelie? Is that what you want?"

She fell silent, stricken.

He leaned forward, putting his hands on his knees. "You know the lieutenant's right. He protects his own."

The loyalty in his voice moved her, and she didn't know what to think.

"How can we finish this, so that we can leave?" he asked quietly.

She was silent for a while and then whispered, "I don't know. Amelie and I are not a pair of trained military investigators. We're only seers, and we cannot solve anything unless we're allowed to use our abilities. You heard Captain Keegan. Unless he gives us a freer hand, I'm not even sure what to try next."

Rurik appeared to be considering this. "So Keegan is the problem?"

Things were more complicated than that, but, yes, Keegan was at the heart of it.

"I don't want to see any of them when they come out," she said, changing the subject. "Will you take me back to my tent?"

"Of course."

*   *   *

After Rurik had left her inside the tent—and headed back for the barn—Céline busied herself, straightening up and making the bed. Time seemed to pass slowly.

Just as she finished, Amelie came in through the flap and stood near the entrance uncomfortably. She was holding a few red apples in her hands. "I got these at the provisions tent. I thought you might be hungry."

Céline pretended to continue making the bed.

"I'm sorry I let Rurik carry you out of there," Amelie added.

"That's what you're sorry about? That Rurik had to carry me out?"

Glancing over, she saw Amelie wince, and she regretted her words. "Oh, Amelie . . ." Walking over, she drew her sister further inside. "Forgive me. I'm just upset." She hesitated. "Is it . . . is it done?"

Amelie nodded. "Jaromir made sure it was quick. That's why I stayed, too."

Céline sighed quietly, no longer certain what was right or wrong. Perhaps it had been the right thing to kill Ramsey. It just seemed so unfair.

"Rurik thinks we need an outing," Amelie went on. "He says a few of the men told him there's a small meadow not far to the east. He and I are going to lead all four of our horses there so they can graze for a few hours. He says it's not good for them to live on a diet of straight grain."

"He seems to know a good deal about horses." Even as the words left Céline's mouth, it seemed odd to be speaking of outings and horses when a man had just been killed while tied to a stake.

"His father is Prince Lieven's gamekeeper, but I think he grew up with horses, too." Amelie reached for her red cloak. "Why don't you come with us? At the moment, there's nothing we can do here."

Céline glanced at her supply box. "I promised some of the miners that I'd come back today. There are a few people I need to check on."

"Oh . . . do you want me to stay and help?"

"No, no. You go with Rurik. He needs your help more. I just want to look at a few of the children with coughs and some of the men suffering in their joints."

"You're sure?"

Céline could tell from Amelie's voice that her sister would much rather be outside with Rurik, away from this camp, sitting in a meadow and letting the horses graze. But Céline found herself looking forward to some time away from all her traveling companions—even Amelie.

"I'm sure. You go ahead."

As Amelie slipped out, Céline wondered what Jaromir was going to do with his day, but she didn't wonder for long. Donning her own red cloak, she slipped the apples into the large front pockets. After gathering up the soiled wool dresses from their journey, she hefted her box of supplies. Once she had everything in her arms, she headed out, walking north through the tents and to the path through the trees.

As the path emptied into the open area of the miners' encampment, she couldn't help being struck by a feeling that the camps were almost separate worlds, joined only by a small stretch of cleared ground between them.

She looked right to the shacks and huts and then left to the collection of covered wagons. Her gaze stopped on the largest wagon, with its painted shutters.

Gripping her box, she headed left, wondering how her reception was going to be after last night. Several of the Móndyalítko milling around outside glanced her way, and she smiled in greeting. As she reached her destination, Mercedes opened the door and looked down at her with an unreadable expression.

"I'm sorry about Mariah and Marcus being dragged to the soldiers' camp last night," Céline said immediately. "I had no idea that was going to happen."

Mercedes's expression seemed locked in a quiet brand of eternal anger, but she nodded. "I know you didn't. Marcus told me." Her eyes moved to the supply box. "And even if you had, I'd be a fool to turn you away."

Her black-brown hair hung loose this morning, making her look younger. She motioned with one hand. "Come on up. Marcus is off hunting, but I'll have word spread that you're here." She reached out. "Let me put those gowns with the wash."

"Where's Mariah?"

"I don't know. I rarely know where that girl is off to. She's as wild as a deer."

Céline climbed the few steps, passed off the gowns, and stepped inside. She took off her cloak and began setting up at the table as Mercedes prepared to head out.

"I'd like to see the boy with the broken arm," Céline

said, "and certainly that older man with the swollen finger joints. I want to send some of this monkshood home with him."

The afternoon progressed from there, and burying herself in work proved a good outlet for Céline. She lost herself in helping others.

She was pleased to see her rose petal cough syrup had done well for the afflicted children, and Mercedes had managed to find a few small bottles so that some of the mixture could be sent home.

The boy with the broken arm was in discomfort, but that was to be expected with a newly set bone, and as he complained more about the bandages itching than anything else, Céline thought him on the road to recovery. His father thanked Céline three times—to her embarrassment.

She spent the remainder of the afternoon massaging more of the monkshood into sore or swollen joints, and again Mercedes went out and scavenged some small containers so Céline could send the liniment home with those suffering the worst.

As the sun began to wane, after the last patient had been seen, both women sank into chairs. Céline reached into the box and pulled out a pouch.

"Do you think you could manage one more thing," she asked, "and get us some hot water?"

Mercedes leaned forward. "What is it? Some other herb I haven't seen you use?"

"No." Céline smiled tiredly. "It's spiced tea. For us."

"Spiced tea? We haven't seen tea in over a year. I'll be right back."

As Mercedes went outside, Céline took the apples from the pocket of her cloak and found a knife. She sliced them into pieces and cut out the seeds. When Mercedes returned with small pot of boiling water—from the fire outside—and produced two mugs, Céline made them tea.

As Mercedes looked down at the tea and sliced apples, some of the anger in her face faded as sorrow took its place. "You make me remember so many things I'd forgotten. You make me ashamed of what I've come to accept."

Céline pushed over a mug of tea. "Marcus says he's going to take you out of here in the autumn. When he's finished out his brother's contract."

Mercedes looked over. "He told you that? I mean . . . I knew his plan. He's just normally not one for talking." She sat and picked up an apple slice. "We should have left years ago. I should have shown some spirit and shouted the roof down. Just before coming here, we'd hit . . . hard times, very hard times. Hearing of this place, it seemed wise for the men to sign contracts and try to earn some money. The captain back then was a fair man. But a year went by, and some of our men, including my father, signed new contracts, and then we were locked in for another year . . . and then another."

"Your father is gone now?" Céline asked softly.

Mercedes nodded. "Died from a fever, and we had nowhere to go. I could see that Mariah was growing into a wild thing, with no sense and no purpose, and yet we stayed." She lowered her eyes. "When I was a girl, my mother once told me that if you drop a frog into hot water, it will jump out. But if you put a frog into cool water and then slowly, slowly heat the water, it will stay there until it dies. I let myself become the frog."

"What else could you have done? The rest of your people were here."

"I should have fought harder for Mariah. When Keegan came last spring, I shouldn't have let him near her." The anger in her face was returning. "I'd given up the fight by then. But you . . . you make me remember things, that helping others, that decency, that a life worth a fight, those things all still matter."

Céline had no idea what to say. She badly wished to help Mercedes and Mariah . . . and Marcus. She simply didn't know how yet.

"Well," she said finally. "I think you've done the best you could with the hand you were dealt."

Mercedes shook her head but didn't answer.

Céline stood up. "I should be getting back or my sister will come looking for me." She leaned over and touched Mercedes's arm. "I'll be back."

Mercedes looked up. "I believe you."

Jaromir spent most of the day frustrated and annoyed, and without the correct outlet, by the time the sun dipped low, he was on the edge of seething.

The whole ordeal in the barn had left him more shaken than he'd admit to anyone. Though he remained convinced that killing Ramsey had been the right decision, that didn't make it any easier. Céline was right in that Ramsey was as much a victim as the soldier he'd killed in the night.

But . . . at present, his main concern was Amelie. Céline might fight him on moral issues, even to the point of occasionally challenging his decisions, but he knew how to handle her and he always won.

Amelie was openly disobeying his orders—and doing so in front of the men.

That had to stop, and it had to stop now.

He'd let her leave the barn and walk away with Rurik, but he knew that Rurik was planning to take their horses to a nearby meadow to graze, so he decided to wait and catch Amelie alone. He had no wish to embarrass her. He simply needed to impress upon her the absolute necessity of obeying his orders in their current situation. He'd been charged with protecting her, and he'd not allow her to endanger herself.

However, after waiting a short time, he'd gone to visit her tent and found it empty. A short while later, Guardsman Saunders told him that she'd gone off with Rurik, to help him with the horses, and that Céline had last been seen walking toward the miners' encampment with her box of supplies.

This left Jaromir facing an entire afternoon with nothing to do besides think and stew and grow angrier with Amelie. Near dusk, he was standing outside the women's tent, waiting with his arms crossed.

And that was his mood as Amelie came walking back after her excursion. Watching her approach, he couldn't help thinking how pretty she looked in her pale blue dress, with her short black hair swinging back and forth as she walked. Her skin glowed, as if the afternoon away had done her good.

She stopped at the sight of him. "Rurik is putting the horses away," she said. "Are you waiting for him?"

"No." He motioned toward the flap of her tent with his chin. "In there."

She tensed, but this only irritated him more, as if *she* needed to be cautious of his behavior instead of the other way around.

"I want to talk to you," he said.

With a wary expression, she walked into the tent, and he followed.

Inside, she turned to square off with him and crossed her arms as well. A small voice in the back of his mind told him he was handling this badly, and he knew her well enough not to take her head-on like this, but he couldn't seem to stop himself.

"You disobeyed a direct order last night," he started, letting anger leak into his voice. "Worse, you tripped the man I assigned as your escort, and you took his weapon!"

"I saved your life! I'm the one who reached you and Céline. I'm the one who clubbed the wolf with the butt of that spear I 'took.'"

"Saved my . . . ," he sputtered. Was she really delusional enough to believe he couldn't have handled that beast by himself? "My job is to protect you, and our position here is uncertain at best. Do you understand how much your behavior has undermined my authority?"

"Your authority? So far, you haven't done a damn thing besides let Captain Keegan walk all over us and tie our hands."

"When I give an order, you *will* follow it!"

Amelie's eyes narrowed. "I'm not one of your soldiers!" she shouted, uncrossing her arms and clenching
her fists. "And I'm not some gypsy girl you can order
around the way Keegan orders Mariah!"

His head jerked involuntarily as if she'd slapped
him. "The way Keegan orders . . ." He trailed off, so
stunned he couldn't finish the sentence, and for just an
instant, he thought he saw a flash of panic and regret
cross her face.

It didn't matter.

Without another word, he turned and strode out of
the tent.

CHAPTER EIGHT

As Céline made her way down the path between the encampments, then broke through the trees to see the collection of the soldiers' tents, a low male voice caught her attention. She looked over to see Corporal Quinn quietly giving orders to the men who were about to take duty on watch.

His manner with them was so different from Captain Keegan's. He spoke to the men with authority, but also with respect and an awareness of the strain they must be under. Young Guardsman Graham was in the group, looking as miserable and lost as he had at midday.

As Graham began to walk away, Quinn stopped him and said, "I've covered your post. You take the night off."

This small act of kindness moved Céline, and she wondered how Quinn had ended up as a mere corporal serving under a man like Keegan.

Quinn was a much better leader.

This got her wondering about several things, and she changed directions to intercept him. Looking at him, her curiosity grew. He was the type of man that princes often sought out for service, tall and strong, like Jaromir, with clear eyes and a direct but easy manner. His sandy blond hair was cut just short enough not to look cropped, but not so long as to become tangled. She had a feeling he didn't do anything by accident.

"Good evening, Corporal," she said. "It has been quite a day."

He nodded uncertainly. "I'm sorry about that scene in the barn."

She was not up to giving him absolution, but neither would she make him feel worse, so she changed the subject. "It cannot have escaped your attention that Captain Keegan is hindering our efforts, despite Prince Anton's letter. I was wondering . . . could you tell me how the captain managed to receive this assignment? He appears to despise nearly everyone and everything here, as if the assignment is beneath him."

If Quinn was taken aback by her question, he hid it well. However, he also appeared to be considering whether or not he would answer her.

"I regret having to remind you that it was your prince who engaged my lord," she added. "I'd like to know what we're up against as far as cooperation goes."

At that, Quinn shook his head. "Honestly, I don't know why the captain has been so reticent to approve your few requests. I had good reason to worry about taking one of those beasts alive, but I understood why you asked, and I wished you'd learned more." He paused. "He should let you read the men. We can protect anyone you point out, and he knows it."

Though his last statement was close to disloyalty, it gave her hope.

"How did he end up here?" she asked again.

Quinn sighed. "He volunteered, as a payment. The previous man in charge here, a Captain Asher, died of a fever, and Prince Lieven could find no one willing to replace him. My captain . . . he ended up in an awkward position over a gambling debt he couldn't pay, and our prince asked him to volunteer for this duty. At the time, Lieutenant Sullian and I were serving under him . . ."

"And so you ended up here, too."

He nodded.

"What was Sullian like?" she asked.

"Too softhearted. Nothing like the captain. Don't get me wrong—he was a good man, but he didn't belong in the military. I think he was the second son of a second son and had little choice."

"The morning we arrived, Keegan mentioned that he was hoping for a replacement. Has he officially requested one?"

"Yes. He views this assignment as an insult and a punishment, and he feels he's paid his dues."

As Céline digested that, Quinn began to move away from her. "Forgive me, my lady, but I need to check in with him."

"Of course. Thank you for talking to me."

After bowing slightly, he strode off.

But Céline's mind was reeling. How badly did Keegan want to be replaced? Did he want it badly enough to do something desperate in order to sabotage his position here? Could he be infecting his own men? The problem with that theory was that he didn't strike her as unusually clever, and the question of how such a thing could be done continued to rear its head. Some kind of poison wasn't likely. Of course it was possible, but she was too experienced an apothecary to find it probable. Yet . . . if it was something arcane, then what?

As she walked through the camp, her thoughts were so busy that she barely noticed when she'd arrived at her own tent.

Passing through the flap, she saw Amelie sitting on the bed. Dusk had set in and the candle lantern on the table was glowing.

"Oh, you're back," Céline said, glad to have her sister to bounce ideas off. "How was your afternoon? I just had the most interesting talk with Corporal Quinn."

Amelie didn't answer.

"He told me Keegan was forced to volunteer to accept a commission here due to an unpaid gambling debt," Céline went on.

No answer came.

Turning, she realized her sister hadn't said a word since she'd walked in. "Amelie?" Walking to the bed, she was startled by Amelie's bleak expression. "What's wrong? Are you ill?"

"I'm fine."

"You're not fine. Tell me what's wrong."

"Leave me alone."

Céline couldn't believe her ears. In their entire lives together, Amelie had never spoken to her like that. Not once.

"Whatever it is, you should share it with me," Céline said. "You and I don't keep secrets from each other."

"Don't we?" Amelie's eyes flew up to her face. "What about you on our journey here? You told me nothing happened between you and Pavel. That was a lie, and you know it."

The weight of everything came pressing down on Céline: the ugly poverty of this place, her inability to discover or solve anything, the senseless deaths that continued to occur, the thinly hidden fear of the soldiers—that any one of them might turn into a beast and start killing the others at any moment. It was all too much. Always before, no matter what happened, she'd had her sister, and right now, she felt alone.

Sinking onto the bed, she whispered, "I didn't tell you because I was embarrassed."

"Embarrassed?"

"Back in Sèone, I knew Pavel had feelings for me, and I used him in our last investigation. He was angry . . . so angry that he frightened me on purpose, and then I managed to avoid him. That second night of the journey, he caught me . . . and pinned me against a tree."

"What?"

"It's all right. Jaromir stopped him, but I can't imagine what he must have been thinking when he walked up and saw us. I was just so embarrassed and I couldn't bring myself to tell you, too. I'm sorry."

"Céline," Amelie breathed.

Now that she'd started speaking of these things, Céline couldn't seem to stop. "I know things are much better for us in Sèone, but sometimes I can't help feeling they were simpler back in Shetâna when it was just you and me. I'm so grateful to Anton and Jaromir for all they've done for us, but now both those men have become our friends, and they *matter*. I don't know how to be friends with men, and yet I'm terrified of losing one of them or hurting one of them."

Amelie hung her head. "Oh, Céline. I said the most awful thing to Jaromir. It was . . . it was so awful. I almost can't believe I said it."

"You quarreled with him?"

Amelie nodded, and her face shone with misery. "I wish I could take the words back. I wish I'd never said them." She choked once. "I hurt him."

Céline put both arms around her sister and pulled her close. "He'll understand. He knows you have a temper."

"This was more than temper. You didn't hear it. I compared him to Keegan."

Still holding Amelie, Céline realized what a cut that would be to Jaromir, but she was glad that she at least knew what was wrong.

"Let's make a pact," she whispered. "No more secrets no matter what. We vow to tell each other everything."

Amelie gripped her back. "I promise."

Before Céline could say more, an unfamiliar voice called from outside, "My lady?"

She didn't know which one of them he was calling for, so she answered, "Yes?"

A soldier who'd been serving at dinner last night

came through the flap carrying a tray, and she realized it was fully dark outside.

"I was asked to bring you dinner," he said, moving in and setting the tray on the table. "Do you need anything else?"

"No, we're fine. Thank you."

He left as quickly as he'd entered, and Céline walked over to look down at two bowls of stew, fresh bread, and two goblets of wine. "Well, I guess we won't be dining in the captain's tent tonight." That was a respite at least. She wondered where Jaromir and Rurik were eating.

"Do you think you could come to the table and eat some supper?" she asked Amelie. "We've not had much today."

Somehow, they both managed to swallow some of the stew and bread. They had only the single candle lantern for light, but it provided enough.

"So what's our next step?" Amelie asked, perhaps looking to speak of something else.

Céline had already given this some thought and could come up with only one conclusion. They were going to have to find a way to coerce Keegan into letting her read the men. At present, they were dead in the water until she had a new avenue to pursue.

But before she could answer, the sound of running feet came from outside the tent.

"Lady Céline!"

She knew the voice. It was Quinn. Without asking permission, he burst through the tent flap.

"Come quick!" he called. "The captain's in pain. I think he's dying."

When Jaromir and Rurik's dinner was delivered to their tent, Jaromir took it as an insult—that Keegan was deliberately avoiding him. In his current mood, Jaromir realized that he probably would have taken almost anything as an insult, but he wasn't wrong about Keegan. For some reason, the man didn't want Amelie or Céline reading any of the soldiers here, but sooner or later, he was going to have to agree. It was just a matter of time.

Unfortunately, the captain seemed determined to drag out the time as long as possible.

Because he was hungry, Jaromir ate the stew and bread and drank the goblet of wine. Rurik ate with him but had the good sense not to try to make conversation. Jaromir didn't feel like talking, not after what Amelie had said to him.

However, when they'd finished, Jaromir stood up. "I'm going to go speak to Keegan."

Walking out, he ignored the women's tent and made his way directly to Keegan's enormous tent toward the back of the encampment. Only a few steps outside, he heard a sound that gave him pause: a groaning like someone in pain. This was followed by a gagging sound.

"Captain!" a voice cried inside.

Grasping the hilt of his sword, Jaromir swept inside, uncertain of what he'd find.

It took him a moment to absorb the scene he walked in on. There was no one transforming into a wolf. Instead, Keegan was on his knees, gripping his stomach with both hands and gagging like he was trying to retch but couldn't. Quinn knelt beside him with an anxious, helpless expression.

"Lieutenant!" Quinn called. "He just collapsed. I don't know what's wrong."

Hurrying over, Jaromir dropped down beside them. The captain looked ill indeed, choking and groaning, fingers digging into his own stomach. He began to fall to his side and Jaromir caught him.

"Run and get Céline," he told Quinn. "Hurry."

Quinn ran.

Keegan's distress was increasing, and his eyes rolled back in his head. "It hurts," he managed to say.

"What did you eat?" Jaromir asked.

Looking around, he saw dirty bowls and the remnants of supper on the table, but it looked to be the same stew and bread and wine that Jaromir and Rurik had eaten. By way of answer, Keegan groaned louder and doubled over in Jaromir's arms. There was nothing to be done but wait.

Thankfully, Quinn was quick, and only moments later, he ushered both Céline and Amelie through the tent entrance. Jaromir couldn't bring himself to look at Amelie, but right now, Céline was the one he needed.

Céline rushed over and looked down. "Can you carry him to the bed?"

Quinn came to help, and between the two of them,

they got Keegan to the back of the tent and onto his bed. Céline wasted no time.

Sitting on the bed beside him, she looked into his eyes, pulling down the lower lids, and she felt his skin. When he gagged again, some of his dinner began to come up.

"Amelie, get a basin for him," Céline called. Then she looked at Quinn. "He's been poisoned."

"Poisoned?"

As Jaromir had, Céline looked over at the table. Quinn followed her gaze.

"How long ago did you eat?" Céline asked.

"I don't know." Quinn sounded rattled. "Within the hour."

"But you ate in here, and you both ate and drank the exact same things? Were you served wine from the same pitcher?"

Both Céline's onslaught of questions and the idea that his captain had been intentionally poisoned was breaking through Quinn's normal shielded demeanor.

"Of course we were served from the same pitcher and we ate the same . . ." He stopped. "No . . . the cook sent in a plate of mushrooms, fried in butter. They are a favorite of Keegan's, but I don't care for them."

Céline jumped up. "Mushrooms? You're certain? That was the only thing he ate that you did not?"

Quinn's eyes shifted back and forth as if he was trying to think and failing.

"Quinn!" Céline nearly shouted. "You have to be sure. Various poisonings are treated quite differently. If it was mushrooms, we have no time to waste."

"Yes." He nodded, sounding more professional. "That plate of mushrooms is the only thing he ate that I did not."

Céline started for the tent flap. She'd come with Quinn so quickly that apparently she'd not thought to bring her box. "I have to run back to our tent, but I'll need boiling water, a lot of it, and as fast as you can."

Then she was gone.

Jaromir glanced at Amelie, but to their credit, they moved into action. There was a campfire burning outside, and he called for an iron hook, while Amelie fetched a cast-iron pot of water, and they set it to boiling.

Céline wasn't gone long and came running back with her box. Dropping to the ground by the campfire, she opened the box and took out a jar.

"I need a large mug," she said.

By now, several of the off-duty soldiers, Rurik among them, had gathered and were asking questions, and one of them handed Céline a mug, which she filled with hot water. Then she opened the jar and measured several spoonfuls of a powered substance into the hot water and stirred it, blowing on it at the same time to cool the worst of the heat. She was moving so quickly, Jaromir had trouble following her actions.

Jumping up—without spilling a drop—she hurried back into the tent.

He followed.

Quinn was still at his captain's side.

"Get him up," Céline ordered. "He needs to drink all of this."

"What is it?" Quinn asked, lifting Keegan up into a sitting position.

"A strong purgative. It will make him vomit."

Jaromir felt rather than saw Amelie at his side, and they both watched the unpleasant scene that followed, in which Keegan tried to drink the concoction, then choked harder, and Céline doggedly forced the rest of it down his throat. She spilled some on her dress and his shirt. Watching her, Jaromir marveled at her calm, at her capability in an ugly situation. Her brand of courage might be different from his—and even from Amelie's—but it was a sight to behold.

"Be ready with that basin," Céline told Quinn. Looking back at Jaromir and Amelie, she added, "This is going to be a long night. The only way to save him is to get the mushrooms out of his system before they fully digest. That means we're going to need to make him throw up and then throw up . . . and then throw up again until nothing but juices come from his stomach."

She turned back to Quinn. "If you cannot face this, no one will think the worse of you. Amelie can assist me."

He blinked and then shook his head. "No, I'll help."

As those words left his mouth, Keegan rolled and began retching in earnest. True to his word, Quinn was ready with the basin.

"Amelie, keep mugs of boiling water coming," Céline said, holding on to Keegan to help lean him over the basin.

"I will," Amelie answered. But she didn't go outside to the fire right away. Instead, she leaned closer to Jaromir and whispered, "I'll see to the hot water. Maybe you should have a talk with the cook and ask him where those mushrooms came from. We don't want the trail going cold."

He glanced down at her. So far, he'd been fully focused on helping to save Keegan, but she was right. Now that Céline had taken charge, and she had assistance . . . it was time he talked to the cook.

Although Amelie had assisted Céline many times, by the second round of Keegan's purging, even she was growing queasy. It was a messy, nasty business, but she understood that it had to be done.

Worse, after all this, they probably wouldn't know if he'd live or not until tomorrow. It would all depend on how much of the poison had gone into his system before Céline had gone to work.

As Amelie kept the hot water coming, she expected Jaromir to leave and go hunt down the cook, but he didn't. She was thrown slightly off-kilter when a soldier dragged a balding, overweight man into the tent, and the poor man began sputtering.

"What is the meaning of this?"

Jaromir stood near the bed and turned to focus on the man's expression as he saw the scene before him. Then Amelie understood. Jaromir wished to gauge the cook's reaction.

"Captain?" the man asked, watching Keegan being held over the basin. "What is happening?"

"You're Volkian, the cook?" Jaromir asked coldly.

"Of course I am. What is happening here?"

"Captain Keegan was poisoned by a plate of mushrooms that you sent over."

For a second, Volkian's face was blank, and then horror began to dawn. "That I . . . oh, no, sir."

"You didn't send the dish?" Jaromir's voice seemed to get only harder and colder.

"I . . . ," Volkian stammered. "Yes, I sent it over, but I have several assistants going back and forth between where the oven is stationed and the front of the supply tent. They often bring me whatever is most available."

That struck Amelie as an odd arrangement, but she let Jaromir continue with the interrogation.

"So someone brought you the mushrooms?" Jaromir asked.

"Yes, but I didn't see . . ." The cook drew in a deep breath, perhaps trying to calm himself. "I was busy at the stove, seeing to the final touches of the stew. When I went back to my chopping table to fetch a bit of parsley, someone had left a pile of mushrooms. I assumed one of my assistants had brought them, and I remembered how much the captain liked them fried in butter."

He sounded plausible, but Amelie could have sworn she saw the slightest twitch of his eye at the words "someone had left."

He knows, she thought. *He knows who brought those mushrooms.*

For some reason, he didn't wish to tell.

Jaromir did not appear to have caught the twitch. "You're telling me you have no idea who left a pile of mushrooms on your chopping table, and yet you served them to your captain?"

Volkian raised both hands in the air, palms up. "As I said, I have several assistants bringing me ingredients. It is a common practice, and I gave it no thought."

Jaromir pointed to Keegan. "Well, if he dies, you'll have a good deal to think about."

The cook went pale.

By morning, Céline's opinion of Quinn had risen even higher. The man certainly had backbone. He'd held the basin and followed her every instruction for hours.

Amelie had kept up with the boiling water, and Jaromir helped out where he could, and not long past the mid of night, Céline was sure she'd purged Captain Keegan of anything in his stomach. After that, they were all in wait-and-see mode, so she'd sent Amelie and Jaromir off to bed to get some sleep. Quinn had insisted on staying.

Keegan was so weakened by that point that he was unconscious and no longer groaning, so Céline and Quinn spent the remainder of the night quietly sitting at his side. But Céline's mind was not still, and she continued going over and over everyone who had a motive to kill the captain. Unfortunately, the list was long, and the possible motives were convoluted.

First . . . what if he indeed was a murderer—for that was how she'd come to think of whoever might be intentionally turning these soldiers into wolves—and someone had found out and, instead of accusing him, had decided to kill him? Keegan had a strong motive for wanting to shut down the mining project, even if he lost face in doing so. He hated it here and wanted out.

However, even if he was not the one behind these recent tragedies, there were a number of people who would be glad to see him dead: Marcus and Mariah for two. Both of them had a reason to wish to be free of him.

In addition, there was a whole camp full of panicked soldiers. What if one of them assumed they'd be transferred and replaced should their leader die? Had that not happened once before?

The list of suspects was overwhelming, but she kept turning them over in her mind through the night until one other possibility occurred to her.

Just past dawn, Jaromir and Rurik came into the tent, and Jaromir leaned over the bed. He looked as if he hadn't slept well, with dark circles under his eyes.

"How is he? Will he live?"

Céline reached up absently and rubbed the back of her neck. "I don't know for certain, but I think so. His breathing is even, and he's been sleeping normally for the past few hours." She paused. "But he'll be weak and ill for some time, possibly up to a month, and he won't be fit for command while he's healing."

At that, Quinn looked up, and a quick flash of alarm crossed his face. She wondered why. Did he fear a clear lack of leadership?

Jaromir hadn't seemed to notice Quinn's flash of alarm, and he nodded to Céline. "All right. But you both need to get some sleep. I'll sit with him."

"Where's Amelie?" she asked.

"I left her sleeping in your tent," Jaromir answered tightly.

Glancing at Rurik, Céline tried to stand and wobbled. "Guardsman Rurik, would you walk me back? I'm so tired I can barely stand."

Rushing forward, Rurik took her arm. "Of course."

She let him lead her out, and she took a deep breath. The fresh air smelled good after sitting with Keegan all night.

"The lieutenant said you were something to see in there," Rurik told her as they walked. "He said he'd trust his life to you before any court physician he's ever met."

"Did he?"

That was unusual. Jaromir wasn't one to pay compliments. But Céline had other things on her mind, and she noticed two small empty tents to their left.

"Rurik, stop a moment," she said, stepping between the tents.

"What? Are you that tired? Do you need me to carry you?"

As soon as they were out of sight, she turned on him. "I'm going to ask you something, and I want you to tell me the truth. Jaromir will find out anyway, and it's better for you if he hears it from me."

They were standing close enough that she could see his light freckles clearly, and she noticed his eyes were green.

Before he could speak, she asked, "Did you leave those mushrooms for the captain's cook?"

Rurik's mouth fell open.

"You've wanted out of here since before we arrived," she rushed on. "And yesterday, you asked what was standing in my way, and I told you it was Keegan. You were off all afternoon with Amelie, through the forest and in a meadow. While she was resting or watching the horses, you could have slipped off, picked enough mushrooms, and hidden them. You were both back today before me, and then you went to stable the horses. You'd have had time to get the mushrooms onto the cook's chopping table. What if we'd been invited to the captain's table? Amelie loves mushrooms in butter. You could have poisoned her."

Rurik closed his mouth and shook his head. "I never!" He took a step back. "I'll not deny there was a moment or two when I thought everyone here might be better off if that captain was dead, but I wouldn't kill him. And if I did, I wouldn't do it by poison! I don't know one mushroom from another, and poison is a woman's weapon."

Céline was skilled at reading faces and voices and gauging reactions. At one time, her profession had depended upon it.

He was telling the truth.

She reached out and touched his arm. "I'm sorry. I had to catch you off guard. I had to know."

He exhaled through his nose and glanced away, still offended.

"I really am quite tired," she said. "Could you take me to my tent?"

As they moved on, something he'd said kept echoing in her mind.

Poison is a woman's weapon.

Amelie stirred and opened her eyes.

She was in the bed inside their tent, fully clothed,

and Céline was sleeping quietly beside her—also fully clothed. Frankly, Amelie wondered that she hadn't woken up when her sister crawled into the bed, as Céline's hair and clothing smelled . . . rather strong. After all, she had been up through the night tending a retching captain. She wasn't going to smell like a rose.

Carefully, Amelie slipped out from under the covers and made her way to the tent's flap. Her sister didn't stir. Amelie knew that Céline didn't care to sleep during the day, but exceptions must be made.

Besides, Amelie had a task that was best handled alone.

Judging by the sun, she guessed it to be midday or so, and she wondered how Captain Keegan was faring. Had the man lived through the night? She assumed so. Otherwise, Céline would have awoken her with the bad news. Not that Amelie would have considered Keegan's death much of a tragedy, but Céline and Quinn had worked hard to keep him alive.

And this morning, Amelie had decided it would be best to track down the poisoner.

Several of the soldiers milling about glanced her way, but no one tried to speak to her. Yesterday, Rurik had shown her the provisions tent, and she walked right to it.

It was huge, even bigger than Keegan's.

The front section was filled with barrels and crates and casks sent from Castle Pählen.

Ignoring the front, Amelie walked around to the back of the tent. Before entering, she crouched and drew the dagger out of its sheath in her boot. She didn't expect much trouble with this first visit, but still . . . it was better to be safe than sorry.

As she walked through the back entrance, the first thing she saw was a large wood-burning stove with a vent above it in the top of the tent. The bald cook, Volkian, was sitting in a chair beside it with his face in his hands.

Amelie cleared her throat, and he looked up.

Upon recognizing her, he jumped to his feet, moving faster than she would have expected.

"What are you doing here?" he demanded. "I told your lieutenant everything I know last night."

"No, you didn't." She kept the dagger hidden in her hand, gripping the hilt with the point upward and the flat side against her wrist. Walking closer to the cook, she tilted her head. "Who brought you those mushrooms?"

"I don't know. I've talked to my assistants and no one will own up."

"You talked to them this morning? So if my lieutenant goes and talks to them, they'll tell him that you already questioned them yourself?"

Panic flickered across his face.

"I knew you were lying last night," she said, "but I didn't say anything. Tell me who brought you the mushrooms, and I'll keep quiet. Stick to your current story, and I'll go tell the lieutenant I *think* you're lying. He'll believe me. My sister and I are Prince Anton's seers."

His breathing grew labored.

"Trust me," Amelie went on. "You'd be much better

off talking to me. He always gets results, but I don't think you'll like his methods."

In defeat, Volkian sank back into his chair. "It was the gypsy girl."

"Mariah?"

"I'm not sure of all their names."

"The young one with the black hair?"

"No, her elder sister."

"Mercedes?"

He nodded. "Yes, that's her name." He put his face into his hands again. "What a fool I am. I was trying to get the stew ready to serve, and she just appeared. But Captain Keegan has an arrangement with one of their young hunters, and those gypsies are always bringing venison or fowl or rabbits for the captain's table."

"And she told you that she had some mushrooms?"

"Not at first. First she asked me if you or your sister would be dining with the captain. He'd already told me to have your supper served in your tents, so I told her no. That alone should have gained my attention. But then she showed me the mushrooms and reminded me how much he loves them cooked with butter. Her sister . . . well, her sister knows the captain."

Indeed, Amelie thought dryly.

"He's been complaining about a lack of variety," Volkian went on. "But I don't have much to work with! I thanked her and fried up the mushrooms. Fool." He looked up. "Do you understand how it will look to your lieutenant, to Corporal Quinn, if they find out I accepted mushrooms from some gypsy girl? I'll be lucky if I'm only dismissed."

Yes, Amelie could see his dilemma, but at present, she had no intention of giving away Mercedes, not until she knew more. And that meant protecting the cook.

"Listen," she said. "You keep up your courage, and I'll keep your secret."

He studied her cautiously. "Why would you do that?"

"Because I like those gypsies a lot better than I like your captain."

Turning, she walked out of the tent.

Although Jaromir had never been one for just sitting, at the moment, he was glad for having taken on the task of sitting at Keegan's bedside. Hopefully, Céline, Amelie, Rurik, and Quinn would get some sleep while he sat here alone.

It gave him time to think.

Keegan had not yet awoken, but his breathing was still even. His complexion was a sickly shade of gray-green, and Jaromir did not doubt Céline's assessment that the man's recovery time would be long.

However, this left Jaromir with some decisions to make, and he considered what paths were open to him. In the end, though, he could think of only one way forward if he was to solve whatever was happening here, stop it, and get the silver flowing again.

The rear tent flap opened, and Quinn stuck his head inside.

"How is he?"

"I thought you were getting some sleep."

"I couldn't."

Quinn's genuine concern caught Jaromir off guard,

as he'd not seen much of a connection or loyalty between the two men.

"I think he'll live," Jaromir said, "but Céline is right, and he'll not be fit to command for some time."

The anxiety on Quinn's face grew more pronounced as he came inside to stand near the bed. "Does that mean we'll be recalled and replaced?"

"Not yet." Jaromir paused. "As the only available officer, I'm taking command of the camp."

He waited to see how Quinn would accept this news. Officer or not, Jaromir didn't serve Prince Lieven. However, he did serve Prince Lieven's son—and thereby the House of Pählen. If Quinn accepted him, the others would follow suit.

His concerns proved to be groundless. Quinn leaned against the bed in open relief. "Yes, sir."

Amelie left the provisions tent and walked straight to the miners' encampment. Upon breaking through the tree line, she turned left and headed toward the largest of the covered wagons. An old man sitting outside with a smokeless pipe in his mouth nodded a greeting. She nodded back.

When she reached Mercedes and Mariah's wagon, she paused out front at the sight of the clothesline; both her green wool dress and Céline's lavender one were hanging there and appeared to be nearly dry. Every last speck of mud and blood had been removed, and the dresses looked new.

Mercedes was a skilled laundress.

Unable to put the reason for her visit here off any

longer, Amelie climbed the few steps up to the back door of the wagon. In spite of what the cook had told her, she needed to know for certain whether Mercedes was the one who'd poisoned Keegan . . . and she needed to know why. There were a number of possible reasons for Mercedes to want him dead, but those reasons had existed well before now. Why had she finally acted? And did her reason have anything to do with the Pählen soldiers being turned into mad wolves? Could Mercedes be the one behind that as well? Had Keegan learned something, so she'd decided to get rid of him? But if that were the case, why wouldn't she simply infect him next? Why switch to poison?

Amelie had many questions, and if Mercedes wouldn't talk to her, she had her own methods for learning the truth.

Raising a hand, she knocked lightly. "Mercedes?"

The door opened almost right away, and Mercedes looked out. Her posture was tight but not overly anxious.

"Are you alone?" Amelie asked.

"Yes, Mariah is off searching for berries. I was just about to go and join her."

Amelie pushed her way inside and closed the door.

"What do you think you're doing?" Mercedes demanded, backing up.

"Céline was up all night trying to save Captain Keegan, but you probably already know that."

Mercedes watched her carefully, and Amelie wouldn't make the mistake of underestimating this woman. She might be slender, but she didn't look weak.

"I haven't told anyone," Amelie said. "Not Céline or the lieutenant. I just want to know why you did it."

"Did your sister succeed in saving the captain?"

"Yes."

Of course Amelie didn't know that for certain yet, but if Keegan were already dead, she'd most likely have heard about it.

Mercedes turned away, closing her eyes.

"Why now?" Amelie pressed on. "If you were going to kill him over what he's been doing to Mariah, you'd have acted before this."

Opening her eyes, Mercedes spun back. "What do you know of our lives? Of what brought us here? Of how years of suffering can deaden a soul? You . . . with your fine wool gowns and your lieutenant and your meals at the officers' table. Get out! At heart, you're nothing like your sister, and I don't owe you anything."

Without warning, Amelie closed the distance between them and grabbed Mercedes's hand, gripping hard. She expected fierce resistance and was caught off guard when Mercedes gripped back, leaning forward.

"Do you want to see?" Mercedes whispered angrily.

Fearing this was a trick and that Mercedes might try to break away, Amelie reached out with her thoughts for the spark of Mercedes's soul. She felt it right away and focused on the events of last night, on what led up to the mushrooms finding their way to the cook's table.

"No," Mercedes breathed in her ear. "If you want to see, you'll see it all."

The first jolt hit and Amelie gasped, bracing for another, but she didn't let go. As the second jolt hit, she found herself rushing through the gray-and-white mists, flying backward in time with Mercedes. Effortlessly, almost without choice, she felt her spirit meshing with Mercedes's, intertwining with Mercedes's, until she saw through Mercedes's eyes. But unlike ever before, her consciousness remained separate and aware.

The mists cleared, and she found herself kneeling on a riverbank, looking down into the dead face of a beautiful woman.

Listen . . . , a voice whispered inside her mind.

CHAPTER NINE

Mercedes: Five Years in the Past

THE DEATH

The first time I experienced fear and sorrow in the exact same moment was the day I found myself looking down into the face of my dead mother.

I couldn't believe it. It happened so fast.

She'd been standing beside me, my father, and Mariah, on the bank of the Vudrask River, just outside the city of Kéonsk. She was smiling and looking forward to all the pleasures of the Autumn Fair. Even in her late forties, my mother was lovely, small and lithe, with black eyes and a mass of black hair. She wore white peasant blouses and brightly colored skirts and silver bangles on her wrists. Everywhere she walked, the heads of men would turn to follow.

That morning, we'd just arrived outside Kéonsk, to set up for the fair, and we'd walked over to see the rushing river. There were barges coming and going, loading and unloading, and it was always enjoyable to watch the activity.

A merchant was trying to get a team of young horses to pull his wagon closer to the bank, and two dogs beside them broke out into a snarling fight. The horses bolted, coming straight at us. My father pushed me and grabbed Mariah, and my mother was struck full force by one of the horses as it tried to stop itself at the top of the bank.

She was knocked into the water, and my father cried out.

Men began to hurry over, but she was in the current facedown and did not appear to be moving. My father jumped into the river. Mariah and I ran along the embankment, calling to her, but it was a good distance until Father was able to reach her and pull her out.

She was dead, her face white, her hair soaked, her eyes closed.

Standing beside me, Mariah stared down, and in my shock and sorrow, I was hit by a sense of fear. My mother's name had been Moira, and she was the leader of our small group of Móndyalítko. We depended on her for many things.

And in a blink, she was gone.

Kneeling on the ground, my father, who was called Jude, let out a shameless sob. Mariah continued staring down in silence.

I asked, "Father . . . what are we going to do now?"

He didn't appear to understand my question, as I do not think he fully understood that it was my mother who had managed everything . . . everything for our family community for my entire life. His tears were all shed for the loss of a beloved wife, but I saw the larger scheme of things.

And I was afraid.

THE FAMILY

Our traveling group consisted of four wagons—one for each family—eight horses, one good-natured milk cow, and a varying number of chickens.

My mother was from the line of Marentõr.

And as an eldest surviving daughter, she was the undisputed leader of our small branch. Since my father, Jude, had married into our kin and joined with us, he took her family name, as was the custom. For some reason no one could remember, her grandmother had believed all children born into the line should be given first names starting with the letter *M*.

Mother believed in following such traditions.

Although our immediate family consisted of only four people, we had the largest wagon, and we always led the way.

The second wagon housed my mother's younger sister, Miriam, her husband, Landrien (who had also married in), and their two sons, Mikolai and Marcus.

The third wagon belonged to my mother's elderly uncle Marten and his wife, Leticia, along with their son, Micah, and his wife, Katlyn, and their three young children, meaning seven people were packed into one wagon, but they seemed to manage.

The fourth and last wagon had once belonged to a second cousin of my mother's, who, for reasons never revealed to me, had been shunned by her closer kin and joined up with our group before I was born. Her husband's name was Shawn, and between them, they'd brought five sons into the world, and she'd died giving birth to the last one. My mother, of course, could not turn Shawn and the boys away, so they'd remained with us. However, this family did not follow the traditions of naming children with the letter *M*, and the two oldest boys, Payton and Orlando, had proven to be a great trial to their father—and thereby my mother—as they neared manhood. Both young men had a tendency to be light-fingered. This, coupled with their mutual lack of wits, had been occasionally troublesome in our travels.

My own father was not above theft in a pinch, but he never got caught.

At the time of my mother's death, I was nineteen and Mariah was eleven. Without Mother, our group numbered twenty people.

Everyone stood in shocked silence when my father told them what had happened on the riverbank . . . that my mother was gone. But I was the only one who truly appeared to grasp the full implications of her sudden absence.

My mother was known as "the Great Moira."

She was not Mist-Torn and possessed no inborn abilities. In our family community, Marcus had been the only one born with a Móndyalítko gift. He was a shifter, and a fine hunter as a result. We were proud of him, but his gift was a secret, known only to us and other Móndyalítko. He could not be used to earn money or gain fame. But even without a Mist-Torn among us, we managed quite well.

Mother was a palm reader, the best I'd ever seen.

She knew how to make someone else feel like the only person in the world. She knew how to shine her light and give someone else hope and joy and peace. She knew how to make other people feel good about themselves and to do it in a way that was natural and believable.

This might not seem like such an unusual gift—but it was.

Every autumn, large numbers of farmers, merchants, and Móndyalítko converged upon the city of Kéonsk for the fair, far too many to be allowed inside the already crowded city.

Wagons, tents, and market stalls were set up outside, overseen by a city administrator called Master Deandre. He was lord of the fair, and like everyone else, he adored my mother. Not only that, but he was a shrewd businessman also, and he was well aware just how many people would line up outside our wagon to be read by the Great Moira.

Because of her, our small group from the line of Marentõr was considered important and quite a draw for the fair, as some people came just to see her and then would spend money at the merchant stalls. Master Deandre always kept a prime spot for our four wagons, just outside the west entrance of the city. Nobody could miss us there.

Of course other members of our group had skills and talents, and we put on shows as well. Aunt Miriam and I could sing. Even at eleven, Mariah could dance beautifully. Something about the way she moved was mesmerizing. Mikolai and Micah could both play the violin, sometimes staging dueling duets, and my father was astonishing at card and magic tricks—which he mainly used as entertainment as opposed to fleecing people out of their money. We'd put out hats and people would toss in coins.

But my mother was the one people came to see, and she earned the lion's share of our income.

In addition, she was wise and careful with money, and she kept the family accounts. We would all work the fair for the last month of autumn, and then she'd take the earnings and find good bargains on supplies: food, bolts of cloth, thread, paint for the wagons, herbal medicines, grain for the horses, new tools . . . anything we might need. Even after, she always ended up with a surplus of coins.

Once the fair was over, and we were well supplied, we'd head east to our winter destination: Belfleur Keep.

When I was just a girl, a lord named Camden had fallen under my mother's spell, and he'd invited us to spend the winter in the courtyard of his keep. He was unmarried, but he loved to entertain friends and family in the winter months, so he often had numerous guests.

We went to serve as entertainment, and this became a tradition.

Every winter, we'd roll into the courtyard, and Lord Camden would welcome my mother like a lost jewel, kissing her hands with moisture in his eyes. He stabled our horses and let us all eat from his kitchens. We lived in our wagons, but if the weather grew too cold, we were allowed to come into the keep and sleep in the great hall by the fire.

As payment, my mother would spend many evenings doing readings for his guests after dinner. Her mere presence always meant he had people coming and going, and he was never lonely in those long, cold months. The rest of us worked, too, singing and dancing and playing music and performing magic. Mariah had never known what it was like to be cold or hungry in the winter, and I had only a few vague memories from childhood.

But again, I'd always understood that our welcome and our comfortable, safe winters at Belfleur Keep were all due to my mother. It never occurred to me that this realization had not dawned on my father or Aunt Miriam.

Not until after my mother was already dead.

THE DESCENT

The first sign of trouble came swiftly. Aunt Miriam went to speak with Master Deandre, to tell him of our tragedy and to gain permission to begin setting up in our usual spot outside the west gate.

He expressed sorrow over the death of my mother,

and he offered Aunt Miriam sincere condolences, which she accepted. But then . . . he told her that we could not set up just yet, as there had been a few delays with preparations for the fair.

He came to us that night and related, with deep regret, that he'd already allotted our spot to another group of Móndyalítko from the line of Renéive, who were traveling with a Mist-Torn seer. He said the city had already made this decision before our arrival in order to alternate the entertainment nearest the front gate—to keep it fresh.

I knew he was lying.

Father and Aunt Miriam were dumbfounded when we were shown our new location at the outskirts of the fair among the wagons of shabbier Móndyalítko and farmers selling old apples to those who could not afford better.

"What are we going to do?" I asked my father again.

He shook his head in confusion. "Do? We'll do what we do every year. We'll stage shows and put our hats out for coins."

I wanted to clench my fists. He still didn't understand.

Aunt Miriam took over as head of the family—as was her place—but she was not my mother. The elders in our group had long since grown complacent without realizing it. In fairness, my father, Aunt Miriam, and Uncle Landrien did attempt to organize some shows for us to perform, but on the outskirts of the fair, almost no one saw us, and no one had any money to toss into our hats.

Then . . . Aunt Miriam announced that we would walk farther inside the fair and perform where there were more people.

So we did.

Unfortunately, the arrangement of the Móndyalítko families and wagons had been carefully orchestrated, and after receiving a few complaints, Master Deandre visited to politely ask us to perform only in the area where we'd been placed.

Several of Shawn's boys were put in charge of the horses and our cow. When we ran out of grain, they began leading the animals out anywhere grass might be found. Eight horses and a cow required a good deal of grass.

By midmonth, we were spending the few coins we earned on food for immediate use, and I had a terrible feeling that very little was being saved. By the end of the month, we were living on boiled oats for breakfast, nothing for lunch, and eggs from our own chickens for dinner . . . and we had little to feed the chickens. Our cow did provide us with some milk, but she was growing older.

Poor Mariah was so confused and lost. She'd never suffered hardship, and she missed our mother so much. I tried to give her what comfort I could.

There was no one to give me comfort.

As the fair ended, it was finally time to head east for the winter, to Belfleur Keep. Mariah was so happy, she clung to me.

"I can't wait to eat warm bread and sausages in the keep's kitchen again," she said. "And to sit by the fire in the hall and to play with Lord Camden's dogs."

I smiled and nodded and held her close. My beautiful

little sister. I did not want to voice my fears and spoil her happiness. Though I had a bad feeling about what was coming, I convinced myself that I could be wrong.

We left Kéonsk with few supplies and no grain for the horses.

The journey east took us just over a week. Out on the road, it was safe to send Marcus hunting at night, and he kept us supplied with rabbits and pheasants, but feeding twenty people was no easy task for him, and we all grew accustomed to small portions.

When we finally rolled up to Belfleur Keep, I could see the stark relief in both my father and Aunt Miriam. I knew they were both shaken by our change in circumstances at the Autumn Fair, and they were desperate for Lord Camden's hospitality.

Aunt Miriam now drove in the lead of our group, and she led the way to the south side of the courtyard, where we had wintered for the past thirteen years. We all climbed down to stretch our legs and begin setting up. Shawn's boys had not even begun unharnessing the horses when Lord Camden emerged from the keep, coming out to greet us. A collection of small spaniels ran around his feet, and Mariah's face broke into a smile at the sight of them, but I held her back.

"Wait," I said. "Aunt Miriam needs to speak to him first."

My aunt glanced at me, and then she headed across the courtyard to intercept Lord Camden. I could see his face from where I stood, and he frowned slightly at the sight of her coming toward him. He began casting his gaze around, and I knew whom he sought: my mother.

Aunt Miriam went to him and began speaking softly. I could see only her back, but she was using her hands as she spoke. Lord Camden's face froze, and he staggered backward. I thought he might fall. Aunt Miriam reached out for him, speaking faster. I couldn't hear her exact words, but I could hear her rushed voice.

Lord Camden looked ill and appeared to be trying to get control of himself. He breathed deeply a few times. Then he shook his head and said something that made her entire body stiffen. Aunt Miriam's voice rose, and I knew that was a mistake. My mother would never have raised her voice. She would have charmed him. I did not inherit her ability to charm, but I had seen it in action many times.

"What's wrong?" Mariah asked.

I didn't answer.

Lord Camden shook his head again and said something else. For a moment, his eyes moved toward us, stopping on Mariah, who was a small replica of my mother. Then he turned and walked back to the main doors of the keep. His shoulders were shaking.

Slowly, Aunt Miriam turned and walked back to us.

My father's face was stricken. "He has refused us?"

Aunt Miriam seemed beyond speech at first, and finally she said, "I told him that we would be able to entertain his guests all winter. I promised we would put on as many shows as he wished. But he says his pain at Moira's loss is too great. He says that seeing us would be a daily reminder of his sorrow. He wants us to leave today."

"Leave?" my father repeated. "And go where?"

Everyone in the family appeared stunned except for Marcus and my great-uncle, Marten.

With his pipe clenched between his teeth, Great-Uncle Marten made a sound of disgust. "What did you expect? Moira spent years making sure you needed her, depended on her, and you followed her like children. Performers like the rest of us can be found traveling down any road. *She* was the one Camden wanted here. We're all just baggage. She made sure of that, and you let her."

So I wasn't alone in my realizations or fears—although I didn't care for some of the implications he was making about my mother.

"What's wrong?" Mariah asked again, gripping my hand.

Everyone fell silent, but we had no choice other than to climb back into the wagons and roll out of the courtyard. Mariah wept quietly, and the sound broke my heart.

Throughout that winter, I thought that life for us could not possibly become worse.

We couldn't survive in unpopulated areas, as we were performers and we required people to entertain. I had no idea of the low opinion that many fief lords and town magistrates had of vagabond travelers. Often, we'd barely set up camp outside a town or large village when soldiers or a local constabulary would come to chase us off.

Mariah heard many words she'd never heard before. These men called us filthy gypsies and *tzigän*—meaning "vagabond thieves." The term "Móndyalítko" meant "the world's little children," and this was all Mariah had ever known, to be adored and protected as the small image of my mother. I watched her change that winter from a joyful little dancer into a frightened child, hiding inside herself.

Both my father and Aunt Miriam proved almost useless. They seemed lost and adrift without my mother. I came to depend on Marcus, who was a quiet sort, but he kept us alive by hunting all night. I made sure he was left alone to sleep during the day. Some of the other men did try to hunt as well, but it was not their trade, and they weren't shifters like Marcus, so they brought back very little.

Deer were scarce that winter, and even Marcus could hunt down only so many rabbits and pheasants—again, not enough to support twenty people. We had a difficult time finding grass for the horses, especially when we were never allowed to remain in one place for very long.

Near midwinter, the chickens stopped laying, and so we began to eat them.

Firewood proved a problem as well. For thirteen years, our men had not had to seek firewood in the winter. Much of what they managed to bring back was too wet and too green to burn, so we began piling it in the wagons where we could to try to dry it.

It didn't snow much in eastern Droevinka, but it did freeze, and we faced many cold nights huddled beneath blankets in the wagons. I think these nights were hardest on Great-Uncle Marten and his aging wife, Leticia.

One of my own bleakest moments occurred when

Mariah came to me and whispered, "What about my birthday?"

I felt like I'd been kicked in the stomach. Mariah had been born in midwinter. Back at Belfleur Keep, Mother had always watched the moon and picked a day to celebrate Mariah's birth. Lord Camden would order something special to be made for dinner, and he always gave Mariah a new gown as a gift, and she would dance for everyone—and be adored.

But now . . . what could I do for her?

With a smile, I hugged her thin shoulders. "I've not forgotten." Even though I had.

The next day, we camped near a dried-up cornfield. I slipped away and gathered up some husks. While I was there, I rejoiced at finding a small patch of onions that someone had neglected to dig up in the autumn harvest. I dug up every onion I could find. Then I went back to the wagon, found some scraps of cloth, made Mariah a corn-husk doll wearing a dress, and hid it.

To my eternal gratitude, Marcus brought down a deer that night.

So, for the following evening, I was able to produce a large pot of venison and onion stew for the family. I somehow turned this into a celebration for Mariah's birthday, and I gave her the doll. A full stomach of meat and onions did everyone good, and Mikolai played his violin while Mariah danced for us around the fire.

She went to bed happy that night and kissed me twice.

A week later, our cow died, and although this meant there would be no more milk, the men butchered her and we lived on the meat.

As spring came and the trees burst forth with green leaves, I welcomed the warmer air and marveled that we had somehow all managed to survive. The world looked brighter to us again, as it was now time to head southeast toward our late-spring and summer destination.

And we all knew that no one would turn us away.

The prince of the House of Yegor owned vast lands of apple orchards and berry fields, so many that he could not employ enough peasants to handle the harvest—and the strawberries began arriving in late spring. Years ago, he had let it be known that if any of the Móndyalítko were willing to work the harvest, they were welcome to camp in a large meadow about half a league from his castle.

At least fourteen Móndyalítko caravans came every year, my own family among them.

It was a pleasure for us to live among our own for the damp spring and warm southeast summers. We harvested strawberries first, then raspberries, then blueberries, and then apples in the early fall. We were asked to pay nothing in rent for our stay, and we were allowed to keep a portion of the berries and apples we picked—and also to fish in any of the area's numerous streams and to set snares for rabbits.

This entire yearly cycle had become a rhythm so comfortable to us that we'd forgotten anything else: late spring and summer in the southeast meadow of Yegor, the Autumn Fair in Kéonsk, and winter and early spring inside the safe walls of Belfleur Keep.

Though now some of this rhythm had been lost to

us, we could all at least look forward to our journey to Castle Yegor.

However, as we arrived and rolled into the meadow, already filled with other wagons, I could feel a change in how we were observed. The line of Marentõr in general was not viewed as prosperous, but previously, my own family had commanded respect and even envy. My mother had seen to it that our horses were well fed and groomed and that our wagons were always in good repair, with freshly painted shutters. Our group was always well dressed, with enough supplies to help other families in need. In addition, we had Marcus, and there were other groups who longed for a shifter of their own.

As we set up camp in our usual place that summer, I felt the first tinge of shame. Our horses were thin and unkempt. The harsh winter in the forests and fields had left our wagons dull and in need of repair, and we had no money for paint. We ourselves were thin and shabby, and we did not have enough to feed ourselves, much less to share.

Some of the families who had envied us in the past now snubbed us and pretended we didn't exist. But others were kind—especially those to whom we had once been kind—and they brought us oats and honey and eggs. Mariah seemed to become more herself again at the prospect of being among a larger number of our people, and I got a campfire going and made her some scrambled eggs.

Things improved from there. Our men caught trout in the streams, and soon the strawberry harvest began.

We worked hard, but in my spare time, I washed and mended clothes; my father, Mikolai, and Marcus did what they could to repair the wagons; and Shawn and his boys cared for the horses.

Shawn's two oldest sons, Orlando and Payton, soon became my main concern. They were eighteen and nineteen, and I had observed them more than once looking into other wagons at food and silver trinkets. I spoke to Aunt Miriam and asked her to give them a stern warning about the dangers of stealing from our own people. We could be banned from the meadow for life. Thankfully, the young men only looked and did not touch, and in the end, they caused us no trouble.

The summer weather was warm, and the harvest was plentiful, and by autumn, Mariah was running and laughing with the other girls and no longer hiding inside herself so much. I was glad to see this, for I remembered that at her age, I'd fostered great curiosity about the other families, especially the line of Fawe, who came every year. They were among the most prosperous of the Móndyalítko, as they tended to give birth to an unusual number of Mist-Torn seers. Some of their people had wheat gold hair, and their seers were always born with lavender eyes.

I was sorry when the harvest ended.

But for the last month of autumn, we headed back to Kéonsk.

By this time, my father and Aunt Miriam had no illusions regarding how far we'd fallen, and they didn't argue or complain with Master Deandre when he placed us way at the back of the fair again.

We earned what money we could, and fool that I

was, I assumed that now that my father and Aunt Miriam and the other elders had finally grasped our situation, they would be busy making a plan for winter.

We certainly couldn't wander from place to place as we had last year.

But that's exactly what we did, and the winter became a blur of cold and hunger. Although none of our people died, we arrived in the meadow of Yegor the following spring looking every inch the "filthy gypsies" we were so often called. Mariah had completely retreated inside herself and did not come out. She didn't run or play with the other girls. Only one family took pity on us and brought us a few oats and eggs.

The strawberry harvest began, and we all did our best to work, but we were in a weakened state. Marcus and Mikolai both fished and set out snares instead of picking berries, and I thought that as with last summer, a bit of sunshine and decent food would put us all to rights soon.

Then one night, just as the raspberry harvest began, Orlando and Payton were caught red-handed stealing from the wagon of a Mist-Torn seer from the line of Renéive.

My father and Aunt Miriam begged, but the rules of the families were clear and no exceptions could be made. We were told to leave and not to come back.

I was numb. We had lost our last place of true safety.

Worse, I experienced a moment of irrational fear that Marcus might leave us. Any of the groups would have taken him. But of course he didn't, and I don't know where that fear came from.

We wandered again until the last month of autumn and then headed back to Kéonsk. At end of that year's fair, my father and Aunt Miriam announced that something drastic must change and that they had come to a decision. I felt a single moment of hope that they'd found us someplace safe to spend the winter. Then, when I heard their decision, I bit the inside of my mouth. Their plan was . . . uncertain at best.

"We've heard that the House of Äntes is more accepting of our people," Aunt Miriam announced, "so we will travel north and west, to Enêmûsk. We can find a place inside the city to set up and put on our shows. We should at least be able to earn enough to feed ourselves and the horses."

While this sounded far better than the hardships of last winter, I wondered where they'd heard of this tolerance of the Äntes. I'd never heard such a thing. Also, the winters in the northwest provinces were much colder than those in the east, and should this plan fail, I feared we would be wintering in ice and snow.

Marcus caught my eye, and I knew he was thinking the same thing.

But neither he nor I had a voice in these decisions, and so we headed west first and then north, arriving at Enêmûsk just as the weather began to turn.

To this day, I don't know who had given my aunt and father such foolish advice, but the Äntes soldiers guarding the front entrance to Enêmûsk looked at us with such disgust that I put my hands over Mariah's ears to stop her from hearing whatever was about to come from their mouths.

It was vile.

In the midst of their insults, they made it understood that we would not even be allowed to roll our wagons inside the city. They informed us that the Äntes did not suffer any vagabonds or beggars and that we'd best be on our way if we knew what was good for us.

I'll never forget the look on my father's face. Some of the life went out of him that day, but I was beyond pity, and for the first time I felt anger toward my mother. Had Great-Uncle Marten been right? Had she intentionally made the rest of us dependent upon her? Had she enjoyed feeling so necessary? Why had she never tried to teach Aunt Miriam or me how to read palms? I had no answers.

That winter almost cannot be described.

We were driven away from every place we tried to make camp, and Marcus found it difficult to hunt in the snow. By midwinter, four of the horses had died. The men managed to butcher a bit of stringy meat from one of them, but we were driven off in the morning by a group of soldiers, forced to leave the other three lying in the snow. This was hard on Shawn's younger sons, as they loved our horses.

Mariah did not mention her birthday. She was too cold and hungry to remember it.

About a moon later, poor old Leticia died, and I think Great-Uncle Marten was too hungry to mourn her. Within a few days, Micah and Katlyn's youngest child died.

Mariah had become a shadow, and I feared she was next.

Then one night, we managed to make camp outside a village, and my father and Uncle Landrien went in to see what the prospects might be for us putting on a show. I found this rather a stretch, since few of us were capable of performing, and we looked like the walking dead. I wondered if the men simply planned to find a tavern and perhaps beg a mug of ale.

But when they came back, they gathered us together and delivered unexpected news.

"We were just told of an encampment called Ryazan, to the north, up above Enêmûsk," my father said. "A prince of the House of Pählen owns a collection of silver mines, and there is a shortage of workers. The soldiers overseeing the mines have a large a provisions tent, and they are willing to sell food to anyone who mines for them. We could offer to work and buy food and at least have a place to spend the remainder of the winter."

A chance at work and food sat well with the rest of us, and so we headed farther north and then slightly west. The going was slow, as only one horse now pulled each wagon. We rolled into the Ryazan encampment on the last dregs of our strength and spirit.

From the top of our wagon, I took my first look at what struck me as a sea of tents and men in brown tabards.

THE CAMP

At the time of our arrival in Ryazan, Aunt Miriam no longer even pretended to be our leader. She was barely able to rise from her bunk.

So it was my father, Uncle Landrien, and Mikolai who first spoke with Captain Garrett of the House of Pählen. He came out to meet us, and I stood in the doorway of our wagon, peering out and listening.

Captain Garrett was a wide-shouldered man, with silver hair and a proud bearing. But he was in need of workers, and he spoke to our men with respect. Unfortunately, the bargain he offered was a disappointment.

"Our miners sign a one-year contract," he said, "and they get paid at the end when the contract is fulfilled. We just had a new round of contracts signed in the autumn, but I can sign you on at a slightly reduced wage, and you can work out the rest of the year." He went on to explain that through the year, while working out their contracts, the men could take out vouchers to be exchanged for food from the provisions tent. These vouchers would later be counted against their wages. I could see this for what it was—a way to reduce monetary wages by preying on the miners' need to feed their families. But at the time, I didn't care. It sounded as if our men would be able to get food for us right away.

"However," Captain Garrett continued, "no one is allowed to trade vouchers for provisions until they've worked in the mines for at least a month. We've had a few workers load up on food, work one day, and then disappear."

My father's face fell. We needed food now. We could not last a month.

The captain seemed to understand this—although I'd been watching him count the number of men in our group, along with the boys old enough to work. I knew he wanted us to stay. He looked at our horses, which were all thin and weakened like us, but these last four were otherwise sound.

"I'll buy your horses from you, and you can use the money to purchase provisions to feed your people." He pointed north. "The miners' camp is through those trees. You can get your wagons settled and then bring the horses to me."

For traveling Móndyalítko, the idea of selling our horses was almost unthinkable. They were our life-blood, our method of moving from one place to the next in the rhythm of the year. But we had lost our yearly rhythm, and the desperate state of the men drove them to agree with the captain's offer. Later, I learned that none of the other miners had ever been told they had to work a month before taking advantage of the vouchers. Although Captain Garrett was a fair man in most ways, I thought he might have put us in a position of having to sell our horses so that we could not leave.

At the time, however, I didn't know this.

By that afternoon, we'd settled our wagons in the miners' camp. Our horses had been sold, and we'd been given a good price. Our larders were filled with supplies from the soldiers' provision tent, including oats, lentils, dried tomatoes, onions, tea, wheels of cheese, and a few pails of milk with cream floating on the surface. How cheaply we'd been bought.

Then all the men except Marcus signed contracts to work for Captain Garrett. Marcus didn't wish to sign, and he was excused because we would still need our hunter. I am ashamed at how relieved we all felt simply to have food and a place to camp and the promise of work, even if the men would not be paid in actual coin for nearly a year.

We lit a campfire, and Katlyn and I got to work making a large pot of lentil stew with onions and dried tomatoes. That night, Mariah sat by the fire with a blanket around her shoulders, and I brought her a warm bowl of lentils. She was too hungry to even wolf it down, so she took small bites.

"We can stay here?" she whispered. "We won't have to leave tomorrow?"

I don't think she understood that our horses were gone.

"No," I whispered back, sitting beside her. "We don't have to leave, and I'll make you soft oats with cream for breakfast."

She leaned into me and pressed her face in my shoulder. Maybe we were not bought so cheaply after all.

The next day, the men went to the mines to work, all except for Marcus and Great-Uncle Marten, who was too old. Only one of Shawn's boys had not turned twelve yet, and apparently, any male over twelve was considered old enough to work in the silver mines. So in one fell swoop, Captain Garrett had gained my father, Uncle Landrien, Mikolai, Micah, Shawn, and four of Shawn's sons.

I let Mariah rest that day, and I set about the task of getting a more permanent camp set up. Then I made supper. Katlyn helped me, and she also minded her two remaining children and Shawn's youngest.

Aunt Miriam did not rise from her bunk, and I began to worry that she was more than simply weary. I brought her tea and food, but she couldn't eat.

When the men came back that evening, I had my first inkling that we'd made a horrible mistake.

The Móndyalítko were not born to spend their days underground in the darkness. They need light and air. Though our men had been drawn to the promise of work, they'd not fully considered the type of work for which they were signing on—hard labor in the darkness underground.

I saw fear and desperation in the eyes of my father.

Mariah saw it, too, but her reaction offered no pity. Catching me alone, she asked, "We're not leaving, are we? Father won't give up and make us leave?"

"No," I assured her. "We will not leave."

I fed the men dinner and did what I could to make their evening pleasant with food and a warm campfire.

The following morning, they went back to the mines.

Two days later, Aunt Miriam died in her sleep. Uncle Landrien, Mikolai, and Marcus mourned her. So did Father and I. Poor Mariah was beyond mourning and barely seemed aware that her aunt was gone. The girl was too driven by fear of being back out on the road again.

As that first year passed, I made friends with the wives of the miners who lived in shacks and huts in our encampment, and a few of them taught me to use the food vouchers wisely. The soldiers placed a high price on luxuries like tea, so if I wished for our men to have more real money coming in at the end of their contracts, I learned to purchase only what was absolutely necessary. Of course, the problem with this was that I often ended up making the same things for supper—such as lentil stew. Marcus supplemented our meals with game and venison when he could. But the men were denied even small pleasures like tea. This troubled me, and yet, when I expressed my worries to my father, he told me to continue with my thrifty methods.

Over that year, I watched the life drain from the eyes of our men, and I saw a determination growing in my father that I'd never seen before. I knew he hated it here. He hated those mines. But what was going to happen when the men earned out their contracts and received the wages owed them? We certainly wouldn't have enough to buy horses.

At the end of summer, I asked him, "What are we going to do?"

He studied me for a long moment. "I have a plan, but no one knows except Marcus, and you cannot speak of it yet. Do you swear?"

"Of course."

"I've noticed the soldiers don't guard their horses well, with perhaps one man on the perimeter at night. Once we are paid, after dark, we'll overcome that one guard. We'll take six horses and slip away the same night. We'll leave Uncle Marten's wagon behind. He can ride in Landrien's. Micah and Katlyn and their children can ride with us."

"No." I shook my head. "Captain Garrett will come after us. You'll be hanged for stealing their horses."

"He won't find us." His voice lowered further. "I've

let it be known that we all long to return to Belfleur
Keep in the east. He will believe that we have run, and
he'll organize men to chase us east. But Marcus has
found us a place to hide only three leagues away. There
is freshwater, fish, and good hunting for him. We'll
hide out until the soldiers stop seeking us, and only
then will we begin to move."

This sounded risky, but if Marcus believed the hiding place to be sound, I trusted his judgment.

"Where will we go after that?" I asked.

"Back to Kéonsk. I'm going to speak to Master Deandre about finding us work in the city, even if we end up
mucking out stalls for the Väränji soldiers." His voice
broke. "But we have to get away from here, my girl. This
is no place for us. Those mines are no place for us."

"I know, Father."

I reached out and stroked his arm, truly proud of
him for the first time since Mother died.

Autumn came, and I prepared for our dangerous
departure. I said nothing to Mariah. I knew she would
fight me. She was going on fourteen, and for her, this
place meant food and stability.

Finally, the day arrived when our men were paid,
and I knew Father and Marcus were going to unveil
their plan to the other men. I wasn't entirely certain
why Father had waited so long, but I think he feared
that the younger men—Mikolai, Payton, and Orlando—
would feel the same as Mariah and would not want to
go back on the road. Perhaps he felt that if he sprang it
on them when they all had money, they would be more
likely to take a chance.

After the hour when their work had ended that day, I waited for them all to come home . . . and I waited. No one came.

Katlyn, Mariah, Marcus, and I grew worried.

Then one of the miners' wives came to tell us that on payday, once a year, the men were excused at noon, so they could make the walk—several hours—to a large village somewhere between Ryazan and Enêmûsk, where they would use their money to have a mug of ale and buy supplies they could not get here. They would stay the night and come back in the morning, and then they would see Captain Garrett and sign new contracts.

I didn't believe my father would do this, and that if he had gone with our men, it was only to explain his plan.

But the next day, just past noon, he walked slowly up to our wagon, and I could see the defeat in his face. Marcus ran up to him, and I had never seen Marcus desperate before. He hated this place, and he'd believed we were leaving.

"What's happened?" he asked.

"They wouldn't agree," my father answered hoarsely, "not even your father. They said stealing horses from the soldiers was madness, and we would be caught and hanged. They spent their money, and they all signed a new contract."

Marcus stumbled backward. "And you?"

"I . . . signed as well. I cannot leave the family."

Marcus's features twisted in bitter disappointment. Turning, he ran into the forest. But by now, I knew he'd be back. He wouldn't leave the family either.

And so we began our second year in Ryazan.

Somewhere along the way, I began to stop caring about many things. Like a number of the older miners, Uncle Landrien began having problems with his joints, until he could barely close his hands without pain. I knew I should have pitied him, but I was beginning to have trouble just making it through the days with my washing and mending and cooking, each day blending into the next.

I never thought I would miss traveling, miss the road, but I did. In my entire life, I had never been in one place for so long. Our men stopped laughing. They stopped singing and playing their violins.

Captain Garrett was replaced by another man named Captain Asher, along with a new crop of soldiers who served under him. Asher didn't have much to do with us so long as the silver in the mines kept flowing—and it did.

In that second year, a small part of me began to worry more about Mariah. She rarely spoke, and she seemed to spend much of her time off by herself. She resented helping me with the washing or the cooking, and it was easier for me to do it myself than to try to force her. She was growing up wild, but I couldn't seem to bring myself to care.

I watched my father fading before my eyes.

The following autumn, most of our men signed their third contract, but Uncle Landrien could not. His joints had grown so painful from the cold and the damp and the relentless work in the mines that he could barely walk.

Orlando and Payton both married girls from the miners' camp, thus grounding themselves forever.

Marcus continued to hunt for us, but he seemed to speak less and less.

The following winter, Mariah turned sixteen. She was hauntingly beautiful.

Not long after, my father caught a fever, and he died.

All of these things began to feel as if they were happening in someone else's life, that I was just an observer. One day blended into the next.

Then, in the spring of our third year in Ryazan, Captain Asher died, and his replacement was not long in arriving. His name was Captain Keegan, and I felt a wave of fear the first time he visited the miners' encampment. He looked at my family and me as if we were filth. I could see the disgust in his eyes, but his eyes stopped for much too long on Mariah, moving up and down her slight body and exquisite face.

He didn't say a word. He just turned and walked away.

He had a handsome lieutenant named Sullian serving with him, along with a corporal named Quinn, who both struck me as fair men, and I hoped perhaps we would end up dealing with them more than with their captain.

But a week later, Keegan came back . . . to see me.

"I've done some checking," he said, "and you and your sister have no man working in the mines. The rules are clear, and they were written for good reason. Women who have no men working in the mines need to clear out and make space."

"We're not taking up any space," I argued. "This wagon belongs to us. And we do have men working in the mines, my cousin Mikolai and my second cousin Micah."

"Those men aren't part of your household, and your father's dead. You'll need to clear out. Take your wagon if you can buy a horse somewhere."

He walked away. I couldn't believe it. He was ordering Mariah and me to leave.

When I told Mikolai and Marcus, of course they came to our defense, and Mikolai went to speak with the captain, to tell him that Mariah and I were part of his family. He came back grim faced and said that the captain had told him that since he was not a husband or father to us, he didn't count, and we would have to leave.

We had no horses, and we could not take our wagon. With the possible exception of Marcus, I didn't think any of our men would go with us—and even he might not leave his father. What would become of us?

I spent the next two days in fear, thinking that soldiers might come at any moment to drive Mariah and me out of camp, but they didn't.

Instead, Mariah came in late, opening the door to the wagon and slipping inside long after dark.

"We don't have to leave," she said.

"What?" I asked in confusion. "I don't think that captain will change his mind."

"I'm not going *anywhere*!" she spat at me, and then I could see that she was upset, her small hands trembling. "I've made a bargain with the captain. You and I can stay, and in exchange, Marcus will give him wild game for his table, and I will give him . . ." She trailed off.

I went cold. "You'll give him what?"

She turned away, and reality hit me. This was what he'd been after all along. This was why he'd threatened to banish us: to place her under his power.

I should have been outraged. I should have taken a knife and gone after him. But I didn't.

"We can stay?" I asked.

"Yes."

I wasn't even relieved. I didn't feel anything.

That day blended into the next.

CHAPTER TEN

Somehow, Amelie drew her hand away. She couldn't watch any more of the events that led up to the state of Mercedes and Mariah's current life. While doing readings, her targets were not normally actively involved, but this one had been different. She'd felt Mercedes with her, almost speaking to her, all along.

"I'm sorry," she whispered. "I couldn't watch anymore."

Mercedes just sat there with bleak eyes, and Amelie realized what it must have cost her to relive all that.

"So . . . ," Amelie said, "not long after that, the first attack happened? The soldiers started turning into wolves?"

Mercedes nodded slightly. "Mikolai was killed the first time it happened, and Captain Keegan threatened to make his father complete his contract . . . if we wanted the wages. Uncle Landrien's joints are too painful to work in those mines, so Marcus signed on to take over for Mikolai, which is exactly what Keegan expected to happen." She sighed. "But then the attacks continued . . . and this last one that occurred inside the mines proved too much. Even desperate men will refuse to work if they fear something more than starvation."

"You left those mushrooms for Keegan, didn't you?"

"Of course I did."

"Why now? If Keegan has been at Mariah for months, what made you decide to try to kill him now?"

"Your sister," Mercedes answered quietly. "She woke something inside of me. Right after she left me last night, I went out and picked the mushrooms and ran them to the cook. He was just finishing the stew, and he knows the captain likes mushrooms fried in butter. But I made sure that neither you nor Céline would be sitting at the captain's table last night. I'd never do anything to hurt one of my own people."

"What about Quinn? Or Jaromir? Did you ask about them?"

"I don't care what happens to them. I just want Keegan dead."

Though Amelie didn't blame her for hating Keegan, she could not condone Mercedes's callous disregard for Jaromir or Quinn.

"Listen to me," she said. "I'll do something about Keegan. I'll make sure he leaves Mariah alone and that you're both allowed to remain with your family. But you need to promise me you won't try anything else. You have to trust me."

"You won't give me away? You won't tell your lieutenant?"

"No. I won't tell anyone but Céline. She and I don't keep secrets. Do you swear to stop, to let me handle this?"

Mercedes nodded again.

Amelie stood up. "I need to get back."

Though she had established who'd poisoned Keegan, she was no closer to resolving the true reason she and Céline had come here—to find out why these soldiers were turning into mad wolves one by one. But she didn't believe Mercedes had anything to do with it or knew anything about how it was being done.

Still, there was much to consider.

After heading out the door, Amelie walked through the miners' camp back toward the path leading into the trees, and a single word from Mercedes's story rose in her mind. Several times Mercedes had referred to Marcus as a "shifter." He'd always before been mentioned as a hunter, but this designation as a shifter seemed to give him importance. The word was vaguely familiar, and Amelie thought she'd heard it somewhere before.

Could it be a Móndyalítko reference to one born with a special ability for hunting? Or did it mean something more?

Stopping, she turned and looked at Mercedes's wagon, wondering if she should go back and ask. But . . . she'd already put Mercedes through too much today and thought it best to just find out on her own.

Jaromir remained sitting at Keegan's bedside, by himself, well into midafternoon. He'd told Quinn to leave, instructing him to get some rest. The captain groaned and rolled a few times in his sleep, but Jaromir took that to be a good sign, suggesting that Keegan had not fallen into deep unconsciousness.

Footsteps sounded from the front section of the wagon, and he looked over in annoyance, prepared to order Quinn to bed if necessary, but the visitor was not Quinn. Instead, Céline came into view from around a hanging tapestry.

Her hair was damp and hanging loose down her back. She wore her red cloak, but he could see a shade of dark pink beneath the opening in the front.

Smiling tiredly, she lifted the hem of her cloak a few inches to let him see the skirt of her evening gown.

"I feel ridiculous walking around camp in pink silk, but my tan wool is spattered with everything the captain ate yesterday, and it smells terrible. I took it off and washed my hair, and I had nothing else to put on."

He couldn't help smiling back.

She looked around. "Is Amelie not with you? I thought to find her here."

"She's not in your tent?"

"No, I woke up alone . . . and I can't believe I slept out so much of the day. But I'm sure she's not far. Perhaps she's gone to the provisions tent. I'll take a look at the captain and then check there."

However, she didn't move. Instead her mouth opened once and closed again.

"What is it?" he asked.

"There's something I've been wanting to tell you, and we've had no time. It could be nothing."

Growing annoyed again, he half turned in his chair. "Tell me."

"Yesterday afternoon, when I was coming back from having tended to the miners, I ran into Corporal Quinn, and we had a rather . . . frank conversation about Captain Keegan."

Jaromir sat straight, at full attention now.

"Apparently, Prince Lieven had trouble getting any of his officers to take up a position as commander here. The last captain died, and the prince could find no one willing to replace him. Quinn told me that Keegan ran into difficulties over a gambling debt and was coerced into volunteering as a result." She walked closer, looking down at the sleeping captain. "Quinn's exact words were, 'He views this assignment as an insult and a punishment, and he feels he's paid his dues.'"

"What are you suggesting?" Jaromir asked, but he already knew . . . He'd already had his own doubts about Keegan.

"Quinn says that he's requested a replacement several times, but no action has been taken."

Jaromir put his hand to his chin, thinking. Keegan had also staunchly refused to allow either Céline or Amelie to read any of his soldiers, and as he appeared to care little for his men, perhaps this reticence was due to the fact that he was hiding something.

"Do you want to read him?" Jaromir asked.

"I'd like Amelie to read him first. Whatever he's protecting, I think we'll think find it in his past."

A groan sounded from the bed. Keegan rolled and opened his eyes. He looked up at Jaromir blankly for a few seconds, and then moved his gaze up to Céline.

"Water," he croaked through dried lips.

"Of course," Céline said, hurrying toward a basin and filling a mug.

"Give that to me," Jaromir said, standing up. "I'll take care of him. You go and find Amelie."

Céline checked the provisions tent first, and upon not finding her sister, she headed back to their own tent, thinking perhaps Amelie had already returned there. As Céline walked up, she saw her dark-haired sister coming toward her from the direction of the miners' camp—wearing a pensive expression.

"Are you all right?" Céline asked.

"Let's go inside."

"Jaromir sent me to get you. He has a task for you."

"Soon enough. I need to tell you something."

Concerned and curious, Céline passed through the flap into their tent, and Amelie followed.

"Mercedes poisoned Keegan," Amelie said as soon as they were inside and alone.

"What?" Céline gasped.

"It's true. Listen. She let me read her."

And with that, Amelie began to spill out a story of hardship that became increasingly difficult to hear, the story of what brought Mercedes and her family not only to live here, but to end up trapped here. Putting off Jaromir for now, Céline didn't interrupt or rush her sister. She listened to everything Amelie had to say.

"And after Keegan threatened to banish Mercedes and Mariah," Amelie finished, "Mariah sold herself to him. That's why they've been allowed to stay."

"He's a monster." Céline furrowed her brow. "And so Mercedes just tried to poison Keegan now?"

"She says you woke her up."

Thinking back to her last conversation with Mercedes, Céline felt an unexpected wave of guilt. Had she induced Mercedes to try to murder Captain Keegan?

"You can't tell anyone," Amelie said. "I made a promise that I wouldn't tell anyone but you, not even Jaromir—especially not Jaromir—and that I'd think of something to help Mariah. Mercedes says she won't try it again, and in the end, not too much harm was done. Will you help protect her?"

"You know I will."

"There's something else," Amelie continued, her eyes growing more thoughtful. "Mercedes referred to Marcus several times as a 'shifter.' I know I've heard that word before, but I can't remember where."

"It was Helga." Céline remembered the speech. "Inside our guest room at Castle Sèone when she was telling us about our heritage. She said that Móndyalítko don't have wealth or power in the same sense as the princes and lords. She said, 'But they have their own bloodlines of power, the shape-shifters, the Mist-Torn, and the like.'"

Amelie's body tensed. "I remember that now. Shapeshifters? Do you think Marcus has some natural-born power like ours but that lets him change his shape?"

Céline sank into a chair. "Oh, Amelie . . . I forgot to tell you something. I swear I wasn't keeping it a secret. With all that's happened since, I . . . forgot."

"What?"

"Our first night here, Marcus was standing outside the tent. I was so tired, it almost didn't seem real, more like a dream, but he let me read him, just for a moment, and I felt the strangest sensation. Instead of observing, I seemed to be inside another body, and I was running swiftly through the forest . . . on all fours."

"On all fours?"

"Keep your voice down. Someone outside could hear."

"Céline, if Marcus can change himself into something that runs on all fours, he just made it to the top of our list of people to investigate. He hates these soldiers, and he certainly has a motive to get rid of them."

"So what are you saying?" Céline asked. "That he's somehow infecting them with his own natural ability—if he even has one? We're only guessing here. Do you think you or I could pass our gift to someone else and then twist it so the person goes mad?"

Amelie frowned. "I just think we need to pursue this."

"Agreed. And we will. But right now, Captain Keegan has moved to the top of Jaromir's list."

"Keegan?"

"Yes. Come with me. I'll tell you on the way."

As Amelie walked into Keegan's tent, the afternoon sun was already sinking, and she was disturbed by how much part of her wanted this corrupt captain to turn out to be guilty of the crimes here. She was hoping to do a reading and expose him as a false leader who was somehow destroying his own men in order to get himself relieved of an unwanted command.

While she didn't view herself as a vindictive person, she wanted to see him punished. Thankfully, the better part of her fought against such instincts. She needed to keep her mind clear to be able to focus on the reading, on seeing the critical scenes of his past.

As she and Céline approached the bed, she looked down, and a different part of her wavered briefly. Corrupt or not, the man looked so . . . ill.

Worse, Jaromir stood there with his arms crossed, and she still couldn't manage to meet his eyes. During the crisis last night, he and she had worked well together, but they hadn't looked at each other, not after what she'd said to him in the tent. How could she have said such a thing? Why did such terrible things come out of her mouth every time he made her feel backed against a wall?

Captain Keegan's bloodshot eyes were focused on Céline. "I'm told I have you to thank for my life," he said hoarsely.

"I'd have done the same for anyone," she answered. "But you'll be in bed for weeks, possibly longer. Mushroom poisoning takes a toll."

He didn't argue. Perhaps he felt as bad as he looked.

"I've assumed temporary command," Jaromir said, "in the absence of another officer."

Keegan's eyes rolled toward him. "Have you sent a messenger with a request for a replacement for me? Surely you can't remain until I'm fit again. Your own prince must need you."

"I will remain as long as I'm needed here and until I complete the mission for which I was sent," Jaromir answered coldly. "In that regard, I've authorized this lady to do a reading of you." He motioned toward Amelie.

Keegan's eyes widened. "No. I refuse." He tried sitting up and failed.

"You have no choice," Jaromir went on, "and unless you allow her to touch you, I'll hold you down."

The captain's greenish skin went pale. "Where's Quinn?"

Jaromir ignored the question and closed the short distance between himself and the bed. Without any hesitation, he leaned over and pinned Keegan's arms. "Amelie?"

"You can't do this!" Keegan cried weakly. "I order you to stop."

Amelie hated doing readings like this. Jaromir had once ordered Corporal Pavel to hold down a traitorous court physician at Castle Sèone and then told her to read the man in order to gain evidence to prove his guilt. It had been . . . uncomfortable.

But she wasn't about to turn back now. Kneeling by the bed, she tried to shut out Keegan's weak protests. Touching the back of his hand, she closed her eyes and reached out for the spark of his spirit. On the walk over here, Céline had related that Jaromir wanted to know Keegan's secrets, his reasons for having volunteered to take this command—something more specific than gossip about a gambling debt.

A simple gambling debt wouldn't be enough to coerce a man like Keegan into overseeing what he would consider a pack of shabby miners. It had to be more.

And if so, how far would he go to be relieved of this unwanted position?

With her eyes closed, she cleared her mind and continued focusing on Keegan's spirit, reaching back in time to whatever had brought him here to Ryazan. The first jolt hit, and she braced herself. The second jolt hit, and the tent around her vanished. She was swept backward through the white-and-gray mists. This time, she kept herself carefully separated from Keegan. She needed to view only as an observer, to see what was happening to him and around him—not to mention she was sickened by the thought of being inside his head and seeing through his eyes.

The mists kept rushing as she was drawn backward, and when they cleared, she found herself standing in what felt like an underground chamber lit by a few lanterns. There were no windows and the walls were made from stone. A man in a long tunic with a heavy blue gem hanging around his neck stood behind a long table. He was counting money into a bag.

Captain Keegan, Corporal Quinn, and a handsome man with thick hair stood on the other side of the table. Amelie studied the third man for a moment. His expression struck her as . . . fragile, as if he could be easily hurt. He looked out of place in his dark brown tabard and armor.

"All right," said the man in the long tunic as he finished counting. "That's it." He held out the bag and pushed a piece of paper across the table. "Captain Keegan and Lieutenant Sullian, please sign at the bottom to verify that you've accepted this season's pay for your men."

"We've done this before," Keegan answered in an unfriendly tone, as if he didn't care for the man, who was probably Prince Lieven's treasurer.

Amelie realized the third soldier was Lieutenant Sullian, who had transformed into a wolf and been killed before her arrival in Ryazan.

Both Keegan and Sullian signed. Keegan hefted the bag of coins, and all three men walked toward the door. Amelie stepped aside even though she knew they couldn't see her. She wasn't actually there. She was simply witnessing an echo in time.

But why was she watching Keegan receive the payroll for his men?

The room vanished, and she found herself standing outside in the open air, in the courtyard of a castle. Soldiers in armor and brown tabards milled around, and she spotted four of them crouched down and playing a game of dice.

New voices drew her attention, and she turned to see Keegan, Sullian, and Quinn all walking into the open courtyard. Keegan was still carrying the bag of money with his men's wages inside.

He stopped at the sight of the dice game, and Lieutenant Sullian's face took on an anxious expression.

"Sir," Sullian said, "we need to see the horse trader from Miltaná about those new geldings."

But Keegan ignored him and continued watching the game. Amelie observed Quinn and Sullian glance at each other in alarm.

A moment later, Keegan took a number of coins from the bag he carried. "This is my own wage." Handing the bag off to Sullian, he walked over to the game. "Room for one more?"

"Of course, sir."

The soldiers made room, and Amelie moved closer. She never played dice—as the games all seemed to depend on luck as opposed to skill—but she knew the one being played. It was simple, called Thrice Thrown. One of the soldiers functioned as the counter, and he didn't take part in the game. The players all agreed on the amount of the bet first, and everyone gave him their money. Then each of the players took three rolls and whoever ended up with the highest count of their three rolls won all the money.

Amelie found it foolish, but she knew many soldiers who enjoyed the random simplicity. It took no thought and passed the time. Sometimes instead of money, they bet extra chores or night watch duty.

"Shall we say two silver pennies?" Keegan suggested.

The other players hesitated. That was a large bet for normal guardsmen, but one of them shrugged. "Why not? Tomorrow is payday."

"Sir?" Quinn asked.

Keegan gave him a hard look. "Yes?"

"Nothing."

All the players took their turns, and Keegan lost. He did have the second-highest total for his rolls, but it was a winner-take-all game. A few other soldiers noticed Keegan playing, and they wandered over. On the next round a few more joined in.

Keegan won the next two rounds, and his eyes glinted.

Then he began losing.

Two of the initial guardsmen dropped out when the newcomers began playing for higher stakes.

Lieutenant Sullian's appearance of anxiety was increasing. Walking over, he touched his captain's arm. "Sir, the horse trader? He's waiting."

"In a moment," Keegan answered. "I just need to win my money back."

Amelie had seen men like Keegan before. Once they started, they couldn't seem to stop. They always believed they would win the next round of dice or the next hand of cards.

The courtyard vanished, and she found herself in the mists again, moving forward, just a little. The mists cleared, and this time, she was standing inside a stable. Keegan was leaning forward with his hands on knees, as if he was about to be ill.

"What can I do?" he said. "Master Terlone is coming tomorrow. He said if I don't settle my account, he'll go to Prince Lieven."

Both Sullian and Quinn looked on in concern.

Sullian was still carrying the bag with the soldiers' payroll. "Could you not give some of your purchases back to him? The pewter goblets?"

"He won't take them!" Keegan snapped. "And I cannot give a season's worth of wine back. It's already been drunk." He stood and ran his hands over his face. "The prince cannot find out how much I owe. I'll be ruined."

"You know I'd give you my wage," Quinn said. "But I send almost everything I earn home to my parents."

"And I owe for my own wine bill and that new saddle I purchased," Sullian said. "Sir . . . if you'd only come away when I asked you. You wouldn't have lost everything."

Amelie began to understand why she was here now. It seemed Keegan had lost an entire season's worth of wages in that dice game, and he owed a merchant for wine and other luxury items he'd bought on credit.

"Don't mother me!" Keegan half shouted. "I have to do something. The prince cannot hear of this." His voice was desperate.

"Wait . . . ," Sullian began. He hesitated and then said, "Quinn, what about that game of Hard Tens you promised to deal tonight? Could you get the captain in? He's better with cards, and he could win his wages back."

Keegan stood straight, his eyes filling with hope. "Hard Tens?"

Sullian nodded. "With Prince Damek here on a visit, a few of his officers asked Lieutenant Tanner to put a game together, and Tanner asked Quinn to deal."

"Can you get me in?" Keegan asked Quinn.

"No," Quinn answered. "We'd have to stake you, and what if you lose?"

"I won't lose!" Keegan's features twisted into what looked like an expression of pain. "Please . . . please. I promise that if you help me this time, it won't ever happen again."

Quinn glanced away, as if he couldn't bring himself to even look at his captain. "All right. I'll speak to Lieutenant Tanner."

The scene in the stable vanished, and Amelie saw

only a blink of the mists before they cleared and she found herself in another small, windowless room. This one contained a round table, with six men sitting around it. There were goblets and pitchers of wine on the table. Candle lanterns burned from small square tables in the corners.

Right away, Amelie noted Captain Keegan and Corporal Quinn. In addition, there were three officers wearing the black tabards of Damek's guards and a middle-aged man in a brown tabard. She assumed he must be Lieutenant Tanner. Sullian wasn't there.

Quickly, Amelie realized she'd not come in time to observe the beginning of the game. From the state of the table and the men, she guessed they'd been playing cards for a while. One of Damek's officers and Lieutenant Tanner had the largest piles of coins sitting in front of them. There were almost none in front of Keegan.

Quinn was dealing.

Again, although Amelie had rarely played Hard Tens, she knew the rules. It was another simple game, though this one involved some strategy. Before play, all the kings, queens, and jacks were removed from the deck, leaving only forty cards.

The dealer dealt every player two cards, one faceup and once facedown. The players could glance at their facedown card and then make bets. After that, a player could stand with what he had or ask for another card . . . and more if he wished.

The goal was to come as close to a total of twenty in any combination, with two tens as the best possible hand. Any player with two tens won, and in the rare—but possible—event that two players were dealt two tens, they split the pot of winnings.

The dealer's job was simply to deal. He didn't take part in the game otherwise.

Amelie could tell from the strained expression on Quinn's face and the look of desperation on Keegan's—along with his small pile of coins—that Keegan had not been lucky tonight.

A new hand was dealt.

Amelie walked up behind Keegan. He had a two of clubs showing. She leaned down as he peeked at his hole card: a ten of diamonds.

Men began placing bets, and by the time they were finished, Keegan had put in almost every coin he had left.

One of Damek's officers raised an eyebrow. "Looks like a do-or-die hand for you, Captain," he said dryly.

Keegan didn't answer and nodded to Quinn that he wanted another card.

Quinn dealt him the ten of hearts. Keegan closed his eyes. He'd gone over.

As the hand finished and the men turned over their hole cards, Lieutenant Tanner won with a combination of nineteen. Gathering his winnings, he shrugged. "Hard luck, Keegan, but it looks like you're out."

Keegan's forehead was perspiring. "No . . . wait. Just give me a moment, and I'll be right back."

Quinn looked up in alarm as Keegan fled the room, and a few of the visiting soldiers shifted uncomfortably.

"I do so pity a fellow who doesn't know when to stop," one of them said.

But not long after, Keegan came hurrying back . . . carrying the bag with his men's payroll. He was going to bet with his men's wages? In spite of her low opinion of Keegan, Amelie had not thought even him capable of that.

Quinn was staring at him as he sat down.

But Keegan glared across the table. "Deal the cards, *Corporal*."

The small, dim room vanished, and Amelie was rushing forward on the mists again.

When they cleared, she was in a great hall with walls of stone and a hearth large enough to stand in.

Captain Keegan was down on one knee, on the floor with head bowed.

Amelie looked to see a muscular man with graying hair and a proud bearing sitting in a chair on a dais up above the captain. He wore a loose red jerkin accented by gold thread. Three jeweled rings on each hand adorned his fingers.

His expression was unreadable.

"I don't know what to say, my prince," Keegan said. "The act is unforgivable."

Amelie's eyes flew back up to the dais. She was looking at Anton's father, Prince Lieven. He looked nothing like Anton, who was slender, with soft dark hair and narrow features.

"It is unforgivable," Prince Lieven said, and his voice echoed through the hall. "In all my years, I've never heard of a captain gambling away his men's wages. You've broken a sacred trust. How will any of them send money to their families? Once this news is out, you will lose your office, and no man will ever serve under you again."

Keegan's body flinched, as if he'd been struck, but he didn't raise his eyes from the floor.

Prince Lieven was silent for a long time. Finally, he said, "Though the act is unforgivable, it is not beyond repair. Would you be willing to do a small service for me? If so, I would replace your men's wages, and no one need know."

Keegan's head snapped up. "A service?" he breathed.

"Yes, I require an officer to go north and oversee the silver-mining operation in Ryazan. If you would be good enough to take on the command, I will see that your men are paid."

Keegan's jaw twitched, and he went pale.

Amelie realized he must have known something of Ryazan, of the desolate place he was being sent.

"Of course, if you would rather not . . . ," the prince said casually, as if it didn't matter one way or the other.

"I'll go, my prince," Keegan said quickly. "With gratitude."

He had no choice, and even he was wise enough to see that.

The prince nodded. "Good. The flow of silver is important to the welfare of our province here. You and Lieutenant Sullian may take a few days to prepare, and you will leave at the end of the week."

Keegan's eyes were hollow, almost as if he'd been given a death sentence, but it was still better than public humiliation and being stripped of rank.

"Yes, my prince," he managed to say.

The great hall vanished, and Amelie was swept forward on the mists again, with a mix of thoughts churning in her mind. She expected to leave the visions behind now and find herself back inside Keegan's tent, sitting next to Jaromir.

But instead, when the mist cleared, she was standing out in the open of the soldiers' encampment in Ryazan, still an observer. What could she need to see here? Dusk was nearing, and looking around, she could see Captain Keegan's large, new tent had been set up, but other elements of the camp were different, and several of the smaller tents were missing, as if Keegan's men were still getting situated and settled.

Keegan and Sullian both came striding through the camp toward her as evening campfires were being lit. She could hear them talking.

"It's not so bad, Captain," Sullian was saying. "We've only been here three weeks, and I've already managed to sign on new miners. Production is up, and the prince will be pleased."

Keegan grunted. "There's no need to try to put a good face on this. We've been banished, and it's my fault. But we won't be here long. I'll find a way to get us back to Castle Pählen."

Sullian paused and lowered his voice. "Sir . . . some of the men seem to know *why* we were assigned here. I don't know how they learned of it. Neither Quinn nor I would breathe a word, but I fear it may undermine your authority."

"You let me worry about that. I can handle the men."

He seemed about to say more when Amelie heard a choking sound. Both Keegan and Sullian turned their heads at the same time she did. A young soldier who'd been building a campfire suddenly began retching with force, struggling to draw in air at the same time.

"Guardsman!" Sullian called, hurrying over to help.

But the soldier collapsed, his mouth contorting in pain. His chest began to expand, and his hands began to change. Fur sprouted from his skin as his clothing began to split, and his fingers were turning into claws.

His face was elongating.

"Sullian!" Keegan shouted, grabbing his friend and pulling him away.

As he did so, Amelie looked at Keegan's face. Somehow, she knew she'd come to this place in time to watch him and not the soldier who was transforming.

Savage snarls exploded from her right, but she kept her eyes on Keegan.

"What is that?" someone cried.

Staring, Keegan was stunned, absolutely shocked by the scene before him. He had no idea what was happening.

"Get the spears!" Sullian ordered.

"Sir!" another soldier shouted. "It's running toward the miners' camp!"

"After it!"

The scene vanished, and Amelie was in the mists, rushing forward. When they cleared, she was back in the captain's tent, looking down at his green-tinged face. Jaromir sat on one side of her, still holding Keegan down, and Céline stood on her other side toward the end of the bed.

The first emotion to hit her was anger as she realized what her last vision had meant.

"Amelie," Jaromir said, as he let go of Keegan. "What did you see?"

Jaromir had never seen Amelie come out of a reading so angry.

"It's not him!" she spat. "Whoever is doing this to the soldiers, it isn't *him*."

Keegan was staring up at her with wide, bloodshot eyes, as if he feared what she was about to say.

"He gambled away his men's payroll," she rushed on, "and that's how he ended up here."

"Gambled away . . . ?" Jaromir had never heard of such a thing.

"But the final memory I saw was of the first soldier who turned . . . at least I think it was the first soldier." She jammed a finger in the air toward Keegan. "He was stunned, confused. He didn't have any idea what was happening." Her chin dropped. "It's not him."

"Of course it's not me," Keegan croaked. "You thought it was?"

Jaromir fought to absorb everything Amelie was saying, but her agitation and clear disappointment bothered him the most. Did she want Keegan to be guilty?

Céline stepped closer, putting her hand on Amelie's shoulder.

"Let's go someplace and talk alone," Céline said quietly.

Amelie didn't rise. She leaned forward, putting her face directly into Keegan's. "I know who poisoned you," she bit off.

"What?" Jaromir cut in, unable to escape the feeling that he was rapidly being left behind in this exchange.

Amelie ignored him and continued speaking directly to Keegan. "It's someone who cares for Mariah, but it could be anyone. It could be one of the Móndyalítko. It could be one of your soldiers or a miner who's fallen in love with her. It could be *anyone*. I've stopped them for now, by promising I'd speak to you and tell you to leave Mariah alone. Keep your distance, and you'll be fine. But if you ever, ever touch her again or you threaten to banish her and her sister, you won't live through the night. Do you understand?"

Keegan's eyes were locked on her face, and his breaths were shallow.

Without waiting for an answer, Amelie stood up and walked out of the tent. Céline and Jaromir looked at each other for a second or two, and then Céline turned to run after her sister.

"No," Jaromir ordered, rising to his feet. "You stay here with him. I'll go."

Céline's brow wrinkled uncertainly. "Lieutenant?"

He raised one palm in the air. "I'll be patient, but I need to talk to her. You stay here."

Turning, he strode out of the tent after Amelie. Upon emerging, he looked both ways, just in time to see her disappearing into the forest around the encampment. He followed and caught up quickly, finding her leaning over with one hand against a tree. He'd known she disliked Captain Keegan, but he'd had no idea how much. It would not do for her to *want* any specific person to be guilty. They were here to learn the truth.

"Amelie," he said softly.

She whirled at the sound of his voice and seemed genuinely surprised to see him standing there. Did she think he was just going to let this go?

"Who poisoned Keegan?" he asked.

It had occurred to him for an instant that she'd been bluffing back in the tent, telling Keegan a lie to keep him away from Mariah. But then Jaromir realized Amelie wasn't capable of that level of deception—Céline, yes, but not Amelie.

She watched him approach.

"Who?" he repeated.

"I can't tell you."

Despite his promise to Céline, he felt his temper rising. "Amelie! I'm in charge of both protecting you and solving this situation for Prince Anton. If there's a poisoner in the camp, I need to know who it is."

"It's not my secret to tell. And it has nothing to do with these soldiers turning into wolves. I can swear on that. It's over, and it won't happen again."

His eyes searched her face. In all his life, though he'd seen women more beautiful than Amelie, he'd never known anyone so pretty. Her sweet, pale face, silky black hair, and lavender eyes pulled at him every time he looked at her. She might be prickly on the outside, but he knew this was a shell she'd created for her own protection.

In addition, she made him think of home, of Castle Sèone. He missed it, and she was the only thing here that felt familiar.

Leaning in close enough that he could see flecks of yellow in her irises, he said, "Tell me who it is. I'm asking you." Given his gentle manner and that he'd asked instead of ordered, he fully expected her to give him a name.

She shook her head.

For a second, he couldn't speak, and his anger rose again. "This isn't a game! You tell me who it is right now, or I'll—"

"You'll what?" she demanded. "What do you think you're going to do, Jaromir?"

Her eyes flashed and she was breathing hard, and without thinking, he grabbed the back of her head and pressed his mouth over hers. He expected her to shove him away, but to his endless wonder, one of her hands gripped his sleeve, and then she was kissing him.

Amelie almost couldn't believe what Jaromir's mouth felt like as it moved against hers. She'd never kissed a man before, and whatever she'd expected, this wasn't it. She could feel power flowing from him, from the strength in his jaw and the strength in his arms, but he wasn't hurting her. The kiss felt . . . good. She gripped his sleeve, lost in the moment, and moved her mouth against his, drinking him in.

Pressing her against the tree, he slipped his tongue between her teeth, and she almost gasped. He pulled away slightly.

"Amelie," he whispered.

Then he was kissing her again, and she didn't want him to stop. She'd never felt anything like this. She put her other hand against his chest, and he moved one hand to her waist as he kissed her more deeply.

And then . . . without warning, a flash appeared in her mind of his last mistress, a lovely, haughty, wealthy young woman named Bridgette. Amelie had learned through the other soldiers that Bridgette was never allowed to visit Jaromir's apartments until she was sent for—which was always the arrangement with Jaromir's mistresses. For about six months, Bridgette had slept in his bed whenever he sent for her, and when he got tired of her, he'd cast her aside like baggage and never once looked back.

For the span of another breath, Amelie clung to the sleeve of his shirt and kissed him with force. But she knew she couldn't do this. She couldn't become another one of his obedient mistresses until he got bored.

Putting the flat of her hand on his chest, she pushed. It was the hardest thing she'd ever done.

"No," she said raggedly.

At first she couldn't move his body, and she pushed harder, slipping out of his grip and backing away. "No," she repeated.

His expression was lost, and he took a stumbling step after her. "Amelie?"

Turning, she ran.

*   *   *

Sitting by Keegan's beside, Céline couldn't help feeling relieved when the captain fell back to sleep. They'd not spoken after Amelie and Jaromir left, but she'd fed him water and sponged his face, and finally he'd closed his eyes, giving her time to think.

She was curious to learn more about what Amelie had seen in his memories, but she had greater worries at the moment. They were no closer to solving the situation here than they'd been on the day they'd arrived, and Jaromir and Amelie appeared to be losing their ability to work together.

Céline felt guilty for having allowed Jaromir to be the one to go after Amelie . . . but those two did need to talk to each other. They needed to close the growing gap between them. Getting to the bottom of the horrors taking place in this camp was going require cooperation and collaboration among the three of them.

Sitting there by Keegan's bed, Céline hoped Jaromir would not be so proud, and Amelie would not let her temper get the best of her . . . and that a few moments alone might give them both a chance to reach out to the other.

Footsteps sounded from behind her, and she turned her head just in time to see Jaromir coming around a hanging tapestry. Right away, at the sight of his face, her hopes were dashed.

"What happened?" she asked.

She didn't think she'd ever seen him fighting so hard to keep control of himself, but he ignored her question and was clearly struggling to keep his voice steady.

"I've taken command of the camp," he said, "and now I'm giving the orders." His voice broke slightly. "Céline . . . we have to solve this. We need to end this and go home."

She wondered if he'd ever forgive her for having seen him in this moment of weakness.

"What do you want to do?" she asked quietly.

"Exactly what we did back in Sèone. I'll organize the soldiers, and you start reading. Get me the name of the next victim, and I'll take it from there."

She closed her eyes briefly, thankful that she and Amelie were about to be given a free hand.

"You wish me to look for the next victim?" she asked. "Might it not be better to have Amelie start reading pasts and see if she can't find out who's doing this?"

"How many people can you or she read at a stretch before you tire?"

"Six, maybe seven. Then we need to rest."

"Anyone here could be guilty. There are roughly forty soldiers and over two hundred people in the mining camp. Since only the soldiers are transforming, you can peg the next victim more quickly by reading only them. Once you give me a name, I have a few ideas." He was beginning to sound more like himself now. "Besides, the men are on edge, and you're much better at easing that, and you have just as much chance of hitting on something important while reading a future as Amelie does a past."

Céline hoped Jaromir was not trying to avoid working with Amelie. She glanced down at Keegan's sleeping form. "The captain may have been right about one thing. If I name a soldier, I'll be putting him in danger from the others. We'll have to keep it very quiet."

Shaking his head, Jaromir said. "No, as soon as you read the next victim, I want you to speak up—loud enough that everybody knows who it is."

She wavered, wondering what he had in mind. "But do you promise that you won't use anyone I name as bait . . . like you did the last time?"

"Trust me."

CHAPTER ELEVEN

Although Céline knew Jaromir would act quickly, she couldn't help feeling rushed when he almost immediately began gathering men inside one of the larger tents.

She wanted someone to sit with Keegan, so she hurried back to the tent she shared with Amelie. Thankfully, her sister was there, but less fortunately, she was sitting on the bed, her eyes bleak. Céline decided not to broach a discussion of whatever had happened with Jaromir. They didn't have time, and it might do Amelie good to focus on the larger tasks at hand.

"Jaromir has taken command, and he's given me permission to read the soldiers," she said. "I'll be starting right away."

Amelie stood up. "Oh . . . that's good. What about me?"

"We'll need you soon enough, but he wants me to begin by reading futures. I hate to ask this, but Keegan is alone right now, and I need someone to sit with him. He can barely feed himself water. Can you do it?"

Grimacing, Amelie nodded. "All right."

News that Céline had been turned loose to use her ability did seem to have a somewhat healing effect on Amelie, and she pointed toward the end of the bed.

"If you have time to change, those were delivered a little while ago."

Walking closer, Céline saw her lavender wool dress laid out at the end of the bed, along with Amelie's dark green one. Both appeared spotless.

"Oh, thank the gods," Céline breathed.

"Thank Mercedes. She's the one who washed them."

"Come help me out of this ridiculous silk gown and into something sensible."

Pulling off her cloak, Céline turned so Amelie could unlace her, and not long after, she felt more like herself. She liked the lavender wool. It was warm, and it fit her perfectly, snug at the waist with a skirt that hung straight and was not too full.

Leaving her cloak behind, she headed back out of the tent with Amelie following.

"I'll come to you with any news as soon as I'm done," Céline said when they parted.

Amelie walked toward Keegan's tent, and Céline headed for the large tent where Jaromir had gathered some of the soldiers. Dusk was upon them, and she knew they'd be needing lanterns soon.

Entering the tent, she was somewhat taken aback to see at least twenty soldiers inside. Jaromir was standing near the rear, and he must know she couldn't read all of them. Perhaps he just wanted an audience for what was about to take place. Guardsman Rurik was standing beside him. All heads turned to look at her, and the tent fell silent.

Her first instinct was to cover her nose with her hand. In their current unwashed state, and with so many of them in an enclosed space, they produced quite a stench. They were also frightened—both of one another and of being the next man to transform.

Forcing her hands to remain at her sides, she smiled. She had to help them relax, to trust her. That part came easily to her. It always had.

"Good evening, gentlemen," she said, still smiling. "I know this must seem an odd request, but I do assure you that the lieutenant and I are trying to help, to solve this and keep everyone safe. That is our only goal."

The tension inside the tent eased slightly, and she looked left to see that two sturdy chairs—from Keegan's tent—had been brought in. With her back straight and her head high, she walked over and sat down.

"Lieutenant?" she asked, deciding it was best to appear as if she was deferring to his authority, which she was.

Jaromir motioned to a lean, middle-aged man near the front, and then gestured toward the empty chair. "Guardsman," he said.

This was clearly an order and not a "request," as Céline had delicately put it, but she noticed how quickly the man moved, and that the men here did not seem to mind being organized or ordered by Jaromir.

"Yes, sir," the man said.

They're glad he's taken over, she thought. They wanted someone like him in charge.

However, as the man sat in front of Céline, he suddenly grew anxious again, wiping his dirty hands on his breeches. "Sorry, my lady. I didn't know that . . ."

"It's all right," she assured him. "I just need to touch your hand."

Reaching out, she gripped two of his fingers and closed her eyes. Then she counted her blessings that she didn't have to hide what she was really doing here or pretend to be providing entertainment—as she had sometimes done in the past for Jaromir.

"What are your duties tonight?" she asked with her eyes still closed.

"Tonight? I'll be on watch on the south-side perimeter until the mid of night, and then I'll be relieved."

Céline used her mind to feel for the spark of his spirit, to focus on him in his duties among the night watch and move forward from there. She connected with his spirit right away, but no jolt hit her.

"What about tomorrow?" she asked. "What will your daily duties be?"

"I don't know, my lady. The lieutenant said he was going to go over the roster and reassign some of us. Normally, I'd be helping take care of the horses."

Céline let her focus flow forward, trying to see the future of this soldier tomorrow and beyond, but again, nothing came to her.

Opening her eyes, she let go of his fingers and patted his hand. "I see nothing dangerous in your near future."

He exhaled, as if he'd been holding his breath. "Is that all you need from me, then?"

She nodded, and he stood up. She was about to choose the next soldier herself when Corporal Quinn strode through the open tent flap, looking semialarmed.

"What is this . . . ? I stopped to check on the captain, and Lady Amelie told me—"

"*Corporal!*" Jaromir barked. "May I speak to you outside?"

Quinn fell silent, but he didn't look happy. Céline assumed that although he was well aware that Jaromir had assumed command, Quinn had probably not realized this would entail Jaromir openly countermanding Keegan's previous orders.

As Jaromir stepped past her, he asked quietly, "Can you handle this?"

"Yes."

Both men stepped outside the tent, and some of the soldiers began whispering among themselves. Céline noted a round-faced young man only a few paces away from her. This one had less fear in his eyes, and he was watching her with more curiosity than anything else.

Smiling at him, she motioned to the now empty chair.

Without hesitation, he sat.

Reaching out, she grasped his fingers and closed her eyes. "What are your duties tonight?"

"I don't take watch again until the mid of night shift. Tomorrow is supposed to be my day off unless the lieutenant decides otherwise."

Again, she felt for the spark of the young man's spirit and found it right away. Letting her mind drift forward, she focused on his night watch duties and felt nothing. Then . . . as she moved farther forward, a jolt hit her, and she braced herself.

The soft sounds around her in the tent vanished, and she was jerked into the mists, rushing forward, fearing what she might see. Though she knew she had to do this, it didn't make observing death or suffering any easier.

The mists cleared, and she found herself standing in broad daylight. Looking around, she realized she was in the miners' encampment among the collection of shacks and huts.

"Lianne, we have to tell him. We can't go on like this. It's not right."

Turning, Céline saw the round-faced young man. He was holding hands with a girl . . . and pleading with her. "Let me speak to him, please."

"But, Jadon," she answered, "what if he says no?"

Moving closer, Céline studied the girl. Her homespun gown was shabby, and her features were somewhat plain, with eyes set too closely together and a mouth full of crooked teeth. But she had lovely hair, a rich shade of chestnut that she wore in a neat, thick braid down her back.

More important, she was looking at the young soldier, whom she'd called Jadon, with open affection, and Céline was well aware of the great shortage of affection in this camp.

"He won't refuse," Jadon said. "I'll explain everything to him."

"He won't believe you. He doesn't trust soldiers."

"He will. If he wants to help with arrangements, I'll

marry you tomorrow in front of twenty witnesses, and I'll swear to take you with me when we leave, that I'll always care for you. If he loves you, he'll want something better for you than this place."

"Oh, Jadon," she breathed, moving closer to him.

Leaning down, he kissed her softly on the mouth.

The kiss lasted only a moment or two before an angry shout sounded. "You! What are you doing? Get your hands off her!"

Looking across the encampment, Céline saw an enraged man carrying a pickaxe striding toward them. Jadon's hand moved to the hilt of his sword, but the girl gasped.

"No. You can't fight my father." Her voice filled with pain. "And he'll never listen to what you say now. Run!"

The mists rushed in and Céline found herself back in the large tent, looking at the young soldier—who stared back. All the men were poised and tensed.

"No danger," Céline said quickly, somehow resuming her smile.

But as the soldiers began talking amongst themselves again, she leaned forward. "Your name is Jadon? And you are in love with a chestnut-haired girl named Lianne, a miner's daughter?"

Jadon blinked several times. "How did you—?"

"The next time you visit her near her home, you will discuss how to tell her father of your plans to marry. Whatever you do, do not kiss Lianne. Don't even hold her hand. He will be coming soon, and if he sees you touching her, he won't listen to your case. Stand off

from her a pace or two, and he will be more amenable
to listen. Do you understand?"

He sputtered in what sounded like confusion for a
second or two and then nodded.

Glancing over at the open doorway, Céline saw Jaromir and Quinn both watching her. Jaromir wouldn't
want her wasting time helping two star-crossed lovers,
so she shook her head once at him and then turned
back to motion Jadon out of the chair.

Young Guardsman Graham was in the mix of gathered soldiers, and her gaze fell on him. He was standing halfway behind Guardsman Saunders. Poor boy.
His eyes—one brown and one blue—were still sad.
Such a fragile young man did not belong in the military, and she realized he must have depended a good
deal on Ramsey. The thought of what had become of
Ramsey in that barn unsettled her, and she decided to
get this over for Graham as quickly as possible, so she
motioned to him with her hand.

Most of the men appeared more relaxed now that
they'd seen how the process worked—and they'd seen
two men read and immediately excused.

Graham came out from behind Saunders and approached cautiously, sinking into the chair. "Do I just
sit here?"

"For the most part, yes," she answered, reaching
out. "I need to touch your hand."

His fingers were smaller and more slender than
those of the previous two soldiers, and his skin was
warmer. She closed her eyes. "What is your duty sched-
ule tonight?"

Before he even answered, the first jolt hit her, and she accidentally bit the inside of her mouth. The second jolt hit and she was caught in the mists, being swept forward.

The journey was brief.

When the mists cleared, she was standing outside, in almost utter darkness, listening to the sound of some-one choking. A single hanging lantern on the far side of a tent provided the only illumination, but she looked down and about twenty paces away to see Guardsman Graham kneeling in the dirt.

No, she thought, *Not him.*

Gagging hard, he was struggling to breathe, and she longed to do something, to try to help. Graham cried out as his clothing began to split. Even in the darkness, Céline could see fur sprouting on his hands as his face began to elongate and his chest swelled to an astonishing size.

Within moments, she was looking at an enormous wolf with red eyes. Saliva dripped from its fangs.

The shouts of other soldiers began echoing all around.

The wolf crouched and snarled . . . It charged.

The scene vanished.

"Céline!"

Someone called her name, and she opened her eyes to find herself on her feet, being held up by Jaromir—who was gripping both her shoulders. She was back in the tent.

"Come out of it," he ordered. "What do you see?"

Looking down, she saw Graham in his chair, rigid, as he, too, waited for her to speak. Her first instinct was to lie and say that she simply saw something frightening in her own future—and then find a way to tell Jaromir quietly. She didn't want to expose this young man in front of the other soldiers. But Jaromir had made her promise. He'd told her to trust him.

His eyes were expectant.

Against everything in her nature, she said clearly, "It's him. Graham is turned next."

Just as Jaromir expected, as the words left Céline's mouth, pandemonium broke out in the tent—complete with several men drawing their weapons and Graham looking at the doorway as if he'd bolt.

Jaromir let go of Céline and grabbed Graham by the arm.

"Stand down!" he shouted at the men and then called out, "Quinn! Rurik!"

Rurik was already pushing through, coming to his aid, and Quinn appeared at his side. The corporal had been uncomfortable with Jaromir's rescinding of Keegan's command, but thankfully, he was still following orders.

"Get the boy's other arm," Jaromir told him. "Rurik, get Céline out of here."

Without looking back or wasting a moment, Jaromir headed for the exit.

"To the barn," he told Quinn.

With himself on one side of Graham and Quinn on the other, they rapidly half escorted, half dragged the boy across the camp and into the barn. Once inside, Jaromir closed the barn doors.

Graham was panting in what sounded like panic. "Is she right? Is it going to happen to me?"

In truth, Jaromir didn't know. Céline saw the future, but now that she'd exposed the boy as the next victim, anything could change. They'd proven that back in Sèone. The future could be changed by a single action. However, besides himself, no one but Céline and Amelie knew that a future could be altered, and now that he had a possible victim in his grasp, he needed to see how this would play out.

"Calm down," he ordered Graham. He motioned through the stalls toward the back of the barn. "We're going to tie you to a stake so that you can't hurt anyone, but I swear that we'll protect you unless you . . . change."

Graham swallowed and appeared to be attempting to get ahold of himself. "And what if I do change?"

"Let's cross that bridge if we reach it." Jaromir knew this was a weak answer, but he had nothing better to offer.

Not long after, Céline was back sitting at Keegan's bedside. Darkness had fallen, and several candle lanterns glowed from small tabletops. She was only too aware that whatever Jaromir had in mind regarding poor Graham, he'd never had any intention of discussing it with her, and she was going to have to wait for information. So she'd let Rurik escort her to Keegan's tent, where she'd filled Amelie in—on what little she knew—and told Amelie to go and eat something and try to get some rest. After her sister had agreed and left, Céline asked Rurik to find Jaromir and see if he could learn what was going on.

His rapid agreement suggested that he wanted to know just as badly as she did.

And now . . . she sat tending to Keegan, who continued to drift in and out. She believed he would live, but mushroom poisoning was complicated, with a variety of aftereffects. Keegan's recovery might be a slow one.

As she sponged his face, footsteps sounded behind her. Turning, she hoped to see Jaromir but wasn't surprised when Rurik came into view. He stopped beside a hanging tapestry.

"Is Graham safe?" she asked. "Where is he?"

Rurik hesitated before answering. "The lieutenant tied him to a stake in the barn, and he's made sure word is spreading through both camps."

"What?"

Céline was aghast. She'd had no idea what Jaromir planned to do, but it never occurred to her that he'd tie up the young soldier out in the barn.

Rurik held up one hand and glanced down to make sure Keegan was asleep. "Don't worry. The lieutenant is there in the barn, hiding. But no one else knows that except for Corporal Quinn."

"So . . . ," Céline asked, confused, "Jaromir is guarding Graham himself, in secret?"

"More than that. I think he wants to see if anyone tries to visit, to do anything."

And then Céline began to understand what Jaromir was up to. Graham had been pointed out as the next one who would turn. If someone was doing this to the men on purpose, how would he—or she—react to knowing the next victim was tied up in the barn?

Would the culprit try to slip in and set Graham free to do as much damage as possible? Or . . . if the process could be reversed, would he or she try to stop it from happening in order to discount any more finger-pointing from Céline?

But Jaromir had promised he wouldn't use whomever she named as bait.

Wait . . . had he promised?

Suddenly, she wanted to be alone.

"What does the lieutenant want you to do now?" she asked Rurik.

"He told me to look out for you and Amelie."

"I'm fine here. I think Amelie's in our tent. Will you go and check on her?"

Rurik nodded and vanished.

Full darkness had fallen outside, and Céline fought against her rising guilt over having exposed poor Graham. She should have known Jaromir would try something like this. When he'd said, *Trust me,* she'd assumed he would not put anyone at such risk—much less do something so humiliating as tying the person to a stake. He'd practically lied to her face.

Did he want to finish this so badly he was willing to put her trust of him in question?

A part of her almost couldn't blame him. She wanted to go home, too, to her shop . . . to Anton . . . to all that was familiar. She wanted to leave this place behind.

Keegan's breathing deepened, and he seemed to be in a more comfortable sleep now. That was a good sign.

Céline sat back in her chair and closed her eyes for a few moments.

And in her partially relaxed state, she felt a familiar sensation, like the one she'd felt the first night here after crawling into bed. There was *something* outside, something that called her.

Standing up, she leaned over and felt Keegan's forehead.

He would be all right alone for a short while.

Unable to stop herself, she left the tent.

Instead of using the oversized, makeshift harness—which would not have fit—Jaromir had tied Graham with two ropes, one tied very loosely around his neck and one around his ankle, both finished with stout knots, and the ends of both were secured to a stake. Tying the young man's hands and ankles tightly had seemed a possible option at first, but the physical change these men underwent had proven strong enough to break the links in chain armor, so Jaromir had opted for something from which a wolf might have trouble breaking free. At least it should hold the beast long enough for Jaromir to . . . take any necessary action.

After making sure that Graham had food and water within reach, Jaromir piled up bundles of hay and made himself a hiding place with a vantage point from which he could see the guardsman.

Before going into hiding, he told Graham, "Don't worry. I won't take my eyes off you, and I won't let anyone hurt you. Quinn has ordered all the men to stay out of the barn, on pain of imprisonment themselves."

Graham nodded miserably. He was clearly more afraid of what would happen to him if he began to change.

At present, there was nothing Jaromir could do to alleviate that fear. So he crouched down behind the hay and made certain he could see Graham through a crack between the bundles. Graham ignored the food and water, and after a few moments, he lay down on the floor. A single lantern on the floor—out of his reach—provided the only source of light other than a thin moonbeam coming in through one of the high windows.

Jaromir had nothing to do but wait and observe.

Unfortunately, this gave him too much time to think, and *thinking* was the last thing he wanted to do.

He worried what Céline would think of him when she learned what he'd done with the information she'd provided. Would she ever trust him again?

He respected her greatly and often marveled at her skills as a healer, but she had no capability for making hard or necessary decisions, and that one flaw made her less useful to him.

Worse, much worse, he couldn't get Amelie out of his head. What he'd done in the forest earlier that afternoon was unforgivable. She was young and inexperienced, and she could so easily fall in love with him. He'd thought he could satisfy himself by teasing her and flirting with her and putting any other feelings on a back shelf. But everything about her pulled at him, and in a moment of weakness he'd given in . . . when he knew he'd never be able to give her what she needed: the love of equals.

She deserved a love of equals.

He was already married to the security of Castle Sèone and to the protection of Anton, and he could never allow himself to become involved with a woman unless he was in complete control. Anything less could leave him vulnerable, and thereby leave Castle Sèone and Anton vulnerable.

He should never have allowed himself to start something with Amelie that could not be finished. She could so easily be hurt, and the last thing he wanted to do was hurt her. She mattered to him—much more than he cared to admit. If he were a simple soldier in some prince's forces and she were a simple girl helping to run an apothecary shop, he'd marry her in a heartbeat and spend the rest of his life trying to make her happy.

But he wasn't a simple soldier.

And she wasn't a simple girl. She was Prince Anton's seer.

And Jaromir needed to get a handle on himself damn quick.

If . . . if he could only stop thinking about the fierce manner with which she'd grasped the sleeve of his shirt and kissed him back. He'd kissed more women in his life than he could remember, and he'd never felt anything like that.

Fighting to focus on the task at hand, he squinted through the bundles of hay to gauge Graham's breathing by the rise and fall of his chest. The young man appeared to have fallen asleep. That was probably a mercy. Still, Jaromir desperately hoped this night would yield something, some piece of information that he or Céline or Amelie could explore.

A soft scratching sound caught his attention, and he looked up and to his left. There . . . high in a window, a dark form was crawling over the sill. Jaromir held his position, just watching, uncertain what he was seeing yet.

With a fluid grace, the form leaped from the windowsill, landing lightly on the floor. Jaromir kept still as illumination from the lantern exposed the newcomer.

It was a black wolf.

It looked nothing like the creatures these soldiers had been transforming into. Lean and long legged, this animal appeared to be a normal wolf with glittering amber eyes. Slowly, it walked nearer to Graham, and Jaromir picked up the cudgel he'd brought along in case of nonlethal fighting with any of the camp soldiers. Though his sword was in its sheath on his hip, he left it there for now, as he crouched and prepared to rush.

But he didn't rush.

The wolf wasn't growling or even poised in a hunting stance. It simply approached Graham, lowered its head, and took a long sniff. At the sound, Graham's eyes opened, and he sat up, backing against the wall in confused terror.

Jaromir expected him to cry out, but he didn't. Instead, the fear faded from his face, and the wolf stepped closer, smelling him again, from his feet to his face.

Graham sat there and let it.

Locked in the spell of the bizarre sight before him, at first Jaromir didn't move either, though his mind was racing. What was happening here? Was this how the soldiers were being turned? Was this black wolf coming to them and . . . and what?

That final thought moved him to action. He wanted to solve this mystery so badly he could taste it, but not at the expense of Graham's life. If this creature was about to *do* something to him, it must be stopped.

Without a sound, Jaromir gripped the cudgel and rushed, hoping he could reach the wolf and bash its head before it saw him coming.

Unfortunately, it half spun, saw him, and dashed away, jumping out of reach. Then it leaped to the top of a stall and made a seemingly impossible jump from the top of the stall to the window.

In a flash, it was gone.

Jaromir ran to the stall, thinking he might leap up and jump to the window himself, and then he realized what a foolish notion that was, so he made a dash for the front doors, slowing only long enough to call to Graham.

"I'll be right back!"

Céline walked alone past several tents; then she stopped beside one with a view of the barn.

Why had she come out here?

She didn't know, and she stood there for a few moments watching the side of the barn. Then . . . a dark form appeared in a high window, and it leaped all the way to the ground, landing on all fours. It darted away into the trees, as if it was fleeing from something.

Céline followed where it had vanished, quickly passing into the trees.

Running through the barn, Jaromir cursed whoever had built it without a back door. Racing out the front doors, he ran around the side of the barn where the wolf had jumped.

The creature was gone. The ground below the window was empty.

He cursed again, fighting the urge to run into the forest and start hunting. He couldn't just leave. Graham was tied to a stake inside, and Jaromir had vowed to watch over him for more than one reason.

Turning, he remained outside but closed the doors to the barn—for the moment—as if they'd never been opened, and he called out, "Guardsman?" knowing someone would hear him.

"Sir?"

A moment later, a guard carrying a spear emerged from around the side of the tent.

"Are you on night watch?" Jaromir asked.

"Yes, sir."

"I'm making my rounds, but I haven't seen Corporal Quinn. If you know where he is, send word to him that I spotted a wolf inside the camp." The guardsman stiffened, and Jaromir hurried on, "No, not one of those beasts, just a wolf with a black coat. It ran off when it saw me, but we'll want the men to keep aware. Wolves don't normally come into a large camp like this unless they're hungry."

The guardsman relaxed and nodded. "Oh, yes, sir. I'll pass the word."

The man headed back the way he'd come. Once he was out of sight, Jaromir slipped back inside the barn. He had a feeling that black wolf had come for more than food, but . . . it was just a wolf, and for now, sending an alert was the best he could do.

Without letting herself think, Céline continued walking into the dark forest. She hadn't gone far when two strong hands grabbed her, whipped her body around, and pressed her back up against a tree.

"What are you doing out here alone?" he hissed, pinning her in place.

It was Marcus. But she'd already known that or she never would have come out here. However, along this entire journey, she was becoming rather tired of men pinning her up against trees. That would have to stop.

"What were you doing in the barn?" she countered.

She wasn't afraid of him. She fully believed him capable of destroying these Pählen soldiers. But she was in no danger. Something about him was familiar, a connection she couldn't explain, as if she'd known him for a thousand years. He'd die before he'd hurt her. He'd kill before he'd let anyone else hurt her.

Of this, she was certain.

"What are you?" she asked softly.

"Another side of you. You'd know that if you lived among your own people."

"I'll not stand here and mince words. Did Jaromir chase you out of that barn? What were you planning to do to Graham?"

"Do?" Though he took his hands from her arms, he kept his face close to hers. "You don't think I have anything to do with the horrors taking place here?"

"I don't know. Why did you go to the barn in your . . . other form?"

"To see what I could learn. I'd heard that you named him as the next man to turn, and I wanted to smell him, to sense him, to see if I could understand why this is happening."

"Did you? Did you learning anything."

"No. I only saw, smelled, sensed a filthy, frightened Pählen soldier. But you can rest assured that whatever is happening, it's nothing to do with me. One of those *things* killed my brother."

Studying his dark eyes, Céline badly wanted to believe him, but she wasn't sure. In her life, she'd met some very good actors—she'd even been one. His brother's death could have been a tragic unplanned accident.

His mouth curved up in a slight smile. "You still don't believe me?"

"I don't know you, and I don't know what to believe."

"You know me." Slowly, he leaned even farther forward, giving her every chance to move to one side or the other and pull away.

She didn't.

He pressed his forehead against hers, and again, the action felt familiar, comfortable. "When you saw Graham's future, did you see him change?" he whispered.

"Yes. It was awful."

He stepped back, away from her, and in the moonlight coming through the trees, she got a better look at him. He was barefoot, dressed only in his breeches and shirt, and the shirt was untucked and disheveled, as if he'd thrown it on in a hurry.

"Then watch me and see if you think I have anything to do with those soldier-wolves," he said.

Pulling his shirt off, he exposed his chest and the long, tight muscles in his shoulders and arms. Céline stood watching with her back against the tree.

In the next breath, he was on all fours and the hair on his head began receding as black fur sprouted from his skin. His face elongated and his arms changed into front legs.

Within seconds, Céline was staring at a tall black wolf. He was beautiful. There had been no pain involved—not even any real effort. The change had been quick and natural.

The wolf moved forward, and its back legs stepped out of Marcus's breeches. Céline crouched down and held out one hand. It came to her, licking her hand and then pressing its nose into her cheek. When it pulled back slightly, she looked into its eyes. They were amber now, and not black, but she could see *him* in there.

The wolf was Marcus.

A few moments later, the fur receded and the hair on his head grew, and his snout receded and she was looking into the black eyes of a man again. He was naked but reached back for his breeches. He didn't seem remotely embarrassed.

"I've nothing to do with whatever is happening to these soldiers," he whispered. "I don't care how many of them die, but I'm not responsible. My ability is natural, like yours, and I wouldn't know how to pass it to someone else if I wanted to. Do you believe me now?"

Unfortunately, she did, which meant that with Keegan off the list, she had no suspects at all. However, Jaromir might feel quite differently about this situation.

As if reading her mind, Marcus asked, "Will you give me up to your lieutenant?"

"No. I won't. I don't think that would accomplish anything."

Still holding his breeches in front of himself, he reached down for his shirt. "You should get back to camp and stay there."

She knew he was right, but it felt wrong to leave things like this, as if they had more to say to each other—she simply had no idea what. "Marcus, be careful. Don't let any of the soldiers see you . . . in your other form. Don't give them any excuse to kill you."

Then she walked away, heading back to camp. Once she was among the soldiers' tents again, she went straight into Keegan's and stood over his bed. He was still sleeping easily.

But she hadn't even sat down when footsteps

sounded from behind her, and Corporal Quinn came around the tapestry. Though he looked tired and troubled, he was apparently still his normal capable self.

"I'm sorry you've been left here so long," he said. "I was overseeing the night watch, but I think we're as secure as possible, and the lieutenant is hiding in the barn, guarding Graham." It was a pity he'd chosen to serve under Keegan. He could have gone further in his career by now. "Your man, Rurik, is waiting outside to take you back to your own tent to get some rest."

"Oh . . . are you sure, Corporal? I don't mind sitting with the captain."

"No, you go. I'll sit with him."

Céline wasn't sure she could sleep, but she was beyond tempted by the thought of crawling under her covers and closing her eyes and shutting out the world for a little while.

So she stood up. "Thank you."

As she made to leave, he said, "My lady?"

"Yes?"

"Did you . . . did you really see a vision of Guardsman Graham as the next man to be turned? I don't mean to insult you, but this isn't just a ruse the lieutenant planned to try to lure out whoever is responsible?"

Céline sighed softly. "I don't exactly see visions, but, yes, I saw Graham changing."

"So you can see the future, and your sister can see the past?"

This was becoming tiresome. "Of course we can. Prince Anton would never risk disappointing his father by sending two charlatans all the way out here, would he?"

"No . . . I suppose not. Forgive me."

"Good night, Corporal."

She left the tent and was so relieved at the sight of uncomplicated, good-natured Rurik waiting for her outside that she took his right arm with both hands.

"How is Amelie?" she asked as they walked.

"Asleep," he answered, "but she went to bed fully clothed and told me to suggest the same to you, just in case . . . in case . . ."

Céline nodded, still gripping his arm. "Yes, just in case."

Chapter Twelve

Amelie was sleeping deeply when a sound registered on the edge of her awareness. She rolled onto her side, and the sound came again. This time, she opened her eyes. Before going to bed, she'd left their small lantern glowing, and it still provided some light. The first thing she saw was Céline sleeping beside her, dressed in her lavender wool. Amelie had left on her own light blue gown in the event that something should happen in the night.

Had Céline made a sound that woke her?

The sound came again, and Amelie froze. She'd heard a low growl.

Rolling ever so slowly toward the outside of the bed, she looked into the open space of the tent. Two red eyes stared back at her.

"Céline," she whispered, reaching back to touch her sister. "Wake up."

Céline murmured, "What? Amelie, what did you say?"

"Wake up, but don't move."

The beast crouched on the floor snarled this time, and Céline sat up.

"No!" Amelie cried, but it was too late.

The movement caused the enormous wolf to rush, and on instinct, Amelie grabbed Céline and rolled off the other side of the bed, onto the fur-covered ground.

"Rurik!" Amelie screamed as loudly as she could, hoping he had a spear in his tent. "Rurik!"

Both sisters scrambled backward as the wolf-beast landed on their bed, slavering and snarling and sniffing the air. Its red eyes fixed on them, and it leaped again. Cursing, Amelie shoved Céline aside and then cast about for anything she might use as a weapon.

But she saw nothing except the beast in midair, leaping straight toward her.

Suddenly, it yelped and was knocked aside, and Amelie jumped to her feet. A smaller wolf—black—had knocked the massive one off its feet and was slashing at it with teeth and claws.

The wolf-beast roared in pain as the smaller one got ahold of one side of its throat and held on. Coming back to herself, Amelie made a dash for her boot, for her dagger—the only weapon she had in this tent. Gripping the sheath, she jerked the blade from the boot and whirled toward the pair of snarling wolves rolling on the ground.

"Don't hurt the black one," Céline cried. "It's Marcus."

But as the words left her mouth, the black wolf yelped as the larger one slashed it across the chest, and the massive one bolted for the back of the tent, breaking out underneath the canvas wall, ripping out a tent peg in the process, and leaving a large portion of fabric flapping in the night breeze.

A groan sounded, and Amelie spun around to see Marcus lying on the ground, naked and bleeding from the chest.

"Amelie!" a voice called.

Rurik came running past the tent flap into the tent, wielding a sword. He looked around wildly for something to fight, and his eyes lowered to Marcus on the floor. Céline had dropped beside Marcus and covered the lower half of his body with her red cloak.

"What . . . what's happening?" Rurik asked.

"It was inside the tent," Amelie blurted, "one of the wolves, but Marcus fought it off and it ran out there." She pointed to the loose tent wall flapping in the night air.

"Marcus?" Rurik repeated in confusion, staring at Marcus's naked form and complete lack of a weapon.

But then something else occurred to Amelie, something more disturbing. "Rurik . . . stay here with them. If that *thing* was Graham, then it must have attacked Jaromir to get out of the barn!"

She turned to run, ducking out the new "door" in the back.

"Amelie, you can't go out there alone," Rurik called. "Just stay here with Céline!"

Once outside, she could already hear some of the soldiers shouting to one another, as there was now another beast loose inside the camp.

Jaromir heard the shouting and stepped out from his hay bundles. Graham had been lying on the floor and stood up.

"Sir, what is that?" Graham asked.

"I don't know."

Jaromir heard the barn doors opening, followed by the soft sound of running feet, and he gripped his cudgel tightly. To his amazement, Amelie came hurrying into view, barefoot but wearing her light blue dress and carrying her dagger.

She skidded to a stop at the sight of Graham tied to the stake. "It's not him," she panted, as if speaking to herself.

"Amelie!" Jaromir nearly shouted, wanting answers.

"There's a soldier-wolf . . . a big one . . . loose in camp," she managed to say while still panting. "It attacked me and Céline in our bed. I thought . . . I thought it was Graham, and that he might have killed you."

"It attacked you in your . . ." He trailed off, looking back to Graham.

If the beast wasn't Graham, then whoever was behind all this had changed tactics and turned someone else. That was the only explanation Jaromir could think of.

The shouts outside grew louder, and he heard Corporal Quinn in the midst. "No! Don't let it past the perimeter! Someone stop it!"

A mix of unintelligible shouting followed, culminating in Quinn yelling, "Gods damn it! How could you let it pass?"

"It's gotten outside the camp," Amelie breathed. "Loose in the trees. What do we do?"

Jaromir looked at Graham. "Whenever one of these

things has made it into the trees, what do they normally do?"

"They usually go straight for the miners' encampment."

Jaromir glanced at the blade in Amelie's hand. "Cut him loose."

Céline suffered a few awkward moments while Rurik clearly wondered—but was too polite to ask—what Marcus had been doing naked inside their tent, but she examined the wounds on Marcus's chest, which were not as deep as she'd first feared. His skin was clawed, and he was in some pain, but the wounds were only superficial.

"I need to disinfect these," she said, starting to rise.

"Not now. Later," Marcus said, climbing to his feet with the cloak around his waist.

Rurik was standing guard in the doorway, so Céline leaned nearer to Marcus and whispered, "Where are your clothes?"

"Outside," he answered.

"Can you slip out that new doorway in the back and get them?"

Before she'd finished speaking, he was on the move, and a few moments later, Amelie came running back in the front flap, rushing past Rurik.

"It's not Graham," she called, looking around and then grabbing her boots. "It's someone else. We don't know who yet, but it got outside the encampment."

Céline was struck dumb by both pieces of news.

Marcus ducked back inside the torn back of the tent, wearing his breeches and pulling on his shirt. He handed back her cloak.

"What's happened?" he asked.

"Is Jaromir all right?" Céline asked almost at the same time, finding her voice.

"He's fine," Amelie answered, pulling on her boots, "but he's moving everyone over to the miners' encampment so we can protect those people while we start forming hunting parties."

Marcus was listening intently; then he glanced at the front tent flap.

"Go," Céline told him. "Hurry. We'll meet you over there." She reached down for her own boots.

Jaromir had both Graham and Quinn at his side as he strode through the tents, sounding a full-scale alarm and calling out orders that everyone was moving to the miners' camp to protect the civilians.

"We'll need a few men to get a stretcher and carry the captain over," Quinn said. "I left him alone in his tent. I didn't have a choice."

"Of course you didn't," Jaromir answered. "Use anyone you need."

All the Pählen soldiers responded quickly. Some had been asleep, but they were all soon running toward the path to the miners' camp, and once again, they appeared relieved at the prospect of an officer having taken charge. So far, no one had reacted to Graham's presence, as if they'd also come to expect the unexpected and nothing surprised them anymore. Jaromir still had no idea which of the soldiers was missing or what poor soul they would soon be hunting.

"Jaromir!" Céline called from somewhere behind him.

Stopping, he looked back to see her, Amelie, and Rurik jogging toward him. Rurik carried a sword. Céline wore her red cloak, but Amelie must not have bothered and wore only her blue dress and boots. He waited for them to catch up, and they all pressed onward down the path through the trees, emerging on the side of the miners' camp. A number of Móndyalítko and miners were outside their dwellings, asking the soldiers for information.

Jaromir briefly considered ordering them all back inside their dwellings but decided that could take too much time if they refused. He would do better to get a perimeter guard set up and then form at least two hunting parties.

"We didn't bring enough spears," Quinn said suddenly, looking around, gripping a single tall spear in his right hand. "Over half the men were asleep, and they just came running when we called. I'll need to go back to the weapons' supply and bring more."

With his mouth pursed in thought, he glanced down at Amelie.

"I'll come and help," she said. "You can't carry enough by yourself."

Jaromir turned on her and was about to order her into one of the wagons, but then he saw her face. She was staring back at him with an angry, almost hurt, challenge.

"I can help," she bit off.

His mind flashed back to the sight of her swinging the butt of a spear down on the last wolf's head—and then swinging down twice more. She wasn't a child and didn't deserve to be treated like one. He could give her at least that much.

"Go," he said, handing her his cudgel. "Take this for the trip over."

Her eyes flickered, but she took the weapon and didn't hesitate to start after Quinn when he trotted back toward the path.

Though Jaromir felt a flash of unwanted fear in his chest, along with a desire to grab her from behind, lift her off the ground, and order her into a wagon, he bit the inside of his mouth and turned back to the camp. Amelie couldn't stand to feel useless, and he knew it.

Besides, he had people to protect here, soldiers to organize . . . and an unnatural wolf to hunt down.

Trotting behind Quinn, Amelie took two steps to his one, but she knew he was in a hurry. She wasn't afraid. He looked as strong and fast as Jaromir, and she had a feeling he knew how to use that spear. She had the cudgel, which was good for close-quarters fighting. Between the two of them, she was certain they could handle anything that came their way.

And, though she kept pushing the feeling down, she was grateful to Jaromir for letting her take her place among the soldiers in helping to protect the Móndy-alítko families and other miners.

"Where are the extra weapons stored?" she panted, trying to keep up.

Quinn glanced over his shoulder and slowed his pace. "Forgive me." Then he pointed toward the provisions tent. "In racks along the east wall. It's easier to guard the food and weapons in one central location."

That made sense.

They were only a few tents away from their destination when a snarl sounded, and Quinn jerked to a stop, turning his head and gripping the spear with both hands.

Two red eyes glowed from the brush at the edge of the forest, and the beast snarled louder. Neither Quinn nor Amelie spoke, but she held the cudgel at the ready, waiting for the inevitable charge. But then Quinn shifted positions and the moonlight glinted off the head of his spear.

The wolf's red eyes moved upward, focusing on the spear, and without warning, the beast dashed inside the trees, vanishing from sight.

"No!" Quinn shouted, running toward where the wolf had disappeared. He didn't look back, and Amelie stood rooted to the ground, but he kept running, crashing through the brush, and she realized he was going after the wolf on his own.

Without further hesitation, she bolted, running after him, breaking through the brush herself. Out here, as she had an easier time passing through the trees and brush—due to her smaller size—she had little trouble keeping up with Quinn. Once her wool skirt did get caught, but she jerked it free, wishing for her breeches. Still, the skirt was loose and easy to move in for the most part, and this dress reached only her ankles, so she was in no danger of tripping.

Up a little ways in front of her, Quinn stopped and knelt. "It's bleeding," he said, picking up a leaf.

"Oh . . . yes, Marcus injured its throat earlier. But I couldn't see how badly."

"Marcus? That gypsy hunter?"

Amelie didn't answer. Quinn's tone sounded as arrogant as Keegan's when he spoke Marcus's name.

As Quinn was about to move forward, he paused uncertainly and looked back at her. "I didn't mean for you to follow me."

"You can't fight that thing by yourself." She hefted the cudgel. "Trust me. One good swing, and I can stun it long enough for you to use that spear."

Though he seemed inclined to argue further, he also seemed driven to press on before the trail grew cold, so he turned and moved forward, studying the ground and the surrounding brush. Amelie followed as quietly as she could, but she heard no growls or sounds of a large creature moving in the trees, and she couldn't help thinking of their original mission—to get more spears for the soldiers.

"Quinn . . . ," she whispered, right behind him. "What if we've lost it? What if it's run for the miners' camp and it attacks there? Half the men aren't properly armed."

He was so focused on studying the ground that he barely seemed to hear her. "We haven't lost it," he said absently, smelling a leaf. "This trail is too fresh. I know what I'm doing. I trained with the hunters of Kimovesk, and they are the finest trackers in the nation."

"Kimovesk? That borders Shetâna. Were you serving under Prince Damek?"

She asked this more out of curiosity than anything, as it was not uncommon for soldiers to sometimes move within ranks inside of noble families. But from the back, she saw Quinn's entire body go rigid at her question.

"You know Shetâna?" he asked.

In that instant, Amelie realized that he'd made a mistake in mentioning Kimovesk, and she'd made a mistake in mentioning Shetâna. Quinn believed she was a lady of Anton's court in Sèone, who would have no familiarity with Damek's province.

Turning his head slowly, he looked back at her, and even in the darkness he was close enough for her to see the depths of his light blue eyes. She didn't answer his question, but she was suddenly very aware that he had not intended to give her any kind of clue that he'd ever served under Prince Damek.

Was she alone out here with a man willing to destroy the soldiers who served under him?

Her mind rebelled against the prospect. It *couldn't* be Quinn. He was the only one here who'd even tried to assist Jaromir, the only one in whom Jaromir had placed any trust.

But then . . . he was also the only Pählen soldier who'd known that Jaromir had been hiding in the barn watching Graham. Rurik had told her that much earlier. And . . . the beast tonight had somehow appeared inside Amelie and Céline's tent when Jaromir had been across the camp and unable to protect them.

Had Céline's announcement regarding Graham proven they weren't charlatans? Had Graham indeed been the next intended victim? If Quinn was the one responsible for these horrors, had he then decided to get rid of the two seers from Sèone?

But if so, then why was he so determined in this hunt? He clearly wanted to track down the beast.

Unless . . . he'd known full well that if he ran into the forest after the wolf, she'd follow him. He'd seen enough of her over the past few days and nights to realize that much. What if he'd intended for her to follow him, to help him track down the beast, so he could let it kill her and be rid of at least one sister—the one who could see the past—without calling any suspicion to himself?

No, again, she couldn't accept any of these far-fetched notions.

What possible motive could Quinn, a mere corporal, have for closing down a mining operation?

Unless . . . for some reason, Damek had wanted it closed down, and Quinn was still working for Damek.

"You have a very expressive face," he whispered.

She started to back up. He'd been holding his spear flat against the ground, and he let go of it, freeing both his hands, but Amelie still gripped the cudgel. She'd always depended on the element of surprise, on letting others underestimate her until it was too late, and she had a sick feeling in her stomach that her life was about to depend on this tried-and-true tactic.

So she kept still, waiting for him to make the first move—which would be to try to take her cudgel.

Instead, he swung with his left fist, moving so fast that she had only a second to pull back, and he clipped her across the chin. Even then, the strength in his fist was staggering, and she was knocked aside, hitting the damp ground and rolling.

He was on top of her in seconds, tearing the cudgel from her grip and throwing it to one side.

"I'm sorry," he said, pinning her with his weight and grabbing her by the jaw with one hand. "You shouldn't have come here. I'll make it quick."

Was he going to snap her neck? A mix of fear and rage took hold of Amelie. How could it be Quinn? How could none of them—not she, not Céline, not Jaromir—have gotten a single hint? Falling back on the only defense she had left, she grabbed his wrist with both hands.

Instead of pointlessly trying to pull his hand off her jaw, she demanded, "Why?"

And in a flash, she reached out for the spark of his spirit, trying to rip his awareness from this moment, to trap him in the mists of time. His spirit was strong, and she latched onto it.

Why?

The first jolt hit, and she focused as hard as she could on whatever had brought him here. The second jolt hit, and they were both swept into the gray and white mists, moving backward. Again, she fought to keep pulling him along with her but to remain separate. She didn't want to see through his eyes. She would remain an observer and allow her gift to show her what she needed to see.

He was fighting back, trying to break free, but she held on. In here, she was the stronger one.

Why?

The mists cleared.

CHAPTER THIRTEEN

KIMOVESK: ONE YEAR IN THE PAST

Amelie found herself in a vast windowless room with walls of stone. Small braziers lined three of the walls, providing a good deal of light. Spears and crossbows lined the fourth wall.

It took her a moment to take in the scene before her. Only three people occupied the open space, and all of them stood near a long wooden table. She noted Quinn first . . . but he was wearing a black tabard over his armor. Next, she saw a middle-aged woman with long silver-blond hair. Her face showed signs of fading beauty. She wore rings on all her fingers and was dressed in a robe of purple silk.

At the sight of the third person, Amelie tensed inside the memory. He looked to be about twenty-five or twenty-six, handsome and slender. His hair was long and dark. His skin was pale to the point of being white, and he wore a sleeveless embroidered tunic. He looked like Anton—only with darker, longer hair. But his eyes were cruel as he gazed downward at the table.

Prince Damek.

Strangely, Amelie had never seen him in person, but she'd seen him in another memory and knew his face.

Then . . . her own gaze moved down to the tabletop, and the scene took on an unreal quality. A dead, naked man lay there. He had a mass of black hair, dusky skin, and a silver ring in one ear. His head lay at an odd angle, and his right arm hung down off the side of the table. His wrist had been cut open, and his blood was draining into a bowl.

At his feet, also on the table, lay the body of a dead wolf with a crossbow quarrel still protruding from its rib cage. The wolf was brown with a white chest and one white paw.

Amelie couldn't imagine what any of this meant.

Damek paced, appearing almost anxious. "Lieutenant," he said, "you swear he was in wolf form when you killed him?"

"Yes," Quinn answered impassively. "I broke his neck, and he changed back."

Damek touched the side of the table. "No one else has been able to do this for me," he whispered. "No one."

"I told you I could."

Amelie wanted to gasp as several facts hit her at once. First, Quinn was not a corporal. He was an officer in Damek's forces. Second, Quinn had hunted down and murdered a Móndyalítko shape-shifter.

To what possible end?

Amelie lowered her gaze back to the bowl on the floor, as it was now half-filled with the shape-shifter's blood. The woman picked up the bowl.

"Now I'll need blood from the wolf," she said, "and its fangs, its eyes, and two of its claws."

Damek nodded at Quinn, who pulled a dagger from his belt and started toward the dead wolf.

Fighting nausea, Amelie looked away and saw a burning hearth—large enough to stand in—at the other end of the vast room. An iron hook had been set over the flames, and a small metal cauldron with symbols etched around the outside hung from the hook.

Damek reached out one hand toward the woman. "Lady Saorise, let me carry that for you."

She handed him the bowl with an imperious nod. Amelie had no idea who this woman was, but she focused harder on trying not to look at Quinn as he obtained the requested parts from the body of the dead wolf.

A few moments later, all three of them walked toward the blazing hearth.

Upon reaching it, Lady Saorise stood in front of the cauldron. Damek stood on one side of her and Quinn on the other. Amelie saw a cup with a lip and handle and a metal flask on the floor.

Without hesitation, Lady Saorise took the bowl of blood from Damek and poured it into the cauldron. The liquid hissed as it hit the bottom.

"Now the wolf's blood," she said, "and its teeth, eyes, and claws."

Amelie allowed herself to look at Quinn now. His face was utterly emotionless, but he was holding a bowl of his own. Carefully, he reached out and poured the contents into the cauldron. These additions made less sound.

Lady Saorise pulled at a chain around her neck and lifted a small bottle from the neckline of her robe. She opened the stopper and poured the contents of the bottle into the cauldron.

"Thrice-purified water," she told Damek, "to help the elixir to be absorbed."

He said nothing, but his eyes glittered as he watched in fascination.

Lady Saorise began to chant softly. She placed her hands in the air on each side of the cauldron as her voice gradually grew louder. Amelie couldn't understand a word.

Then Lady Saorise cried out one final, loud, unintelligible phrase, and she swept inward with her hands, holding the sides of the cauldron. Amelie could only imagine how hot the metal must be and the damage it was doing to her palms.

"Rage," Saorise whispered softly. "Madness."

She slumped in exhaustion, and her hands fell away from the cauldron.

"My lady," Damek cried in what sounded like genuine alarm, and he caught her, holding her up. Was it possible he cared for this woman?

A moment later, she stood on her own power. "I am well. The spell is powerful . . . and draining."

"Is it done?" Damek breathed.

Reaching down, she picked up the cup and the flask, and as she did, Amelie saw that her hands weren't burned. They weren't even reddened. Dipping the cup into the cauldron, she poured a now black fluid into the metal flask—without spilling a drop.

"We must test it," she said. "You have a subject?"

Nodding, Damek turned and strode across the room to a side door. Quinn and Lady Saorise followed him. Amelie was drawn after them, but she was flooded with a terrible feeling that the worst of this was not over.

Opening the door, Damek turned to Quinn. "You brought the leather gloves, as I asked?"

"Yes."

Quinn drew a pair of thick gloves from the pocket of his pants, and he put them on.

Upon hearing a rattling sound, Amelie peered around him into a narrow room. A filthy man in rags was manacled by one wrist to the back wall. He looked out in terror at the open doorway.

Lady Saorise handed Quinn the flask. "You only need to place a small amount on his bare skin," she said. "Just wet your gloved finger and touch his skin. The elixir will absorb instantly. But do *not* get the smallest amount on your own skin. You must never be careless. It will affect you as it would affect him."

Taking the flask from her, Quinn wet his gloved right pointer finger with a few drops of the black liquid. Then he entered the narrow room, going straight to the panicked man and smearing the substance on his cheek.

"No!" the man cried, trying to pull back against the wall. "What are you doing?"

Quinn stepped away and looked back toward the door. "How long?"

Amelie almost didn't recognize his voice. He sounded so cold.

"Unknown," Lady Saorise answered. "We will have to wait."

All three of them fell silent, and the only sound Amelie heard was the manacled man whimpering in fear. Inside the memory, it was difficult to judge how much time had passed, but she thought it was less than an hour when the man in the narrow room began gagging.

Though it was difficult to watch, Amelie knew that she was being shown only what was most important, so she looked through a space between Damek's and Quinn's shoulders as they stood in the doorway.

The poor man inside began retching . . . and then his hands began turning into claws and his body began to expand. His jaw elongated and fur sprouted from his skin. Amelie watched, numb, as he transformed into a massive wolf with red eyes, and he lunged, roaring, against the chain on his front leg.

The manacle was tight against his fur, but it held.

"By the gods," Damek whispered in wonder, staring at the mad creature snarling and snapping at the end of its chain. Saliva spattered the floor from its fangs. "Saorise, you've done it." His expression altered to one of someone who suddenly wished to get down to business, and he turned to Quinn. "Kill that thing. We know the elixir works."

Without a word, Quinn walked to the weapons wall, took down a crossbow, and loaded it.

Amelie did not feel she needed to watch this part, and she turned around as he went back to the doorway and fired. The beast inside the room cried out, but she could still hear it snarling. Quinn loaded a second quarrel and fired again. This time, she could hear only panting afterward, and she looked back to see Quinn frowning slightly.

"I shot it through the eye," he said. "They are hard to kill."

Returning to the wall, he took down a heavy spear, and this time he entered the room. Amelie heard a loud sucking sound, and then the room went silent. Quinn reemerged.

"It's dead."

Damek seemed to be growing impatient now, and he turned to Saorise. "My lady, you must be exhausted. Would you like to go and rest?"

"Yes, perhaps. You are pleased?"

He took her hand and kissed the back of it. "More than pleased. I will be up to visit you shortly."

Again, Amelie wondered what these two were to each other—but she received no answers.

As Lady Saorise swept from the room in a rustling of her purple robe, Damek squared off with Quinn, assessing his tall form.

"You do realize this is only the beginning?" Damek asked.

"Yes. What do you want done next?"

"A field test." Glancing over at the table, Damek's lip curled up in distaste at the dead Móndyalítko and the partially mutilated body of the wolf. With one hand, he motioned Quinn back toward the hearth, and both men walked over to stand nearer to the fire.

Amelie followed.

"I'm going to have you placed inside my father's forces as a corporal," Damek said.

"A corporal?"

"Yes, I need someone who will be trusted but not garner much attention."

"So you are offering me to your father?"

Damek smiled, and Amelie found the sight chilling. "Oh, no," he said. "My father would never accept any connection with anyone who'd ever served me. He would doubt my motives. No, I've forged a letter from an acquaintance of my father, a Baron Driesè. Apparently, according to the letter, the baron has a high opinion of you and would like for you to be given a chance in the guard of a royal household."

Quinn frowned. "And you think your father will believe this unselfish act?"

"I do. You see, the baron has done this once before. It is in his nature. My father will accept you. But he and Driesè see each other only every few years at best, and I'll make certain any letters between my father and him are intercepted in the first weeks after your arrival. The ruse will not be discovered."

"So I serve as a corporal. Then what?"

"Your first task is to become trusted by your commanding officer. That's all you need do for now. Later . . . though I've not chosen a time or a place, when I give the word, I will need you to find a way to get your contingent assigned somewhere isolated. You'll then begin to experiment with the elixir. Start slowly, turning a man every few weeks perhaps. Your purpose is to create and incite a complete breakdown of the command structure, to foster such an atmosphere of terror and mistrust that although most of the men will remain healthy and *appear* capable of battle, it would be child's play to ride in and destroy them."

"You're going to attack your own father's men?" Quinn asked, but he didn't sound remotely daunted by the task Damek had just placed before him.

"No, of course not. You are simply carrying out the initial test, but you need to take it to the point where order has broken down, fear has taken over, the contingent could be wiped out with little effort, and yet from the outside, the attackers will appear as the far stronger force. That is the key. I need to create situations where my men always appear as the stronger force. When you've reached that point, you may stop and send me word. I trust your judgment. I only wish to know if this will work to the degree that I imagine."

"And if it does, you will then use it against your real enemies on a larger scale?"

"Oh, yes. I plan to show my father that I maintain the finest fighters in Droevinka, easily able to smash any opposition."

"But why have me try this on your father's men?"

"So that once you've finished your field test, I should be able to swoop in, look the hero as I stop it from happening again, and save the day. We can easily blame someone in the camp." He smiled again. "Not you, of course. I find you far too useful, but I do need to impress my father on every possible front. Later, if he discovers what I'm doing to our enemies, I can say that I tortured the original traitor and gained knowledge of his weapon to use myself—in defense of our family's interests. That will make me look even more resourceful."

"And if I am successful in my . . . field test, you will agree to my reward?"

"To make you vassal of O'Kruge Keep and its fiefs?"

"With me keeping half the rents. And you'll arrange a marriage for me to a noblewoman?"

"That was the agreement. Others have made promises to me, but you're the only man to come this far. If you succeed in the next part of this task, the vassalage and rents are yours, and I will marry you to Lord Chaudoir's youngest daughter. Will that be acceptable?"

"Lord Chaudior?" For the first time, Quinn's icy blue eyes showed a hint of emotion—possibly greed or perhaps just hunger. "Yes, that is acceptable."

As those words left his mouth, the room vanished and the mists rushed in. Amelie felt herself being swept forward . . . and forward until she knew some time had passed. When the mists cleared, she was inside the great hall of a castle, surrounded by a din. More than a hundred people had gathered at long tables for a feast.

Prince Lieven, Prince Damek, and six other well-dressed nobles were seated at a table at the top of the hall, upon a dais. Most of the soldiers in the hall wore dark brown tabards, so Amelie reasoned the scene was taking place at Castle Pählen, and Prince Damek was here on a visit to his father.

Looking down, Amelie saw three men seated directly in front of where she stood: Captain Keegan, Quinn, and the handsome Lieutenant Sullian. Quinn wore the brown tabard of Lieven's forces now. All three men were drinking and laughing, and after only a few moments of watching them, Amelie could not help but note the easy camaraderie among them. Quinn must either be a master actor or so mentally deranged that he could convince himself of the role he was playing.

"A few of Damek's guards suggested a game of dice after dinner," Keegan said. "Under the front torches of the courtyard."

Sullian frowned. "Sir . . . you're in debt up to your ears to Master Terlone already. Maybe you should stay here and dance with a few girls instead. Keep whatever coins you have. The day after tomorrow is payday, and you told me you owe every penny to Terlone."

Keegan's expression tightened. "I can choose my own entertainments, Lieutenant."

Sullian fell silent, but Quinn was looking at the main archway of the hall. A boy of about ten or eleven stood there, peering in.

"Excuse me, gentlemen," Quinn said, standing up. "Nature calls."

He headed toward the archway. The boy saw him coming and quietly put something in his hand before vanishing down the passage. Amelie came up behind Quinn as he opened a note that read only:

The gazebo by the river. At dawn.

The great hall vanished, and the mists rushed in for only a second or two, barely enough time for Amelie to feel much movement. When they cleared, she found herself at the edge of a small river, with a wooden gazebo to her right.

Quinn was already there, and Prince Damek was walking up. The sun was just breaking over the horizon.

"I've chosen the place," Damek said without offering a greeting. "There is an isolated mining camp up north, above Enêmûsk. The captain my father assigned has died, and my father is having a difficult time replacing him, which is no wonder as the place sounds like banishment."

"He won't order one of his officers?"

"With such difficult assignments, my father prefers . . . volunteers. He's a tyrant who hates to appear as a tyrant." Damek paused and crossed his arms. "This mining camp is ideal for our purposes. Can you manage to place your captain in a position where he has no choice but to volunteer?"

Quinn remained quiet for a few moments, as if thinking. "Yes, I can manage."

The gazebo vanished, and Amelie was caught up in the mists, moving forward.

When they cleared, she found herself seeing a memory she'd already experienced. She was back inside the stable, directly following the dice game where Keegan had lost his money on payday.

Just as before, Keegan was leaning forward with his hands on his knees, as if he was about to be ill.

"What can I do?" he said. "Master Terlone is coming tomorrow. He said if I don't settle my account, he'll go to Prince Lieven."

Both Sullian and Quinn looked on. But this time, Amelie noticed how Quinn's eyes glowed. There was no way he could have orchestrated the happenstance dice game in the courtyard, but beneath his false concern, she could see he was pleased.

"Could you not give some of your purchases back to him?" Sullian was saying. "The pewter goblets?"

"He won't take them!" Keegan snapped. "And I cannot give a season's worth of wine back. It's already been drunk." He stood and ran his hands over his face. "The prince cannot find out how much I owe. I'll be ruined."

The rest of the conversation continued as before, only this time, Amelie focused entirely on Quinn.

She did turn to Keegan when he closed his eyes and said, "I have to do something. The prince cannot hear of this."

"Wait . . . ," Sullian began. He hesitated and then said, "Quinn, what about that game of Hard Tens you promised to deal tonight? Could you get the captain in? He's better with cards, and he could win his wages back."

Keegan stood straight, his eyes filling with hope. "Hard Tens?"

Sullian nodded. "With Prince Damek here on a visit, a few of his officers asked Lieutenant Tanner to put a game together, and Tanner asked Quinn to deal."

"Can you get me in?" Keegan asked Quinn.

Again, Amelie stopped listening to the words as Keegan begged. Quinn glanced away. "All right. I'll speak to Lieutenant Tanner."

But as she moved to see his face, she could also see his hidden relief. He must have been the one who'd arranged for the card game with Damek's officers, and he'd probably offered to be the dealer.

The scene in the stable vanished, and Amelie saw only a blink of the mists before they disappeared and she found herself in another small, windowless room.

Again, she was back in a moment she had already seen—the card game with six men sitting at a round table. The same goblets and pitchers of wine were scattered about on the table. Candle lanterns burned from small tables in the corners of the room.

Quinn sat there dealing, and she realized how easy this must have been for him. No one would suspect the dealer in a game of Hard Tens, as the dealer had nothing to win or lose. He didn't need to win here. He needed only to make certain that Keegan lost.

Walking up behind Keegan, she realized at what point in the game she'd come in. He had a two of clubs showing, and when he peeked at his hole card she saw the ten of diamonds. Amelie moved over to stand next to Quinn. No one else even glanced his way, but she noticed he had a card palmed in his hand. The men began placing bets, and by the time they were finished, Keegan had put in almost every coin he had left. One of Damek's officers raised an eyebrow.

"Looks like a do-or-die hand for you, Captain," he said.

Keegan didn't answer and nodded to Quinn that he wanted another card.

Quinn dealt him the ten of hearts, and Keegan closed

his eyes, knowing he'd gone over. Amelie watched the rest of the scene play out, knowing Keegan would jump up, leave the room, and come back with the bag containing his men's payroll.

He did.

Quinn was staring at him as he sat down, and just as before, Keegan glared across the table. "Deal the cards, *Corporal*."

Only this time, Amelie saw the gleam of triumph in the very back of Quinn's blue eyes. No one else saw it. No one else even noticed him.

The room vanished, and the mists closed in, rushing her forward in time.

When they cleared, she was in the Ryazan encampment, and it looked to be in the same state of setup it had been in when she'd seen Keegan's memories. Only now, she was watching Quinn. The early evening was breezy, and he wore a cloak over his shoulders.

He was outside, among the tents, and he glanced through the flap of a deteriorating small one, barely large enough to stand in. But he entered, and Amelie followed to watch.

First, he put on his leather gloves, and then he took the metal flask from the pocket of his cloak. Removing the stopper, he covered the tip of his pointer finger with the black elixir. Closing the flask, he put it back into his pocket.

Emerging, he seemed to choose a man at random, but Amelie could not be sure about that. His gaze paused on a soldier with a crooked tabard. Amelie noted the men were all clean and shaved at this point in time.

"Guardsman," Quinn called. "The state of your tabard is a disgrace."

The soldier turned at the sound of his voice. Quinn walked up quickly and straightened the tabard, and as he did so, Amelie saw his pointer finger brush one side of the man's neck. The black spot left behind vanished into his skin.

"Better," Quinn said, completing his adjustment of the tabard. "Just never let Lieutenant Sullian see you like that."

The guardsman nodded and walked away.

Quinn watched him leave. "Less than an hour," he said to himself. "It begins."

The camp vanished, and the mists closed in.

CHAPTER FOURTEEN

As Amelie came out of the memories, she found herself looking up at Quinn's face, but his expression was faraway. At some point, he'd taken his hand from her jaw and now had both palms pressed against the ground.

She didn't hesitate.

Scrambling out from beneath him, she rolled and pulled the dagger from her boot, holding it in front of herself as she crouched just outside his reach.

His eyes cleared too late. Grabbing for her, he missed, and when he started to rush, he saw the dagger and froze. But she could almost see his mind working, and she feared that in battle he thought too much like she did—always leaning on the element of surprise. He would not do anything that might be expected.

Then . . . balancing herself with her free hand, she felt her fingers touch upon a jagged, good-sized rock.

How long until Jaromir noticed she should be back by now? Probably too long, and he didn't even know where she was. But he'd go to the weapons cache first.

Without looking down, she closed her hand around the rock.

She needed to distract Quinn for a few seconds.

"You did that to Sullian!" she accused. "How could you? He was your friend."

To her surprise, he blinked and answered, "I had to. I'd reached a point where I needed more control. With him gone, even as a corporal, I'd be second-in-command."

Perhaps he'd been playing a part for so long he was hungry to be himself and speak of these things.

"Did you turn a guard right outside our quarters tonight? So the wolf would kill Céline and me?"

"I had to," he repeated. "I'd chosen Graham as the next target. I should have chosen him sooner. He's no soldier. But . . . your sister knew, and if she could see the future, then you might be able to see the past."

"So then you decided not to turn Graham, and you turned whatever poor soul was closest to our tent?"

He didn't answer. She saw a flicker in his eyes . . . and realized he was done talking and about to charge— or do something. He was a trained soldier. A lieutenant. More, he was strong enough that he'd broken the neck of a Móndyalítko shape-shifter. She was good with her dagger but no match for him physically.

Moving as fast as she could, she threw the rock, aiming for his head. It connected with a cracking sound, and his neck snapped back. Darting through the brush, she ran back the way they'd come—toward the provisions tent.

*   *   *

Jaromir immediately set up a circle of perimeter guards around the mining encampment, with men to spare. Once Captain Keegan had been settled inside one of the shacks, Jaromir turned to a more detailed assessment of the weapons on hand. All the soldiers had at least one. About half the men had spears, seven of them carried loaded crossbows, and the rest had swords.

Even in their current situation, the camp was certainly defensible.

But how could Quinn have ordered everyone over here without gathering more spears and crossbows first? The man must have been badly shaken to overlook such essentials. That thought got him thinking that Quinn and Amelie should have returned by now.

They would probably come trotting back at any moment.

It would be best to have the first hunting party set up. Looking around, he noted that too many of the miners and Móndyalítko were still outside their homes, trying to learn what was happening. Several of the men carried pickaxes, and Jaromir welcomed their help, but he thought the elderly, the women, and the children should be moved inside behind locked or barred doors.

Seeing Céline and Rurik only a few paces away, he closed the distance. He could have Céline see to the civilians, and Rurik could help him with a hunting party. Jaromir knew the detailed backgrounds of all his men.

"Rurik," he said, "isn't your father Prince Lieven's gamekeeper?"

"Yes, sir."

"And you've hunted with him?"

Rurik had sheathed his sword, but his left hand now gripped his right, as if the question unsettled him. "Yes, sir."

"Good. I want you to walk the perimeter and pick out five other men with experience as well. Replace them with our surplus guards. I don't want the line weakened. As soon as Amelie and Corporal Quinn get back with more weapons, you can lead the first hunting party."

Even in her red cloak, Céline shivered slightly in the night air, and Jaromir turned to her. "Can you get the women and children to go back inside? Have them lock or bar their doors."

"Of course," she answered.

But Rurik hadn't moved, and a light sheen broke out on his forehead. "Sir . . . perhaps I should stay here. I'm the only man from Sèone you have, and you'll need me to ride for our escort when this is over."

Jaromir stiffened. Rurik had been acting strangely since the morning he'd been ordered to replace Pavel, but now he sounded desperate. Céline was watching him in confusion as well. Rurik was no coward. Jaromir knew him to be a solid fighter who had once saved Anton from a rushing wild boar. Rurik didn't fear hunting . . . so what made him so desperate now?

He's hiding something.

The thought sickened Jaromir that one of his trusted men was keeping a secret . . . but it couldn't be denied. It was all over Rurik's face.

"All right." Jaromir nodded. "Just pick out a party, and I'll have someone else lead it."

Relief passed across Rurik's face, and Jaromir moved like lightning, stepping behind him, pinning his arms, and lifting his feet off the ground.

"Céline!" Jaromir called.

He didn't have to tell her what he wanted.

She came toward them with her hand out.

Rurik went wild, kicking and struggling to break free. "No! Céline! Don't do it. It's not what you think. Don't do it!"

Céline stepped to the side, but she didn't slow down. She knew Rurik would never be able to break away from Jaromir . . . and Jaromir was right about this. She'd suspected something was off about Rurik for days now, but he'd never appeared even close to this desperate before. He was hiding something.

This was hardly the time or the place for a reading, but they were in danger from something unknown here, and no possible clue could be put off.

Reaching out, she gripped his right hand—which was held tightly against his side—and closed her eyes, feeling for the spark of his spirit.

A sensation of panic hit her like a wall. The first jolt hit within seconds, followed immediately by another jolt, and the mists rushed in. She was jerked forward in time so fast that she grew dizzy speeding along the corridor of white and gray.

The mists cleared.

She stood in a great hall. Rurik was kneeling on the stone floor beside her.

Looking up, Céline saw a muscular man with graying hair and a proud bearing sitting in a chair on a dais up above. He wore a loose red jerkin accented by gold thread. Three jeweled rings on each hand adorned his fingers.

"My lord," Rurik said with his head bowed.

"My son's report was vague, as always. That is his way. Tell me, who inside the camp was responsible?"

Inside the vision, Céline's mind raced. The man on the dais was Prince Lieven. She'd never seen him before, as no vision of the future had ever taken her to Castle Pählen. But what was Rurik doing? He appeared to be giving the prince a report outside of what Anton had authorized.

"The criminal was Corporal Quinn," Rurik said. "A spy and infiltrator of Prince Damek."

"And these two . . . seers that my son employs, they uncovered this for Anton?"

"Yes, my lord. Prince Anton is ever resourceful in those he chooses to serve him."

Just as Lieven was about to speak again, the mists closed in, and Céline was jerked away, rushing backward in time. It was the briefest future vision she'd ever experienced.

But when she opened her eyes and she saw Jaromir holding Rurik, she was so shaken and disoriented that she stumbled and fell to her knees and could not stop herself from crying out.

"He's a spy for Anton's father! He's going to tell Prince Lieven all the details of this mission that Anton would not!"

Jaromir roared and shoved Rurik forward.

In one swift motion, Jaromir drew a dagger from the sheath on his belt.

"Sir, no!" Rurik shouted, spinning around. "I'm no spy!"

Céline tried to recover from the rapid, dizzying vision, and she somehow scrambled in between Jaromir and Rurik, blaming herself for this. Jaromir would kill anyone he suspected of betraying Anton, and she knew it. She'd seen a body lying at her feet once.

"Lieutenant!" she cried, holding one hand up.

"I'm no spy!" Rurik insisted. "My father asked me to share anything that would make Anton look better to Prince Lieven. Prince Anton won't report any dark deeds done by his brother, nor ever say a word about his own strengths. My father . . . he thought I should use my position as a messenger to tell Prince Lieven the truth, that Anton is a better leader. I'd never do or say anything to injure him, Lieutenant. You have to believe me."

Jaromir still had murder written all over his face, but he hadn't struck yet . . . and he was listening.

"So, that's why you were so desperate to survive this mission?" Céline asked. "Because Prince Lieven is expecting a report from you?"

Wordlessly, Rurik nodded, but he hadn't taken his eyes off Jaromir.

Then, as her head cleared further, Céline began remembering the more detailed content of her vision.

"Jaromir . . . when Prince Lieven asked for the name of the one responsible for all the deaths here, Rurik told him it was Quinn."

*   *   *

Jaromir turned his gaze from Rurik to Céline.

"What did you say?"

"It's Quinn! Or that is what Rurik was telling Lieven. Amelie is alone with him!"

Rurik was looking back and forth between them in confusion, but Jaromir didn't care.

He had to think.

His instincts told him that Rurik was no traitor. Something would have to be done about him, but he wasn't a traitor . . . and Amelie was alone with a killer.

"Rurik, you stay here and make sure the perimeter holds," he ordered. "Céline, get those people inside. I'm going for Amelie."

Without waiting for a response from either of them, he turned and bolted for the path.

Amelie almost couldn't believe it when she reached the tree line without being caught from behind. She hadn't even heard Quinn coming after her, and she wondered if the rock might have dazed him.

However, now, peering out from the brush into the open camp, she thought that making a run for the path to the miners' encampment would be foolish. It was possible that Quinn had lost her trail and was watching from somewhere along the tree line as well, waiting for her to emerge. Although he claimed to be a good tracker, she wasn't bleeding and it was dark. If she'd gotten a decent head start, there might have been little for him to track.

But he could still be watching for her, and if so, she'd never outrun him all the way to the path.

Looking straight ahead, she saw the front entrance to the huge provisions tent. It was a short run, and there were crossbows and quarrels in there—somewhere along the east wall. She crouched, took a deep breath, and sprinted, running as fast as she could for the open front flap and dashing inside.

Only then did she turn to peek back around the side and see if she was pursued. Again, she was caught in near disbelief. Where was he? He'd struck her as . . . determined.

A crashing sound echoed from within a few paces of where she'd emerged, and Quinn stumbled from the forest, carrying his spear and bleeding from his head. He looked both ways and then fixed on the provisions tent, breaking into a jog straight for the entrance.

Except for a general direction—the east wall—Amelie didn't know precisely where the weapons were stored in here, and Quinn was coming.

Surrounded by barrels and stacks of crates, she came to a fast decision, the only one she could think of. Moving deeper into the tent and down a row of crates, she dropped low and hid herself.

Hopefully, Quinn would run in, go straight for the weapons, believe she was not here, and then run out again, looking for her.

After that . . . she'd have a few options.

Footsteps pounded through the entrance, and she could hear him breathing hard.

After Jaromir ran off, Céline stood facing Rurik, but he wouldn't look at her. His hands were shaking, and it was possible that he blamed her for what had just happened. In a way, she understood.

But she was a good deal more worried about Amelie and hoped that Jaromir would reach her quickly. How could the killer be Quinn? He'd been the only one here in whom Jaromir had placed any confidence.

"Rurik?" Céline asked, hoping he would still be willing to work with her.

Just then, Guardsman Graham came jogging up, carrying a spear, and he appeared distraught.

"What is it?" Céline asked. She didn't hear a disturbance anywhere.

"I . . . I've been searching," Graham answered, "and all the men are accounted for except Saunders. He's the only one missing."

Something occurred to Céline. "Was he on guard near our tent tonight?"

Graham nodded miserably, and Céline felt for him. If the new soldier-wolf was Saunders, that meant poor Graham had lost both his friends.

Rurik glanced at her first and then Graham in sympathy. He seemed to understand the implications as well.

"I'm sorry, Graham," he said. "But the lieutenant left us with orders, and he was right about those civilians. I'm going to check the perimeter. Céline, you try to get those people back inside their homes and tell them to bar the doors."

"Yes," she answered, stepping away. "Graham, why don't you come and help me? I think some of the miners must know you."

She was trying to give him an occupation, but the tactic worked, and he fell into step beside her. They went to the Móndyalítko wagons first, as she thought she might gain help from Mercedes in getting their people indoors.

Marcus was nowhere in sight, but nearly all the other Móndyalítko were outside, looking around. Several of them were armed and surrounding their few children. Perhaps they had not had good luck in the past by shutting themselves away and leaving the fighting to the soldiers.

"Mercedes," Céline said, hurrying up. "We really should get the children inside. It's not safe for them out here."

"Do you think those soldiers can keep that beast out?"

"I think they have a good chance."

Finally, Mercedes nodded and walked over to the group of armed men. Céline looked around and saw Mariah standing off by herself, staring into the forest.

Céline went to her and said gently, "Mariah, come inside."

The girl didn't move or look away from the trees. "They burned Sullian's body," she whispered.

The sorrow in her voice was heartbreaking, leaving Céline puzzled. "You liked Sullian?"

"He was kind." Mariah nodded slowly. "And they burned him."

Céline could not begin to imagine all that this poor girl had suffered, but at the moment, she wanted to get Mariah inside a wagon.

"Come with me. Please."

Mariah's head turned slightly as Marcus came jogging out of the north-side forest. He was still barefoot with his shirt hanging loose over the top of his breeches. There were dark spots on the front of his shirt from the claw marks on his chest, and Céline wondered how badly they were bleeding. She wished she'd thought to bring her box.

He jogged right up to them. "I've done a full sweep above us, and I've seen no sign of the beast."

Coming to a decision, Céline leaned forward and whispered in his ear. "We know who is responsible now, so we should be able to stop it from happening again."

His black eyes fixed on her face.

Just then, a soldier on the west side of the perimeter screamed.

Jaromir ran through the Pählen camp straight for the provisions tent. He barely slowed down as he passed through the front flap, but he knew the weapons were stored in racks along the east wall, and so he jogged through rows of barrels and crates, emerging in a more open area.

There . . . he came to a stop at the sight of Quinn casting around wildly with a spear in one hand and a dagger in the other. He was bleeding from the head.

Amelie was nowhere to be seen.

A cold fear filled Jaromir's stomach, but he fought to keep his face calm.

"Lieutenant," Quinn said.

"What's happened?" Jaromir asked, as if he knew nothing. "Where's Amelie?"

Quinn used the back of his dagger hand to wipe some of the blood off his forehead as Jaromir approached.

"The beast attacked us on the way, and we became separated," Quinn answered.

"And you just abandoned her and came in here?"

"I thought to come in here for more weapons, and then I would look for her." He glanced about nervously.

"More weapons?" Jaromir asked. "You already have a hunting spear and a dagger. How much more could you use?"

Quinn stopped glancing around and fixed directly on him. The tension was thick, and Jaromir decided to drop the ruse. He drew his sword.

"What did you do with her?"

Without a flicker of warning, Quinn swung hard with the butt of the spear.

Céline stood frozen as the scream carried through the night air. The sound of shouting—and more screaming—followed.

Graham dropped his spear and began running toward the flurry of sounds.

"Don't!" he shouted. "It's Saunders."

Before Céline could move or react. Mariah picked up the spear and ran after Graham. With no idea what else to do, Céline turned back and found Marcus gone.

"Marcus!"

No one answered.

Céline ran after Mariah and soon rounded the back of the outer Móndyalítko wagon, reaching the west-side perimeter. The first thing she saw were two dead soldiers on the ground, bleeding from their throats. A spear and a loaded crossbow lay beside them. Any other soldiers who'd been here appeared to have run. She didn't see Mariah.

Only two living creatures now occupied her line of sight in the darkness.

The farthest away was the same massive wolf that had attacked her and Amelie in their tent. Its red eyes glowed, and its jowls were pulled back, exposing its fangs.

A few paces closer to her, Graham was kneeling, facing the beast and holding one hand out in the air.

"Saunders. It's me."

The wolf snarled and charged. Céline wanted to shout, to wave her arms, to do something, anything, to distract it, but the sound caught in her throat, and she couldn't seem to move.

In a blur, Mariah came running from the shadows behind the wagon, past Céline, and she swung with the butt of her spear, catching the wolf directly across the face. The blow barely seemed to stun it, but it faltered somewhat in its charge at Graham, and it only clipped him, knocking him off his feet.

As the beast struggled to halt and turn, a slender black wolf dashed in, smashing against its side and rolling it onto the ground. Two breaths later, Rurik came running up, carrying his drawn sword.

Mariah ran to Graham, kneeling beside him, weeping openly. "It's not him anymore," she cried. "He's not in there."

Then the roar of both wolves drowned out anything else she might have said, and Rurik stood watching the battle of teeth and claws in confusion.

"Help the black one," Céline called to him. "It's Marcus!"

Amelie had watched Jaromir run in, and she'd crawled along behind him without being seen, hoping to use her best and main strength—the element of surprise—against Quinn.

She could hear both men speaking, and then she heard a sword sliding from a scabbard.

"What did you do with her?" Jaromir asked, his voice full of anguish.

Amelie moved from behind a tall stack of crates and peered over the top of a barrel to see.

Before the sound of the words had died, Quinn swung with the butt of his spear and caught Jaromir across the face. Amelie wanted to scream. Jaromir would have expected a straight-on attack, for Quinn to come at him with the point of the spear.

With a cracking sound, Jaromir went down. His eyes were closed.

Quinn flipped the spear upward, gripping its haft up nearer the point, and then he raised it to drive it downward through Jaromir's chest.

Amelie had no weapon but a dagger, and she was well aware that she was no match for Quinn. So she did the only thing possible. She shoved the tall stack of crates beside her, and they fell forward on top of both Jaromir and Quinn with a cascade of crashing sounds.

Darting forward, she ran over the tops of the fallen crates, hoping to reach Quinn and drive her dagger through his throat while he was still dazed. Reaching him in seconds as he lay on the ground, she struck downward with her blade.

But his hand snaked up and caught her wrist. The next thing she knew, he'd jerked her down and was up on top of her, pinning her arms with his knees. This time, he didn't grab her jaw. Instead, his hand closed around her throat. Looking up, she could see anger in the back of his cold blue eyes. He wasn't going to snap her neck. He wanted this to hurt.

His hand closed slowly, and she fought to take in air. The pain wasn't terrible at first, but then it grew unbearable. He went on closing his hand, and the world began growing black.

Céline heard Marcus yelp as the larger wolf snapped its teeth on his shoulder.

Rurik dropped his sword and grabbed a fallen spear, moving closer to the fight and looking for an opening where he wouldn't hit Marcus.

But his action of grabbing the weapon caused Céline to cast about as well, and her eyes fell upon the loaded crossbow lying just outside a dead soldier's hand. The beast must have killed him before he had a chance to fire. Scrambling forward, Céline snatched it up and aimed it at the mass of claws and teeth and fur rolling on the ground. She didn't take her eyes off them, and when the larger wolf suddenly rolled on top, she fired, catching it behind one ear. The creature roared and veered away from Marcus, shaking its head savagely.

As soon as it was off Marcus, Rurik darted in and used both hands to drive the spear downward through its throat, pinning it to the ground in a rush of blood. Rurik stomped down on its front shoulder with his boot and fought to hold the spear in place as the creature bled out and out . . . and finally stopped moving.

Marcus—the black wolf—tried struggling to his feet and then fell. By the time Céline reached him, he was in human form again, naked, panting, and bleeding. He didn't speak as she pulled her cloak off and covered him, trying to check his wounds at the same time. The front of his left shoulder had a deep gouge.

Rurik took his boot off the massive dead wolf, walked over, and looked down at Marcus as if uncertain of what he was seeing. Céline turned her head up and met Rurik's eyes. He was a teller of secrets. That much was known, but perhaps only where Anton's success was concerned.

"He saved us," she said flatly. "You'll keep his secret?"

After a moment, Rurik nodded. Then, as if unsure what to say, he went over to check on Graham and Mariah.

Céline turned back to Marcus. "I need to make sure Amelie is safe. Then I'll get my box and tend to these wounds. This shoulder might need stitching."

He hadn't seemed to hear her, and he was studying her face.

"What you said before . . . about knowing who was responsible, about being able to stop all this, that means you're leaving soon, doesn't it?"

The question threw her, and she wasn't sure what he was trying to ask. "Yes. I have a shop, a life back home."

If anything, his gaze grew more intense. "You mean you have *someone* back home?"

She flinched. Could he see how she was haunted by the trailing wisps of her unexplainable connection to Anton? Looking away, she couldn't answer his question. There was no answer.

Amelie was in agony, and her world was going black.

Then, suddenly, the pressure on her throat was gone and she was sucking in air. Nothing made sense for a moment, but she could hear grunting and crashing sounds, and she tried to struggle up, squinting to see what was happening.

Jaromir and Quinn, both barehanded, were swinging at each other. Where was Jaromir's sword?

Had he seen her being strangled and just rushed in without thinking in order to pull Quinn off?

Quinn struck Jaromir full force in the jaw, snapping his head back, but Jaromir came around and smashed his own fist into the side of Quinn's face. Then, somehow, as Quinn stumbled, he managed to duck up behind Jaromir and make a grab for his head.

In panic, Amelie pushed herself up. She knew what Quinn was doing: trying to get a firm enough hold to break Jaromir's neck. But Jaromir's hand flashed downward toward something on top of a crate, and the next thing Amelie knew, he had slipped around behind Quinn, and Amelie saw what he'd grabbed: a thick piece of twine torn loose from a fallen crate.

In an instant, he had the twine over Quinn's head, and he jerked it taut, using both hands now to cross-pull it closed around Quinn's throat. Quinn bucked wildly, trying to throw him off, but Jaromir held on, pulling tighter, shutting off Quinn's breath.

From where she was half-crouched, Amelie saw fear dawning on Quinn's face. His mouth opened, and part of his tongue protruded, but she didn't look away. She watched as both the fear and the life faded from his eyes.

Jaromir kept twisting and pulling the twine for several moments after Amelie thought Quinn was already dead.

Then he dropped the body and looked over at her.

"Amelie," he breathed.

Jaromir stared at Amelie, who was half-crouched among the fallen crates. He could see angry welts on her throat . . . but she was alive and looking back at him.

He ran her to her, pulling her up against his chest. "Let me see your neck. Can you breathe?"

She didn't struggle in his arms; she just let him hold her.

"It was him," she blurted out. "He's the one who's been turning all the soldiers."

"I know. Do you know how?"

"An elixir . . . a black substance he puts on their skin. He keeps it in a metal flask."

He held her a moment longer to make sure her breathing was normal, and then he leaned her back against a crate.

"A metal flask? I'm going to check his body."

Moving back through the fallen crates, Jaromir didn't see where Quinn might be hiding a flask. He wasn't wearing his cloak, and the pockets of his breeches seemed too snug. But Jaromir searched the body anyway.

"Anything?"

"No."

"Do you know which tent is his?"

Jaromir did. He retrieved his sword and slid it back into its sheath. When he turned to help Amelie up, he found she was already standing.

"Your face is a mess," she said.

He touched his jaw, which had taken several blows— one of which had come from the butt of a spear. "It'll heal."

They left the provisions tent and walked through the empty camp.

"Is Céline all right?" Amelie asked.

"She was when I came after you. Rurik is with her, and all the soldiers. We'll get back to her as soon as we can."

Upon entering the tent he knew to be Quinn's private quarters, he looked around at the sparse furniture, but Amelie walked right to the bed and picked up the cloak lying there.

"He kept it in his pocket." She carefully pulled out a pair of leather gloves, but her expression turned anxious as she continued feeling the fabric of the cloak. "It's not in here. We have to find it, Jaromir. Just a few drops on the skin will turn a man."

A small travel chest sat near the end of the bed. Jaromir walked over and saw a padlock. Drawing his sword, he used the hilt to break the lock and opened the chest.

Amelie stood behind him.

"Oh . . . there." She pointed down.

Seeing the edge of a stopper, he moved an extra shirt and saw a small metal flask.

"Don't touch it," Amelie warned. "There could be some of the liquid on the outside." Leaning over, she used the shirt to wrap the flask without touching it.

"What do we do with it?" he asked, knowing they couldn't just pour it out if there was a danger of anyone or anything touching it.

"We'll take it to Céline. She'll know how to dispose of it properly."

A realization hit him. "This is over. Once we hunt down the last beast, this is finished. You've done it."

They had succeeded, and Anton would be able to report to his father that the issue was resolved and the silver would soon be flowing again. Jaromir felt an emotion he couldn't explain, something beyond gratitude.

"Amelie, you were right back at the castle. You deserve . . . something for what you've done here. If there is there is anything I can do, anything I can give you, tell me."

At first she was quiet, and then she said, "There is."

Within a few sentences, she explained to him what she wanted. As he listened, he didn't completely understand why she would ask for such a thing, but it made him love her more.

"Will you arrange it?" she asked.

"Yes."

CHAPTER FIFTEEN

The next day, Jaromir walked through the soldiers' encampment toward Keegan's tent. He was still having some difficulty believing that Rurik, Marcus, and Céline had managed to take down the last wolf by themselves, but . . . the beast was dead, and Quinn was dead, and Jaromir still had a number of loose ends to tie up.

That morning, he'd sent out two messengers on horseback.

First, he'd sent Rurik back to Castle Sèone with a letter to Anton—along with some strict stipulations. Jaromir had not yet decided what to do about Rurik in the long run, but he was convinced that the young guardsman was no traitor and had thought himself to be working in the best interests of Anton. Of course, Rurik could never be allowed to function as a messenger between Anton and Prince Lieven again, but in their current situation, Jaromir didn't have anyone else to send home, so he'd sent Rurik. First, though, he'd made the guardsman promise to deliver the letter to Anton and then stay put. He was not to leave Castle

Sèone or take a message to Prince Lieven for any reason. Jaromir had made it blindingly clear that Rurik's future in Sèone depended on him following this order. Rurik had agreed and thanked him.

Second, Jaromir had commissioned a Pählen soldier to carry a letter to Prince Lieven.

And now . . . Jaromir arrived at the tent of Captain Keegan, and he paused at the doorway. A part of him was looking forward to the conversation about to take place, and a part of him was dreading it.

Walking in, he made his way toward the back.

"Captain?" he called before stepping around the last tapestry.

"Here."

Continuing on, Jaromir found Keegan alone and sitting up in bed. He'd been carried back and settled the night before, and now he seemed able to eat and drink on his own, though he was still weak, and according to Céline, he would be for some time.

But his expression was a mix of caution and anxiety, and Jaromir wondered how much he'd been told.

"So it was Quinn," Keegan said flatly.

Well, he'd been told that much.

"Yes, and he was working in the employ of Prince Damek."

As those words sank in, Keegan's left hand began to shake.

Jaromir pulled a chair over beside the bed and sat down. "I sent a letter to Prince Lieven this morning."

"You?" The anxiety on Keegan's face grew more pronounced.

"You're not in any state to take command here. I've volunteered to remain here until your replacement arrives."

Keegan just watched him uncertainly, most likely wondering where this was going.

Jaromir leaned back. "You needn't worry. I didn't tell your lord much. Only that the issue has been solved, the silver will be flowing again soon, that you've been taken seriously ill, and that I'll maintain command for now, but that a new contingent and commander must be sent as soon as possible."

"That's all you told him?"

"Prince Lieven has never been one to press for details. He cares about results." Jaromir paused. "And so long as you agree to a request I'm about to make, I'll ensure he doesn't learn anything more."

"What request?"

"I want you to release the Móndyalítko men from their contracts and pay them their full year's wage now. By my count, it's only six or seven men, not enough to matter to the workforce. I've sent word to Prince Anton to send an escort here to take us home once your replacement has arrived and we're ready to leave. In my letter, I also asked him to send four extra horses. You'll let me pick four horses from your barn, for a total of eight, to pull the Móndyalítko wagons."

Keegan's mouth fell open. If Jaromir had just made an offer of marriage, the man could not have been more stunned. "Pay them their full . . . four horses? Are you mad? No! We need every worker back in the mines. Those gypsies aren't going anywhere."

Jaromir raised an eyebrow. "Truly? Then I'll be forced to let it slip to Prince Lieven that you had a spy of Prince Damek's at your side for a year, and you never suspected a thing. I'll let it slip that your incompetence is the reason so many of your men are dead and the silver stopped flowing."

Keegan glared at him in open hatred. "That's a pointless threat. Once your prince learns the truth, he'll be only too glad to tell his father."

"You don't know Prince Anton. While I may not always agree, he feels strongly about never tattling on his brother even when deaths are involved or on the few occasions when Damek has tried to assassinate him." Jaromir shrugged. "Perhaps he's right. As I mentioned . . . Prince Lieven is not normally interested in details, just results." He leaned forward. "But unless you agree to my small request, I'll find a way to make sure a few of those details reach his ears."

"Take the horses," Keegan spat. "And those filthy gypsies. But keep in mind, they've got no place to go."

"You let me worry about that." Jaromir stood up. "I think we're done here."

That afternoon, Amelie and Céline walked over to the miners' encampment to see Mercedes.

After knocking on the door of the largest wagon, they both went inside to find Mercedes at home and Marcus stretched out on one of the back beds. Mariah was nowhere to be seen.

"Leave the door open," Marcus said. "I like the air."

Amelie thought he looked a little pale, but that was

probably to be expected. Céline had been up late tending to his wounds, including stitching up his shoulder.

Mercedes was studying Céline. "So . . . you'll be leaving soon?" She sounded regretful.

"That's what we came to talk to you about," Céline responded, and then she turned to Amelie. "Maybe you should . . . ?"

Amelie gathered her thoughts and positioned herself so that she could speak to both Mercedes and Marcus. "You have been very helpful to us these past few days, and Jaromir sent us with an offer." She thought it might sound less like charity if it came from him. "There's a plot of land outside the walls of Castle Sèone that has gone untended for several years. The tenants decamped to try their luck with a vendor's cart in Enêmûsk. It has a cottage and a small barn. If your family would like . . . you can live there and work the land. Half the crops will go to Prince Anton, and you'll keep the other half to sell or use for your own purposes." For a moment, she kept her focus on Mercedes. "I know it would be a different way of life for you, but some of Prince Anton's tenants have become quite prosperous, depending on which crops they grow."

Mercedes stood with her eyes shifting back and forth as if she was trying to follow something she didn't quite understand.

"But we couldn't make the journey until late autumn, when the men's contracts are finished. And what about our wagons?" she said. "How would we get there?"

"That's all been taken care of. Jaromir has spoken

with Captain Keegan. Your men have been released from their contracts and will be paid their year's wage. You'll be supplied with eight horses, so you can drive the wagons out of here. All of your people have been given leave, including the wives of your younger men. You needn't leave anyone behind."

Mercedes sank onto the bed beside Marcus.

"But you don't have to accept the land," Céline put in quickly. "If you'd rather not turn to farming, you'll still be released from your contracts, you'll be paid, and you can keep the horses."

"If you do decide to take Jaromir's offer of the land," Amelie said, "you can come with us when we leave. We'll take you into Sèone Village first to get you supplied. But there's no rush on a decision. We're stuck here until Keegan's replacement arrives. You have time to think."

Mercedes turned to Marcus, and they locked eyes. Then she turned back to Amelie. "We don't need time to think. None of our people will. We're coming with you."

Footsteps sounded in the open doorway, and Mariah appeared . . . with young Graham standing behind her.

"Coming where?" Mariah asked.

"Home," Amelie answered. "You're coming home with us."

CHAPTER SIXTEEN

Just over three weeks later, in the late afternoon, Jaromir led a contingent of seventeen of his own men, two seers, and four Móndyalítko wagons back inside the inner gates of Sèone.

He'd never been so glad to see the familiar village.

Without stopping, he led the wagons to an open area out behind the smithy where there was enough room for the families to make camp. He figured they'd need some time to rest and buy supplies for winter, and then he could take them out and show them the homestead.

Once the wagons were pulling into position, he dismissed his men, and he watched Céline slide down from her saddle and hand her mare off to one of the guards. Amelie was already on the ground, helping Mercedes to back her team of horses into place.

Jaromir dismounted as well, standing beside Céline and watching Amelie work. They were both quiet for a while, and then Céline looked up at him.

"I know the prince is waiting for a more detailed report . . . but could I give mine tomorrow? I want to go and check on the shop and see my own things and sleep in my own bed."

He paused. He knew Anton would be waiting for a full report, but this was the first thing Céline had asked of him since Ryazan. He owed her at least one night's rest.

"Of course. I'll give him my report tonight, and that should be sufficient for now."

"Thank you."

Amelie was now helping to unharness a team of horses and talking with Mercedes. Then Mariah and Graham came around the side of the wagon to help. Back in Ryazan, young Graham had asked to be permanently released from duty so he could travel here with Mariah, and it hadn't taken Jaromir long to get Keegan to agree.

"You've done a good thing here," Céline said.

"It was Amelie's idea. When I asked her what she wanted, this was it."

"Yes, but you agreed. You made it happen."

He had, hadn't he?

"Well, it looks like Amelie is going to be here awhile," he said. "Can I give you a ride home?"

"No." She smiled weakly and put both hands to her back. "I'd much rather walk."

He nodded and watched her leave. She was an astonishing woman, much stronger than she looked.

Then his gaze shifted back to Amelie as she climbed up on top of a wagon, unlashed a wooden box, and dropped it down into Mercedes's waiting arms.

Amelie.

She'd borrowed some spare clothes and was now back in breeches—with the pant legs rolled up—and a man's shirt, and she appeared much more comfortable. He'd never known anyone like her, all fire and flint and softness at the same time. She could be incredibly selfish in one moment and astoundingly giving in the next.

A strong urge hit him to climb up on top of that wagon and help her unload, to do nothing more than work by her side and spend the rest of the afternoon helping her to get these people settled.

But he turned away, leading his horse up toward the castle. He had a report to give.

Not long past sunset, Céline was in her shop, dusting out bowls and getting her tools ready to begin work again. She'd been gone for some time, and the herb garden would need tending.

Amelie hadn't come home yet.

Though Céline relished the respite of solitude, she wasn't completely on her own. Her orange cat, Oliver—who was normally not demonstrative—was so pleased to see her that he continued rubbing against her legs. A bowl on the floor near the door contained water and another held the remnants of fresh milk. Céline thought that she must do something special for Erin for having tended to him for so long.

However, Oliver's rubbing soon began to make her feel guilty. Though he'd been cared for while she was away, had he been lonely?

"Yes, I'm glad to see you, too." She patted the top of

the worktable. "Come up here for a while. Just don't knock over the candles."

He jumped up, this time trying to press his face against her hands.

In a way, his attention was a welcome distraction, as it kept her mind from drifting back to all that she and Amelie had been forced to see in Ryazan. As before, she thought it might take a little time to recover.

Tomorrow, she would need to go up to the castle and give her report to Anton. Though she welcomed the prospect of seeing his face, the last thing she wanted to do was relive those early days and nights in the mining camp.

The door to the shop opened, and she looked over in mild annoyance. Of course the people here must have missed their apothecary, but she'd just returned, and who would come at this hour?

A man in a cloak, with his hood pulled up, stepped inside and closed the door. He carried a muslin bag in his left hand.

"I'm sorry," Céline said. "I won't be open until tomorrow afternoon at the soonest."

Reaching up with his free hand, he pulled back his hood, exposing a pale face and dark brown hair.

"My lord . . . ," she stammered. "I didn't know . . ."

It was Anton. Had he walked down through the village?

"Don't distress yourself," he said. "Jaromir has told me everything that happened in Ryazan, and I couldn't wait to see you, to thank you."

She watched him come closer, and she had no idea what to say.

"You accomplished something that no one else could," he went on, "and you did it in my name. My father is pleased."

Yes, Céline thought, that had been the reason for all their efforts: to please Anton's father.

He lifted the bag he was carrying and set it on the table. "I feared insulting you by offering you money or jewels. I know you and Amelie did all this for me and the future of Droevinka. Jaromir told me what Amelie had requested, but that you requested nothing. I wanted . . . I wanted to do something." Opening the top of the bag, he exposed a thorny vine sitting in dirt. "It's a velveteen rosebush from Belaski. Helga says that you once told her the petals would make the strongest cough syrup of any rosebush you know, and she also told me that you did not have one."

By now, he was standing close enough that she could feel his breath on her cheek . . . standing too close, really. But, shaken by his thoughtful gesture, she couldn't take her gaze off the vine. A velveteen rosebush.

"Jaromir told me that you need to rest and recover. Don't bother coming to offer a report. I know what I need to know, and I won't ask anything further of you."

Though she was beyond touched that he'd come down here, by his words, by his thoughtful gift, by his manner . . . by his concern, they both knew this was only a reprieve.

"Until something else happens and you need my abilities?" she whispered.

"Céline," he breathed back and started to reach out

for her hand. His hand stopped in midair, and he took a step away. "Again, I cannot thank you enough."

He didn't respond to her question. He didn't need to.

Still, looking up at him, looking around her shop, she found that she didn't mind.

When he called her again, she'd answer.